Katrina Means Cleansing

A Novel of Hurricane Katrina for YA and Middle Grade Readers

C.W. Cannon

47 Journals

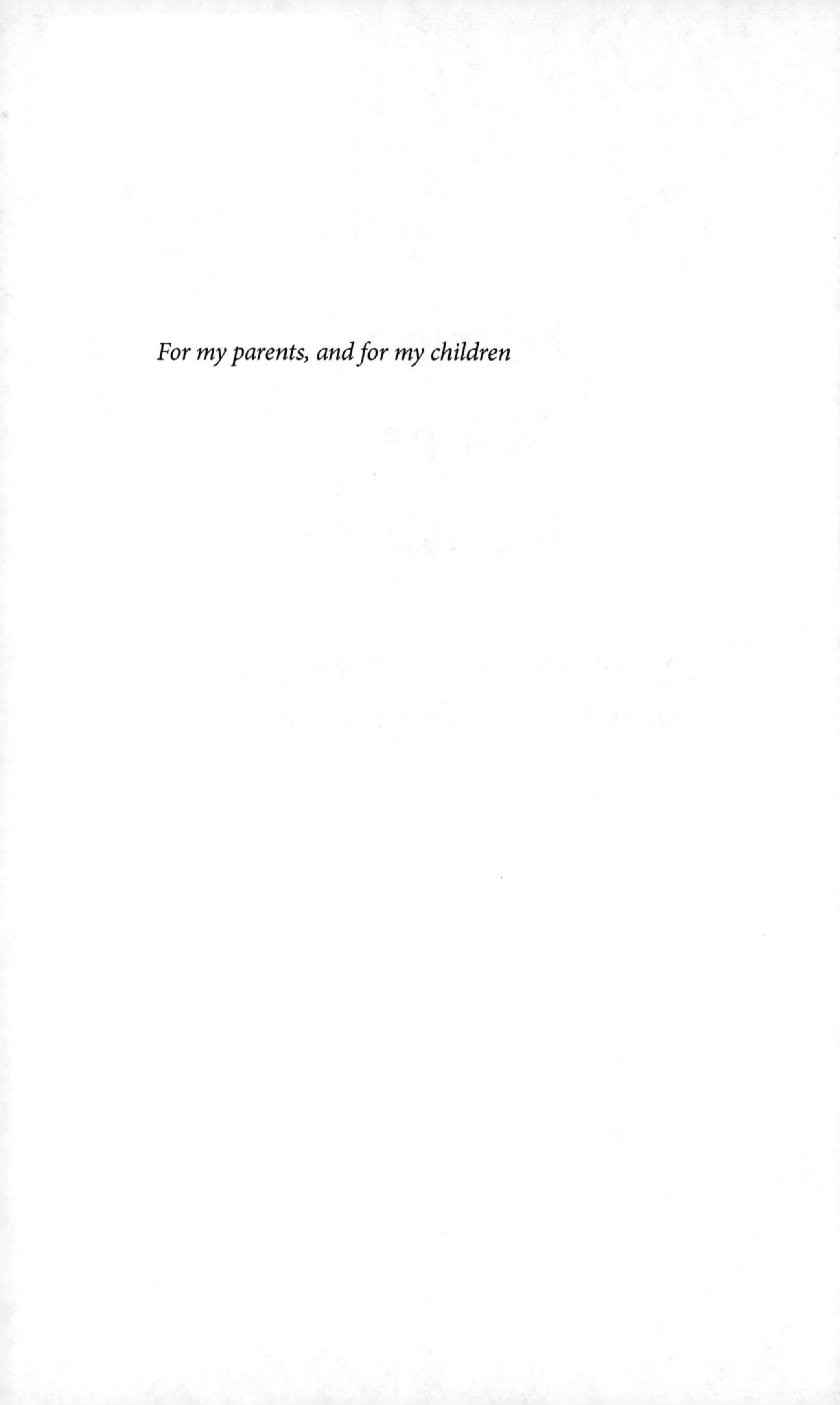

For my parents, and for my children

"The experience of centuries teaches us that nothing is more probable than improbabilities."

—Gayarré, *History of Louisiana,* Volume I

1

Everybody called Rodney Keith DeCuir "Haze," but he wasn't sure when they started calling him that. Since he was too young to remember. The only people who called him "Rodney" were teachers, because he never felt like talking to them long enough to explain how they should call him something different than the name on the roster. Especially this year, there was no way he was going into all that, since it was a new school and he didn't know anybody. His mom was so proud he scored high enough to go to McDonogh 39, supposedly one of the better ones, but he was mainly going for the band. They had a good band where he was at before, too—Douglass, in his district—but grads from 39 were the ones who went on to dance on the field at the Superdome with Southern or Grambling. Douglass kids never went anywhere. Haze intended to go somewhere. As long as he could take his horn, he'd go.

His first day at 39 didn't start well, though. The bus. He waited over a half an hour for the St. Claude bus to huff and puff its way to his stop, and then the driver up and left and went in the corner store and chit-chatted with everybody and their brother for another fifteen minutes. So Haze ended up tardy in a big way.

The front desk didn't go easy on him either. The lady sitting there ignored him for a while and kept squawking away on her cell phone. Then she covered it with her hand and said, "Can I help you."

"Yes ma'am," Haze said, "I'm late. Um, I'm tardy."

"You mean you go here?"

"Yes ma'am."

"And you late on the first day?"

"Yes ma'am."

"If this was a job you know what would happen to you?"

"Yes, ma'am."

 "Mm-mm." Into the phone she said, "I'ma call you later boo." To Haze: "Name?"

"Rodney DeCuir."

"Which one your last name?"

"DeCuir."

"D-E-C-U-I-R?"

"Yes ma'am."

"How long you had that Bob Marley Rasta-man haircut?"

His friends had warned him he might catch attitude for his dreds at 39.

"Since I was a kid," he said. "It's my religion." That's what his cousin told him to say.

The lady behind the desk said "You know a lot of schools don't allow that hairstyle, Mister DeCuir."

"Yes, ma'am, I know." He couldn't resist throwing some attitude of his own: "This one of 'em?"

She ignored the question and wrote something on a slip and handed it to him. "Go on to Room 228, that's Ms. Williams."

When he found room 228 he saw it said "Social Worker" on the door. He knocked, heard her say "enter," like on *Star Trek*, and went in.

She didn't have much of an office. Long and windowless, like it used to be a cloakroom. It was dark, too, because instead of an overhead light, she had a few lamps with dense, dark-colored shades. She sat at a little round table with file folders stacked on it. She had dredlocks, too—long gray ones tied back. She was wearing a big loose linen gown, a dark greenish gray like Spanish moss. She greeted him with a nice warm smile. "Come in, come in," she said, "sit down."

"Yes ma'am." He sat and handed her the slip.

"OK," she said, and stood and pulled a folder out of a filing cabinet and sat again and wrote in the folder. "Did you miss your bus this morning?"

"Yes ma'am," he said, but wondered if she meant a schoolbus and then wondered what he was supposed to say if she asked him his address. He couldn't remember if he was supposed to say his uncle's address or his grandmother's or his own. He thought 39 was a city-wide access school but he wasn't sure.

"Where do you live?"

"Um…where I live?"

She smiled and watched him squirm, but not for long. "Anywhere in Orleans Parish will do."

"Oh," he sighed, "yes ma'am," and told her his real address, where he stayed with his mother.

She nodded and wrote. "DeCuir," she pronounced, then "Rodney." She looked at his face, gazed at it long as if trying to recognize him, then asked, "Did your father go to Jefferson High?"

The question threw him, partly because it wasn't called Jefferson anymore. "Yes ma'am. They call it Douglass now."

"Yes," she acknowledged, "the power to name. Shuffle the symbols if all else fails."

He wasn't sure she was talking to him, since her face was pointed at whatever form she was filling out.

"How is he?"

"He alright."

"I knew him in high school—and from the neighborhood."

"He went in the army." Haze was used to saying this, and it was true, though it was also a long time ago and lots had happened since he got out.

"Is he overseas?"

"Yes ma'am." And then another idea struck him. "He in Iraq."

She looked up at him again, then capped her pen and closed the file. "I'll pray for him."

"Thank you ma'am."

"Can your mother drive you to school?"

"No ma'am. She working when it's time to go. I go on the bus."

His mom worked nights at a hospital.
"Well, try to catch an earlier one, OK?"

"Yes ma'am."

She wrote out another pass and told him first to check in with his homeroom teacher—who would give him his class schedule—and then proceed to first period, which was almost over. He rose to go but she said, "Just a moment," and took his hand, squeezed it and closed her eyes. After a deep breath she said, "Yes—you are Rodney's son."

He nodded, but couldn't think of anything to say, and turned for the door.

"But he ain't in Iraq."

When he turned to look back she was grinning, so he just smiled and moved out the door.

2

Miranda Maitre needed Pepto-Bismol and a stack of fantasy novels to face another first day of school. She wasn't anxious or nervous. She didn't fear failure—certainly not academic failure. It's just that it would take her away from what she loved doing most, which unfamiliar observers might describe as nothing. She liked reading, watching old movies on TCM. Walks in Audubon Park with her ipod. But what she liked most was a kind of meditation. Sitting in her carefully appointed room, in the rickety straightback chair facing the arched window, watching the shadows from the big sycamore outside sigh or heave or dance, depending on the weather. She found summer afternoon thunderstorms especially delicious. First the encroaching darkness, then the windy rage, followed by drizzly denouement, then sunlight again—though a fresher sunlight than before. Almost every afternoon shower that summer found her in her chair facing the tree. But she didn't just plop down and look out the window. She prepared. She combed her long chestnut hair and pulled it back and up and set it with two antique silver combs. She donned a long dark dress and shawl. Made tea—oolong leaves steeped in a ball. Then she sat, gingerly, hands clasped on folded knee. And waited. Sometimes a storm came, sometimes not. In any case, she usually ended up feeling something—something, as she put it, *poetic.* It was an exquisite but fragile sensation, like being so free from mental clutter that you could actually see what was in front of you—until something ruined it like the phone ringing downstairs or a car horn or some guy walking by cursing on the street below.

She had spent all summer getting her room (which she preferred to call her "chambers") set up just right. She had thrown out a bunch of kid stuff, the stuffed bears and—to her mother's horror—the Madame Alexander dolls. She threw out the queen sized bed and replaced it with a twin—another decision her mom couldn't understand. The reason was that she wanted more floor space. She loved to look at those old worn wooden slats, and loved the sound of her high-heeled boots clopping ominously across them, like a big change coming. Besides the bed, she had a single bookshelf, a dresser, two straightback chairs, a small writing desk, a trunk, and three unmatched end-tables—all in varying shades of faded, chipped wood. Long pale cotton drapes remained always tied back from the great arched window, and a rust colored batik sarong hung over her closet door. Besides white, she liked only dark, deep colors, of whatever base. She had a mirror above her dresser and two pictures on the walls. One, on the wall opposite the big window, was a Harper's Magazine print of New Orleans, viewed from a hot-air balloon, in 1885. The other was Emily Dickinson, above the writing desk: the standard portrait, with the somewhat gawky dull stare (from looking within?) and the ribbon around her neck. In the little drawer was an old edition of Dickinson's collected poems. Miranda kept a fountain pen and inkwell, and a sheaf of paper, in the drawer too. (She owned a laptop, but kept it under her bed).

The problem with school wasn't the classes or the teachers. It was the kids. She just never could relate to any of them and was done trying. Her mom was always pressing her to be more social. "Did you meet anyone interesting today?" she would ask, day after day and year after year. Miranda hoped this would be the year she would stop asking. Her dad seemed less worried that Miranda didn't seem to make friends—or want to. "She seems to be very independent," he told her mom, "She'll make friends when she meets people she really likes, and until then, I'll be her friend." But her mom always had a plan to get her in some organization or club. Then Miranda would join, become the secretary or whatever, and still no sleepover invites. The only thing that bothered Miranda was seeing her mom worry that something was wrong with her, like she was autistic or something (they already looked into that, back when she was a pre-schooler). It's not that she was shy. Nobody talked more than she did in class.

At least she could walk to school. It was just through Audubon Park, across Loyola University campus, and then just three more blocks. When the dreaded morning finally arrived, she put on some practical flats, a pair of black jeans, one of her dad's hand-me-down white dress shirts, and headed out the door. She left her hair down in case she wanted to avoid looking at anyone. Her mom asked if she was sure she didn't want a ride and she said yes, she was sure. She wanted to see her dad but apparently he'd been called to the hospital for some emergency. She cued up her ipod to Gregorian Chants and enjoyed watching the morning mist rise off the lagoon in the park. She got to school slightly early—ten minutes before the homeroom bell—so she took a turn around the block. The bell rang right as she approached the side door the second time and she went right into homeroom. She sat in the front like she always did—the teachers were the only people she liked—and listened to the squeals and shrieks of the girls and the "hey dudes!" of the guys. A girl who seemed new sat at the desk next to her and pretended to check messages on her phone. Miranda decided to reach out. "Hi," she said, "I'm Miranda."

The new girl introduced herself and they chatted a bit before the announcements came on and Mr. Chalew, the principal, welcomed every one to another great year at Hennican Prep. The new girl had just moved from Florida. Hurricane

Ivan had messed up their house and they'd moved to New Orleans after the insurance didn't work out. Pensacola was still in bad shape, apparently. Her name was Jess. Miranda agreed to meet her at lunch and they went their separate ways.

Miranda's first class was English, with Ms. Barnigal. She was Miranda's English teacher for a brief while last spring, after the teacher they'd had most of the year suddenly and mysteriously left. That was sad for Miranda because Ms. Godowsky had been one of her favorites. A strange lady with a just slightly strange accent—from Quebec. In the middle of lectures she would just stop and stare, like some ghost had entered the room that only she could see. Then she would say, "OK, back to Earth—where was I?" She wore these retro horn-rimmed glasses and a retro hairdo, up with chopsticks and bangs in the front, but you couldn't tell if she was making a retro fashion statement on purpose or that was just the way she'd always been. She was quite physical with the students, too, would pat them on the head, shoulder, even do playful affectionate little cheek slaps. She talked about characters from books like they were her personal friends. "Gertrude of course knows nothing of Claudius' shenanigans, thinks her son has gone off the deep end, but it's her own fault for being so irritatingly needy that she just shacks right up with the next guy down the pike—her husband's brother, for Christ sake! Ah, what can one do?"

Ms. Barnigal, to Miranda, seemed a bit more like a secretary or maybe principal than an English teacher. "Good morning students! I hope everyone had a leisurely summer, because we will have a LOT of work to do this semester. Starting NOW!" She told them all to take out pen and paper and begin narrating what happened to them over the summer, in five paragraphs.

She padded softly up and down the aisles as the students scribbled. She stopped to chide a few slow starters. "Did

NOTHING happen to you this summer, Michael?" She also interrupted to comment on individual students' appearances. "Joshua, you look a whole foot taller! Is it possible?" And: "Wasn't your hair brown last year, Amelia? Just kidding, the streaks look great!" In front of Miranda she paused—"Miranda Maitre," she mused. "You look a bit plain today." As if in response to the sudden cessation of scratching pencils, she added "Oh, no, I mean it as a compliment!" This got some laughs out of the back of the room.

Miranda realized that Ms. Barnigal was probably making fun of her, that the kids were probably laughing at her. But she couldn't figure out why. She just wasn't able to figure out what went through these people's heads. She shrugged it off and returned to her assigned composition—about finding a mysterious locket in her grandmother's attic and tracing it back to a clandestine romantic adventure in a 19th century French village, on the stormy Brittany coast. But the bell rang before she could complete the tale, and Ms. Barnigal wrested the unfinished manuscript from her hand with a loud "tsk, tsk."

<h1 style="text-align:center">3</h1>

The bandleader at McDonogh 39 was not as friendly as the social worker. He had that drill sergeant style. Haze had walked in all smiles but the courtesy wasn't returned. "What?" the bandleader barked. "Don't tell me you here for beginning band. Beginners already done begun—you done missed it."

"I'm sorry, sir," Haze muttered, face down, "I missed my bus."

"You better take a rocket ship then!"

"Yes sir."

"Yes sir. You got any more vocabulary than that? Look in my face boy, I sound like I'm talking out the ground?"

Haze looked up and saw a broad and well-fed face that wasn't as mean or angry as he'd expected. There was even a little twinkle in it.

"What you play, son?"

"Trumpet."

"You got your own horn?"

"No sir."

"You may call me Mister Brice."

"Yes Mister Brice."

"You got a mouthpiece."

"Yes sir. Mister Brice."

"OK," Mister Brice grinned, "Let's play." He got on an intercom and called another student from one of the rehearsal rooms. The bandroom was empty. Haze assumed the other kids were already practicing in sections. An older kid came in with a trumpet case and opened it.

"You warmed up already?"

"Yes sir," Haze said automatically. But after he slipped his mouthpiece into the horn, he re-thought. "No, Mister Brice, I didn't get no chance to warm up this morning."

"Too busy waiting on the bus, huh?" the bandleader sneered. "If you want to play, you got to play ALL the time. Nothing keeping you from buzzing on that mouthpiece every second of the day. Unless you are in class or the hallway. Now we only got less than five minutes left in this period. And I'm not going to have you being late to your next class on me. So I tell you what we'll do. If you want to be in this band you show up in this room the second after that 3:15 bell ring. I will be here. You hear?"

"Yes, Mister Brice."

The day dragged on unbearably. Like a cashier at the grocery crawling along to punish somebody for copping an attitude. Haze just wanted to skip out and get back to the bandroom and get one of those horns and practice, practice, practice. Just like everybody said you were supposed to do. In between classes he just walked with his head down and buzzed slowly and quietly into his mouthpiece—even though Mister Brice had warned against it. In class he gripped the mouthpiece tightly in his pocket, to keep it warm. At lunch he gave up on the long snaking line in the cafeteria and went out on the blacktop and buzzed away.

The other classes weren't much different than back at Douglass. The history teacher read from the book, after saying they didn't have enough to sign out and take home. The math teacher passed some hand-outs around and instructed the students to work independently and come to him if they had a question.

As requested, Haze arrived back at the bandroom at 3:16. Mister Brice looked up from his desk. "Ah!" He rubbed his hands together. "Mister DeCuir is on time and ready to play.

Very good." He stood and went to the piano next to the desk. "First let's see about your pitch." He struck random notes on the piano and asked Haze to sing them back. Haze did fine until one note was too low. Mr. Brice said, "You singing everything an octave lower, sing it on pitch."

"Oh," Haze realized. Then sang it on pitch.

"Nothing wrong with your ear," the bandleader concluded. "OK." Then he opened a trumpet case and said, "OK, why-ontcha play something for me?" He left the case on the desk and sat in one of the band chairs up front.

"Like…?" Haze ventured, "Like whatchu want me to play?"

"Oh, Flight of the Bumblebee, Shortnin' Bread, your choice."

Haze picked up the trumpet and slipped the mouthpiece in and thought for a second. He started tapping his foot and put the horn to his mouth and played "I'll Fly Away." Mister Brice sat there with his eyes closed but when Haze stopped, he opened them, said, "Huh? What?" and spun his hand like a movie director saying to keep going with the scene. So Haze nodded and did another chorus. Mister Brice stood up and nodded, too, grinning, going, "Uh huh, uh huh," and waving his hand, conducting, speeding up the tempo a bit. As Haze played faster, he played louder, too, and started getting into it a bit more. Suddenly Mister Brice said, "OK, OK," and Haze stopped. "Well, you got the feel. That's good. Now there's just one more matter to attend to." He went to a filing cabinet and pulled out a sheet of music, pulled up a music stand, pointed, and sat down again.

Haze was surprised at how easy the selection was. Some hymn or something. Half-notes and quarter-notes, nothing above or below the staff. When he was done Mister Brice stood up. "Not much feeling on that last one," he grumbled. "But hey, you got the job."

"Thank you Mister Brice."

"We gon' put you in the intermediate band, you not a beginner. You like marching?"

Haze couldn't hold back his first honest grin of the day, and Mister Brice returned it. "Yeah, Mister Watkins told me about you already," he confessed. "You'll do alright, long as you stay with the program."

Mr. Watkins was the bandleader at Douglass. Haze was surprised that these guys actually talked to each other.

"You like that horn?" Mister Brice asked.

"Yeah."

"Well, we'll sign you out that one, then."

<h1 style="text-align:center">4</h1>

Miranda met Jess in front of the cafeteria as planned. Jess was surprised the line was so short. Miranda brought her up to speed: "Cafeteria fare's not quite up to the palettes of most of our classmates." Jess asked if Miranda liked the food. "I'm not sure if 'like' is the right term, but it's OK."

They took their trays out to a bench under a big oak in the courtyard. Their lunches consisted of vinegary salads and red beans and rice. "Monday," Miranda explained, but Jess seemed already to know about the Monday red bean tradition. "It's the same in Pensacola," she said.

"They're OK if you dump enough salt on them," Miranda advised, which both girls proceeded to do.

While Miranda tried to think of something else to say, a boy she was hoping not to run into—Eli Wentzel—walked by. "Hi Miranda," he said, but didn't stop or even slow down very much.

"Who's that guy?" asked Jess.

"Oh, an old friend."

"He's kinda cute," said Jess. "Well, I didn't get a great look at him, but…"

"Yeah, I guess."

"Are y'all still friends?"

"Hmm…what do you mean?"

"I mean, you said he's an 'old friend' and does that mean like friends for a long time or used to be a friend?"

"I meant it the first way," Miranda said. "He's kind of a neighbor, too, lives around the corner from me. We were like street friends or sidewalk friends or whatever when we were kids. Now…well, we still say 'hi.'"

"I had lots of friends in my old neighborhood in Florida. But they kind of scattered after the storm. We lived right by the beach and we would just walk out of our houses and goof around on the beach. You'd always see everybody just by doing that. Never had to call people, make plans, talk to people's parents."

"Sounds like a teen utopia, like a Fox TV series!"

A frown came over Jess' face. Miranda wondered if she'd been too flip.

"I don't know," Jess said, "It *was* really neat. But not like a utopia or a movie or something."

"No shark attacks, huh?"

Jess frowned again as Miranda concluded the girl was too sensitive to have a light casual friendship with. That's all she wanted. If that's what friendship was, she was fine with it. But sometimes kids wanted to get so intense about things. "I'm sorry," Miranda said, "I'm sure you miss it. I didn't mean to make fun."

"Yeah," Jess said, "I guess I just still miss it too much to laugh about it. Like I miss the beach and the sound of the ocean and the smell. And, in a totally new place and school… like I miss my old friends, too, and you wonder if you'll ever make new ones."

"You've already made one!" Miranda exclaimed.

Jess looked warmed and tickled by this, but Miranda wondered if she was not perhaps getting into something she didn't really want to be involved in. At least she could tell her mom she made a new friend that day. After comparing schedules and seeing that they had no classes together besides homeroom, they exchanged phone numbers and went off to fifth period.

Miranda was happy, and relieved, to get back home that afternoon. She loved her house dearly. It was on a corner of leafy Calhoun Street, just a couple of blocks from Audubon Park. It was an eccentric house in the Queen Anne style, with a fanciful turret and lots of gingerbread moldings. The only flaw, Miranda thought, was that it had a smallish decorative porch encasing the front door, rather than one of the big wrap-around verandas that were so common in the neighborhood. On top of the porch was a cozy covered balcony—off her parents' bedroom—that she felt was woefully underutilized. She also wasn't particularly fond of the color scheme. It was pink with baby blue trim, as if her parents had looked forward to welcoming a girl and a boy, but changed their minds after having her. The paint-job looked about that old, too—they would have to re-paint soon, and Miranda hoped she would have some influence on color selection this time. The architectural feature most pleasing to Miranda was the great arched window on the second floor west wall—her bedroom, her studio for dreaming.

Jess called later that night. Miranda heard the phone ring, heard her mom padding down the hall, and then the knock on her door, "Miranda, for you!" She opened the door and took the cordless phone and went back into her room. Her worst fear had come to pass: Jess had called "just to talk." And Miranda had just been getting into this Civil War story she'd been writing. The city—some southern city—had been set alight by marauding troops, and her character had just gone into a flaming barn to save her beloved chestnut mare, Southwind (she wasn't happy with the name but it would do for now).

"Remember that guy who said hi today?" Jess asked.

"Yeah…?"

"He's in my history class."

"Who's the teacher?"

"Who?"

"The teacher? Who's teaching it?"

"Oh, I don't know. Mister…? I don't remember. Kind of an old guy."

Mister Petro, Miranda assumed. Miranda loved him. Quite an eccentric. Spoke in this old-fashioned dramatic accent, flourished his hands during lectures, which were designed like stories. She especially remembered the one about the assassination of Rasputin, all the different ways they tried to off him. Mister Petro did lots of gasping and limping and putting his hand to his brow in that one.

"Anyway, he asked about you," Jess said. "He asked if I was your friend."

"You mean Eli?" Miranda asked.

"Yeah, the cute guy. I think he really likes you. He said y'all used to be close."

"Yeah…we did."

"So what's the deal?"

Miranda wasn't sure what the deal was. She knew he liked her. And she liked him, too, but… "He just kinda wanted to go too fast I guess, got really intense."

"Oh," Jess breathed. "He seems like the intense type."

"Yeah," Miranda agreed. "But I'm just not sure I am."

"Have you like…had a boyfriend?"

"Oh, sure," Miranda said, "I'm sure everyone has had at least one by the time they get to be my age."

"Well, not me," Jess confessed. "Not really."

Miranda really didn't want to have this conversation, so she pretended her mother was calling her. "Oh, Jess, I have to run—I'm supposed to be helping my mom with the Baked Alaska."

"The what? What's that?"

"It's like a resplendent cake."

"Oh…"

She said she'd see her tomorrow and hung up. She sat back down at her writing desk, dipped her pen in the inkwell, but she'd lost her inspiration. She wandered downstairs to see what her mom and dad were doing. Turns out her mom was baking after all—Toll House cookies, though, not Baked Alaska, which, Miranda suddenly remembered, was a baked ice cream concoction she'd had at Antoine's, probably impossible to make at home.

"Who were you talking to?" her mom asked.

"A new girl."

"Do you like her?"

"I guess she's a friend."

Her dad came in from the den, robed and bespectacled and clutching some fat new political biography—he was in domestic heaven. He wanted to know how the cookies were coming along.

"Hey dad," Miranda asked, "You're friends with Ms. Barnigal at school, right?"

"Oh," he said, "I suppose. We haven't talked in a while."

"So y'all used to be friends, but not anymore?"

"You mean Maura?" her mom asked.

"Yes," said her dad.

Her mom said, "Yes, we haven't had her over in ages. Whatever happened to her?"

"Teaching at Hennican," Miranda reminded her.

"Yes, I suppose so."

"But why aren't y'all friends anymore?"

"Well," her dad ventured. "I'm not sure. Nothing definite. We just kind of grew apart, I guess."

"So you weren't like super friends?" Miranda asked.

"No," her dad replied. "Just acquaintances really. Just someone we thought was fun for a while, and then…I guess not anymore."

Her mom said, "Why do you want to know, dear? Is she one of your teachers?"

"This acquaintance concept is intriguing," Miranda

said. "Just someone to pass the time with for a while, but no strings, nothing like…owed."

"But sometimes," her mom cautioned, "acquaintances grow into real friendships. Every friend anyone's got started off as just an acquaintance, a co-worker, schoolmate. You never now where or when a deeper kind of companionship might bloom."

"So you're saying," Miranda guessed, "that I, or people in general, should follow all the leads they get, sort of like looking for a job?"

Her mother frowned, as if disapproving of something in Miranda's tone, but said, "Well, Miranda. Yes. That is what I'm saying."

Her dad looked skeptical but stayed mum.

5

Erik Uglesich endured the first two days of school just fine. No homework was really due yet, and that, at least, was a blessing. But the afternoon of the second day began the downward slide. It was open football try-outs, so he went and ran some reps for the coaches, even though everyone knew the serious players had already been at it for weeks. Everyone expected a lot from Erik on the field, and that level of expectation just jinxed him. With one brother at LSU and another at Louisiana Tech, he was supposed to continue the Uglesich dynasty at Archbishop Leray High School. He loved playing, too, but he couldn't do anything about his body, and his body just wasn't football material, especially not at running back. Not the way they built them these days. It would serve fine for punting or kicking, but those weren't his talents. It took him a while to come to terms, but he finally realized that five feet six and one-seventy-five had no future running, or even receiving, past junior high. He was already so bulked up he could barely blow his nose. One more protein shake and his skin would rip open. He knew his limitations, but others didn't seem to. The coaches gave him a lot of flak for not showing up until the walk-on try-out day. They accused him of not respecting himself. Hardly anybody made the squad from the open try-outs. In fact, the only reason he showed up for them was that he promised his dad. His dad didn't expect him to fill his brothers' shoes (he said), he just expected him to try (he said). So Erik had finally given up and spoken the magic words: "OK, OK, I'll go for the try-outs."

But it was hell on the field that day. Sizzling and steamy,

typical August. But unlike last year, Erik hadn't worked to keep his endurance up all summer. Last year he had given it his all but never got off the bench. This year, he figured, he would endure one afternoon of running around and embarrassing himself, but at least he wouldn't have to go tote Gatorade for the others every Friday night.

He lasted OK through the warm-ups, but running up the bleachers he began to feel queasy. The vague nauseous feeling got worse. They were running a circuit with tires and with a lot of stopping and pivoting when he slowed down, stumbled to the edge of the field, and lost his lunch with the most dignity he could summon (not much). He heard one of the coaches say "Isn't that Justin and Scotty's brother?"

They gave him an icy wet towel and walked him to the locker room with the utmost niceness used for sick weak people. It was fine with Erik, though. He just felt relief that the chapter was over. Football, athletics, they just weren't for him. For fun, sure, but not for bigtime competition.

But he had even bigger problems than that to worry about. Personal problems. Like the slow agonizing wait for his girlfriend to dump him.

That was the first order of business when he got home that day, he was sure. He pulled up the driveway and walked through the garage to the kitchen and, sure enough, his dad said she'd called a couple times already. "Yeah, yeah, dad," he said, "I figured."

""You don't sound too happy about it," his dad said. His dad was in his usual off-duty uniform around the house—t-shirt and boxers, flip-flops at the ready in case he had to go outside for some reason. He was drinking a Bud Light and watching the news on the little kitchen TV, even though they had a big 42-inch flat-screen in the family room.

"No," Erik admitted, "I'm not too happy about getting dumped."

"Oh, that what she's calling for?"

"I'm pretty sure." He popped a Hot Pocket into the microwave and then remembered his stomach probably couldn't handle it right now—so he pulled it out, put it back in the wrapper and returned it to the freezer.

"Wow," his dad said, "you DO got it bad!"

"I know what she's gonna say." Erik pulled a stool to the kitchen counter. "She's gonna want me to go to one of these clubs and I'm gonna say I can't stand it, I'm sick of those places, and she's gonna say that means I don't love her and then she's gonna say something like 'I don't think this is gonna work.'"

His dad laughed. "Congratulations, boy!" He patted him on the back. "You a man now!"

"Where's mom?" Erik asked.

"Hospital."

Erik knew she was probably at work, but he always asked because it was one of those things he'd always asked his dad. Came naturally, felt normal, like scratching an itch, like his dad stripping down to his underwear every time he got home. But Erik was glad his mom was working tonight. He was worried she'd try to make out it was his fault, whatever was going on with him and Ashleigh.

The phone rang again. His dad gestured toward it like saying, "you're up!" Erik took it in the family room. It was Ashleigh, all right. He flopped on the couch and asked her how she was doing.

He was right, she did want to go out that night. To the Funky Pirate on Bourbon Street. "Mallorie's going, and so is Holly, and Holly's new boyfriend's going to be there too. She's says we've got to meet him!"

"But it's like a Wednesday night. We got school tomorrow."

"When did you turn into Mister Serious Student?" she

snickered. "Don't worry, I can't be out late either. Mom says I gotta be back by ten. So definitely by eleven."

"Ugh, OK," Erik sighed.

"Hey, don't put yourself out for me! You don't wanna go, you don't wanna go."

"I don't wanna go," he confirmed. But knew from her silence that she wasn't really A-OK with this option. When she spoke again, she wove in her special sniffly tremor, like on the brink of tears—even though he'd never seen her actually cry in person.

"If you don't want to be seen with me or something, I can't do anything about that. That's your feelings and I can't change them."

But he wasn't going to backtrack and just go along with whatever she wanted anymore, even though he knew the consequences of not doing that. "You know it's got nothing to do with me not wanting to be seen with you. I just—going out all the time doesn't make sense to me. These places are crowded and smoky. You can't even talk. I just like stuff like a quiet night at home more."

"A quiet night at home, huh?" Now she sounded angry. "If you think you can call me up for some quiet-night-at-home hook-up, they gotta name for that kind of date and you can just get yourself some other easy skeezy for that!"

"I don't want to break up or anything." Actually, he realized this wasn't true. It dawned on him then that he did, in fact, want to break up. It just wasn't worth it to him to have the pretty perfect girlfriend that Ashleigh was, if the price was spending pointless money for covers in these clubs and arguing everyday about what was wrong with him that he didn't like passing the time that way. So, yes, he DID want to break up with her, or, more exactly, he wanted a break-up to take place, but he didn't want the onus on him.

"But," he continued, "maybe this is just not going to work

out, I mean, not in the long run."

She said nothing. He could see the look on her face as she sat there, a mix of indignation and triumph as he rolled out the rope.

"I mean," he soldiered on, "I like regular stuff like fishing and barbecuing and crawfish boils. I like going to places like Rocky and Carlo's or Jack Dempsey's, where you don't have to act a certain way. But putting on the monkey suit and standing around in some loud dark smoky club where you gotta shout to hear the guy next to you… And you gotta pay the cover and worry about the fake ID. I'm just never gonna like doing that kinda thing."

Another long silence. He started to feel a sense of dread. Like he'd made a terrible leap without thinking through the consequences.

"You?" Her voice was cracking, but he couldn't tell if it was from crying or laughter. Sounded like both, if that was possible. "YOU are dumping ME?! No *&$%ing WAY, buster!"

"We don't have to look at it like somebody dumping somebody."

"You ARE talking like somebody dumping somebody! All fake nice and considerate. Well, let me fill you in, you LOSER. This relationship has not been working for ME either."

"I'm sorry, Ashleigh."

"Sorry, you'll always be sorry because you can't stick with a *@#&ing thing. You blew off football, you're blowing off me, you're blowing off every chance you had. Because what? Because you like quiet nights at home?"

"Well," he considered. "Kind of." But that wasn't really true. He liked quiet nights out, too, like outside, under the stars, just not crowded loud cramped places in the city.

Now she really was crying. "Don't call me back," she

choked. "I never want to hear from you again." Then click, dial-tone, and she was gone.

Relief was his first sensation, that the phone call was over. But he knew the whole ordeal wasn't over inside him yet. He knew his room upstairs was full of pictures of her, of them together. He knew if he went up there right now he'd break down and sob hysterically and curl up in his bed like she was probably doing. He wasn't ready to go there yet. So he put it off. Like some operation you had to do, an ACL or something you knew was going to hurt but that you didn't have to rush into just yet.

He went to the kitchen instead. There was the little sign next to the microwave: "Whining Will Incur a Five Dollar Surcharge." His dad glanced at him and turned off the news. "You want to talk, son?" he asked.

"No," Erik said.

"You wanna go in the garage and punch the bag?"

"No."

"Some hoops?"

"No," Erik said. "I wanna shoot."

"OK," his dad nodded. He yawned and got up slowly and went into his room and came back in jeans and a shirt. After looking under the mail and the newspaper, he came up with his keys. He slapped Erik on the shoulder and said, "Let's go bag us some overgrown rats. C'mon."

St. Bernard Parish, where they lived, had offered a bounty for nutria tails. Just five bucks a tail, but it was lot more than the price of the bullet. The nutria had gotten to be a nuisance, had been eating into the levees. Erik and his dad had made fifty bucks since the ordinance was passed early in the summer. They threw some gear in the back and drove over to the Forty Arpent Canal, where supposedly lots of the pesky giant rodents were roaming free and burrowing holes everywhere. They brought along Erik's .22 mag and his dad's new

17 caliber HMR. They were both fitted out with scopes. At the foot of the access road that ran along the Forty Arpent levee, Erik hopped out of the cab and into the bed of the pickup. He trained a spotlight along the opposite shore as his dad cruised along slowly in second gear. After a mile or so Erik spotted one. He pounded twice on the top and the truck stopped. His dad got out with the guns.

"You wanna take the first one?" he asked.

"Yeah."

His dad set the guns down in the bed and climbed up. He took the spotlight while Erik slid open the bolt and loaded a shell.

"He's a big'un," his dad said. "Too bad we not getting paid for the meat."

"Maybe he's got an extra-long tail."

The nutria didn't seem too disturbed by the bright spotlight on it. On the other hand, Erik only had one round in his .22, so he'd have to score a hit or it would scamper for sure. He tried to think of the best perch to shoot from, where he'd have some support for his shoulder and some balance.

"Right here, son," his dad suggested, pointing right in front of him.

Erik knelt in front of his dad, who drew one leg up onto the edge of the truck. So Erik was in a neat corner made by the back of the cab and his dad's body. He felt centered, comfortable. So much so that he knew he would make the shot.

"Uh-oh," his dad grunted—the big beaver-like rodent had gotten spooked, started skipping up the bank. But Erik had already been sighting. He adjusted and pulled the trigger. The rifle popped and the quarry jerked into the air, then rolled down the bank and splashed into the reedy marsh grasses lining the canal.

6

Haze's first week of school had gone pretty well. He hadn't been late again after that first day—the St. Claude bus was on a winning streak. But then, he reasoned, so were the Saints. And it was pre-season for both of them, with a trying schedule ahead. Anyway, he was feeling good because he'd made first chair in the intermediate concert band and was first second in the marching band. Thursday afternoon he picked up his uniform and headed back home to the Lower Ninth Ward. He got off the bus at Lizardi Street and walked the two blocks to his house, a double shotgun set a few feet back from the sidewalk. It had once been a shade of dark purple, but now it looked just generally dusty. If it ever had shutters for the tall windows, they were long gone. In between the cracked concrete walkways to the two stoops on either side of the duplex was a patch of sandy dirt and grass. His cousin and uncle were sitting on his stoop when he approached.

"Say blood," his cousin said, "Whatchu got there?"

"That's my band uniform."

"You made the marching band?" his cousin asked in a high voice that Haze knew was a set-up. "You playing or just filling out the '9' on 39? They let you take your mouthpiece on the field?"

Haze ignored him because his Uncle Lionel was dapping him some respect. "OK, then," Uncle Lionel said. "Be looking for you on the parade route."

His cousin, Corey, jumped off the stoop. "Say Haze, "he said, "They got the hard schoolwork over there? With all the homework and all that other &*&%?"

"It's not that hard," Haze admitted. "But you gotta do it."

Corey looked disheartened and Uncle Lionel let out a big laugh. "Boy how you gon' work it out that you never have to work a day in your life?" he demanded to know. "You figure out the secret—and stay alive, too, and not in no jail—you tell me, I been ready to retire since the day you was born. Haze here getting it together."

"Haze getting it together, I'm KEEPing it together," Corey retorted. He pulled a big blunt from his oversized white Dickey workshirt pocket and lit it up. He took a puff and passed it to Haze. Haze reached out for it, then took his hand back. "Naw," he said, "I ain't doing that."

Corey stared in wonder, pointed at him, glanced at Uncle Lionel and said, "Check'im out! The SCHOOLboy don't be doing that. Uh-huh," he nodded. "Well ain't that studious. You worried it gon' fry your brain?"

"Naw," Haze said. "They testing us, if you wanna play in the band."

"Testing you?" Corey asked in wide-eyed wonder. "Whachu mean? They leave Hubig Pies laying on the teacher desk and they got a secret camera?"

"Naw," Haze laughed. "They testing our DNA or some *&^%, ya heard me? I don't know how it work."

"Man," Corey pushed.

"Boy, shut up," Uncle Lionel cut in. "They pissin' this boy, he out the band if he fail."

"They taking my hair."

"All of it?" Corey snickered.

A voice called out Haze's name from the front window. It was his mom.

"Haze, that you?" She appeared at the screen door. "Don't listen to these bums."

"I got a job," Uncle Lionel protested. "I ain't no bum."

"You got a bum job," she countered. "That your uniform

Haze? Come show me."

Haze stepped around Lionel. His mom said, "Lionel, get off my stoop and let my son come up in here. Whatchu hanging on my stoop for anyway? Y'all smoking that stuff on my stoop? Move it on down the street!"

"OK, OK sister." Uncle Lionel gave in and got up. "C'mon Corey, I got some work for you."

"Aw, man!"

Haze dapped them off and they sauntered away. His mom called after them, "Say hi to your mama for me, y'hear?"

Haze went in the house and his mom collapsed on the couch and said, "Let me see that uniform. You gonna try it on for me?"

"Naw," Haze said. "I'm worried I'ma spill something on it."

"Well, you might could," she agreed. "Don't worry, I'm not gon' make you wear it, I just want you to know I'm proud of you."

"Thanks, mom."

"Here, let me get it hung up." She got up and took it, held it up, said "Hm-hm!" and put it in the big chifforobe in her room, where he kept his nice clothes.

He followed her into the kitchen, where she was cooking spaghetti. "What Uncle Lionel doing, mama?"

"Oh, you know, he driving a truck, keeping busy. Doing some hauling."

"How the family doing?"

"He trying to keep Corey in school and he don't wanna go. But Malik doing real well and Trianna and Kimberly OK, too."

But Haze didn't hear the name he was most interested in, and his mom knew it. "That's great," he said. "That they all doing great. How about Corey and Malik and Trianna uncle? How he doing?"

He was referring to his dad.

"They uncle doing the usual. He OK."

Haze nodded.

"He around, Haze. He'll come around. You know he always do."

"Yeah, I know."

What she didn't understand was that Haze didn't really need him to come around. What he really craved was information. He just wanted to know what the man did with his time, and he wasn't really sure. Anyway, Haze had grown at least a couple of inches since the last time the man "came around."

His mom pulled some lettuce out of the fridge and started tearing it into a bowl. "I'm worried about this here storm they say might be coming up," she said.

"They got a storm coming?"

"Maybe. And you know what maybe mean."

"Mean you gotta work."

"You remember for Ivan last year," she sighed.

He sighed too. Then groaned. "Aw, mama, I don't wanna be spending no night in the hospital. I ain't sick."

"You know how I feel about you spending a whole night here alone-"

"Mama, I spend every night here alone—every night you working."

"But I don't leave out till 10 for the regular night shift, and for the storm they have me there the whole day and night."

"Mama, that last hurricane was a chump. Wasn't hardly even no rain."

"I know," she assured him, "I know. It ain't about the storm. It's about you being all alone in here."

"I could stay by Uncle Lionel," Haze offered.

"You know Kimberly ain't staying for no hurricane. She evacuate for a thunderstorm."

"Aw, mama." Haze had no more arguments. His grandmother had passed, a year ago, so he didn't have that option. He just hated hospitals. It made him feel sick just being in one, even if he was just there because his mom was an employee. "Why they need medical records people for a storm anyway?" he demanded. "You ain't fixing nobody broken leg." It's the same thing he asked last year, and he got the same answer.

"You know they need a regular staff, they need all the people work there. I had to sign up for storm duty the day I took the job." She shook her head. "And that was a bright sunny day, else I might not'a done it."

"Well maybe it ain't coming. When it's supposed to get here?"

"We'll know by Saturday for sure what it's doing." She set the salad bowl on the table and sat down and put her hand on Haze's cheek. "My boy," she smiled. "You done got handsome. Denzel Washington from the islands, hee-hee!" Her grin faded, like she was thinking. "I tell you what, my little man," she said, and Haze knew she was going to throw him something. "If it looks like it ain't coming or ain't coming close, or it ain't that big, you could stay here. You can handle it." She patted him on the thigh and got up and went back to the stove.

7

The phone woke Miranda. She knew it was late but she couldn't read her old-timey wind-up alarm clock in the dark. She heard footsteps coming to her door and then a little knock and her dad's voice, "Miranda? You up?"

"I guess," she said, and got out of bed and went to the door. Her dad handed her the phone and whispered, "She sounds distraught."

It was Jess. "O my god I know it's coming."

"What?" Miranda asked. "And what time is it?"

"The storm, the hurricane," Jess warned. "Katrina."

Miranda's second question went unanswered, but she turned on the bedside lamp and saw it was almost midnight. "What, are you staying up watching the weather channel? Is it coming before morning?"

"You think it's funny because you haven't been through it."

"Sure I have. Hurricanes just aren't a big deal here."

"Y'all have just been lucky."

"No, Jess," Miranda tried to explain. "Listen. Remember that thing you liked most about Pensacola?"

"My friends?"

"The beach! Remember?"

"Yes?" Jess said, slowly, as if to suggest 'so what?'

"Well, have you seen a beach in New Orleans?"

"No."

"That's because we're not right on the ocean. We're sur-rounded by land! Well, swamp. Anyway, even a really pow-erful storm would lose some steam over the wetlands and be weaker by the time it got to us. So what I'm saying is…" she had to think for a second. "What I'm saying is that a hurricane just can't do as much damage here in the city as on the beach in Florida."

"Are you sure?" Jess sounded ready to put great store in Miranda's response.

"Sure, I'm sure. All the damage from hurricanes around here is always on the outskirts, like the Mississippi coast or Grand Isle and places like that. Here in the city we get a couple of broken windows, a tree down or two…" She darted a glance through the window to the sycamore outside. It was totally still.

"I just feel like something's following me," Jess said, "like I've done something and storms are going to track me down every year no matter where I go."

Miranda said, "That's a cool idea."

"No, Miranda," Jess corrected, "That's a scary idea."

"But where do you live?" Miranda asked.

"Argonne Boulevard."

"Where's that?"

"Lakeview."

"That's in the city right?"

"Yeah."

"Then you're fine. The only neighborhoods that get flooded in the city are the poor ones. It's sad and unjust, but the middle class areas are on higher ground, or have better pumps or something. So you don't have to worry."

"I don't want to worry," Jess sighed, "believe me. I'm sick of worrying."

"Anyway, why do you even think it's coming this way? On the news before it said it was going to—" she stopped short but it was too late.

"Pensacola," Jess volunteered. "I know. But it can't be. Why would it hit exactly the same place two years in a row?"

"But why do think it's going to end up coming here?"

"Maybe it's y'all's turn finally." There was a slight note of venom in her voice. "A lot of people think New Orleans deserves it."

For the first time Miranda's vague sense of annoyance with her new acquaintance turned into dislike. "Whatever," she said, "I'm tired, I gotta go," and hung up.

Twenty-four hours later the track had indeed veered far closer to New Orleans. Winds had increased to Category 5, the highest on the scale. This meant Miranda had to go with either her mom or her dad, since both

would have to shelter in place at their separate hospitals. For a while she had hoped they might let her just stay alone at home, but the warnings on TV kept getting more and more dire.

"I could invite Jess over," she entreated, "so we wouldn't be totally alone."

Her parents responded in unison: "Forget it."

"Pack your usual bag," her mom said. "We're going to Sinai."

"Dad!" Miranda moaned.

"What?" her dad said, "You want me to say you can stay here alone, or with some friend you just met, for twenty-four, forty-eight hours, no one checking in on you, the whole street evacuated?" His voice rose. "With God knows who roaming the streets and the 911 system suspended!? Pack your bag!"

Her mom grimaced like she always did when her dad yelled. But really they took turns at it. When mom was the one to yell at her, then it was dad's turn to scowl in disapproval.

"Let's just…" her mom started, in her quietest tone.

"Miranda," her dad softened up. "You're just too precious to leave at home. We're lucky that, at times like this, we can actually bring you to work with us so we know you're close. OK? Now it's up to you if you want to go to Sinai or Lake Forest, but those are your choices."

This was the concession Miranda had been seeking. "Well," she ventured, carefully, "I went to Sinai last time…"

"Fine," her dad concluded. "You can come with me."

Now it was her mom's turn to scowl, and to hurl her coffee mug into the sink and stomp out, as Miranda knew she would. She always took decisions like this so personally, like Miranda was choosing one parent over the other. Well, maybe she was, but it wasn't her fault if her mom got so worked up over it.

8

Erik had never seen anything like it on Fleur de Lis Court before. But, of course, the neighborhood—Village Beauchamps—was only a few years old. It consisted of five concentric crescents off St. Bernard Highway, wide concrete drives bordered by wide lawns, long driveways, and five or six different house models, all with an underused brick walkway. Most of the houses were in some subtle shade of stucco, and most had two stories. The Uglesich home was called the "Charles VI." Attached to the multi-car garage on the right was a perfect two-story rectangle with a reasonably pitched roof—not too steep to walk on if repairs were needed. They had added a big deck in the back. And a bamboo stand to separate the yard from the drainage canal behind it. Besides the bamboo, most of the plants in the subdivision were palm trees, not yet very tall.

But Erik hadn't seen what he saw today in his old neighborhood, either: everybody in their driveways loading up their trucks at the same time. Like the whole subdivision had won tailgate passes for Tiger Stadium. Except people were acting more frantic than they would for football, even though they talked down the thing they were running from. "Be just like Ivan," "We probably wasting our time," that kind of thing.

Erik strolled over to his neighbor across the street. Mister LaBruzzo was under the hood of his truck, a 1975 F150. They greeted each other and Erik said, "You staying or leaving?"

Mister LaBruzzo straightened up and looked both ways down Fleur de Lis Court. "Everybody leaving," he said, "Nobody staying for this one."

"That's what it looks like," Eric said. "Looks weird."

"People scared of this one. Calling it the Big One on the news."

"Yeah," Erik agreed. "Mayor Nagin called it the 'Storm We've Always Feared!'"

"Yep."

"I don't know," Erik wondered aloud. "Sounds kinda hyped up to me."

"Prob-ly. Course, nobody wants to take a chance, y'know? You heard what Harry Lee said, huh?"

Harry Lee was the Chinese-American cowboy sheriff of Jefferson Parish, highly respected for being a straight shooter, both with a gun and with his mouth. "Naw," Erik said, "What did he say?"

"They asked him his advice on the radio. He said, 'Haul ass, pardner'!"

"OK," Erik said. "Where you headed then?"

"I got my sister in Tangipaho."

Erik surveyed the street again. "Weird," he repeated. "Like 'Independence Day'."

Mister LaBruzzo looked confused.

"Y'know, that movie? When Will Smith comes out his house and gets his paper and everybody's running and… packing up…?"

Mister LaBruzzo seemed to not approve of movies. "Alright, then," Erik called, and crossed the street back to his house. His mom was slumping over the kitchen counter in her scrubs, watching the news and looking exhausted. She'd just gotten back from the night shift. "Guess you're coming to Lake Forest with me," she said.

Last year, for Ivan, he'd gone with her, too. But she was at Charity then, so he thought at least Lake Forest would be cleaner, more modern, less ghetto.

"Guess so," he replied. He didn't like it but he knew not

to gripe. That's the way it worked in his house. Clear chain of command. He liked it that way, really. It was the opposite at Ashleigh's house. She was a pro at complaining and whining every situation to her advantage. When the phone rang, Erik knew it was her. He said, "I'll get it," even though his mom wasn't exactly racing to the phone.

He took it in the family room, while he flipped through the channels on their big new flatscreen. He knew Ashleigh would love and milk the drama of the day, and she was. "What's going to happen?" she wanted to know, her voice vibrating with the thrill of it all.

"People leave for a couple days. Come back. We'll probably get Monday off, hopefully Tuesday, too."

"But they say it could be the *Big One*."

"That's what they said for Ivan, Georges," Erik yawned. "What are y'all doing?"

"Going to Destin. Dad's loading up the car now."

"Destin? What if it changes back to Florida?"

"Dad doesn't think it will. He says it's our turn. Camille and Betsy were a long time ago, and now it's our turn again."

Erik remembered the Betsy and Camille tales well. Their parents and all their parents' friends had their Betsy stories. About going into the attic with an axe and hacking through the roof. That's when they all lived in the Ninth Ward, though, and it wasn't a hurricane that drove them out.

Village Beauchamps wasn't old enough to have a hurricane record. Erik thought it was a shame that he couldn't stay and score his own stormy adventure story. They had a second floor. A generator. A boat. Instead he'd be stuck in the hospital with the sick people. And no job to do. Just told to stay out of the way like a kid. But there was no point dwelling on it— would just make him needlessly mad and make it all worse.

Ashleigh wanted to talk about their relationship. Erik didn't. He said, "Don't worry about it Ashleigh, I'll call you in a couple days, when y'all get back." The truth was he was already done with it. He'd already gone up to his room and ogled the pictures of them together and curled up and cried. The job was already done. Why go back and do it all over again? "Have fun at the beach," he said.

"Remember when you went with us last summer? When we snuck out?"

"Look, I gotta help my mom get ready."

"Love you—"

"Talk to you soon, bye babe."

His mom had already gone to her room to get some sleep when he got back to the kitchen. On the news—it would be all news all the time now until the storm passed—they were showing the evacuation routes, already starting to bunch up. The interstate would be a parking lot in just a couple of hours. So some people, he figured, including Ashleigh, had it worse than him. Nothing could be worse than being locked in a metal cage with bickering parents on a highway to nowhere.

9

Haze stuffed his backpack with a change of clothes, a math textbook, a notebook, a trumpet book called 'Lip Science', and his Nintendo DS, and climbed into the passenger seat of their old clunky Ford Escort. His mouthpiece was in his pocket. The distant low rumble of hurricane winds had been going on since early that morning, but there was hardly a breeze you could actually feel yet. Every now and then one big gust would come out of nowhere and knock over garbage cans and flip open unsecured shutters. But then it would go back to the dead stillness where you couldn't even imagine a storm was anywhere near.

They didn't talk on the drive to the hospital. Haze was still angry that his mom had finally made him go when she had said earlier he could stay home. The hype on the tube had been too much. Especially when Mayor Nagin had come on that morning—Sunday—and announced a mandatory evacuation. His mom called on the Lord and Haze noticed a wave of real worry cross her face. "They've never done that before," she said. "They must know something they not telling us."

The area around Lake Forest hospital seemed safer than their own. Haze's mom breathed a sigh of relief on the New Orleans East side of the Industrial Canal Interstate 10 bridge—called the "High Rise"—as if the hurricane were on their heels and for some reason couldn't cross over to this part of the city. "The old neighborhood was no place to be during Betsy," she explained. "We had water up in the house. Me and your auntee was scared to get down off the bed 'cause they had rats swimming around in that dirty water. We was on that bed for a few hours before that water went down. And then the mess—"

Haze had heard it all before. Every time a storm made it into the Gulf, the Betsy stories got pulled out of the trunk and dusted off. Haze noticed one time how all the houses in his neighborhood seemed to lean in one direction. Uncle Lionel said Betsy's winds had done it, and joked how they needed another storm from a different direction to knock them back straight again.

Lake Forest looked more like a regular American neighborhood from TV. Black Brady Bunch neighborhood. None of the houses leaned because they were all made of brick. Cream brick, yellow brick, red brick, brown brick. Single story with sliding glass doors in the back and picture windows facing front. Lots of pools. On the other hand they were built right flat on the ground instead of up on bricks like the houses in their neighborhood. "That's 'cause it don't flood around here," his mom told him.

Lake Forest Boulevard itself was more industrial. Warehouses, a couple strip malls, their favorite Chinese buffet. His mom pulled into a Beauty Mart parking lot across the boulevard from the hospital. "They ain't gon' be checking," she said. The store was closed and boarded up already. The only other car was an abandoned Buick Riviera with four flat tires and a busted-out passenger window.

"Why aintcha park in the hospital lot?" Haze huffed, exasperated.

"You pay for my sticker, I'll park in the lot."

"But you work up in there, mama!"

"I work up in there!" she hooted. "That don't mean you get to park for free!"

They went into the ER reception area and his mother dropped her bag behind one of the four computer stations facing the waiting room and said "c'mon," and led him through big automatic double doors down another hall to an elevator. They got out on the second floor and saw a very different paint job than the one downstairs—bright blue, with clouds, and pictures of Mickey, Dora, Spiderman. The pediatric wing. Haze groaned with recognition.

"Why they gotta put us in the kiddie hospital?" Haze complained.

"'Cause you a kiddie!"

The real reason was the suite-style rooms, to accommodate visiting family members longer term. Or it was the big vending lounge at the end of the hall, which included a dispenser of apples and bananas (when stocked). Or maybe they always assumed some employee would bring the little bitty kids who could enjoy the play area with the blocks, puzzles, plush books, etc. It took up about a quarter of the room and was padded and cordoned off by a row of big vinyl rectangles. It made a comfy chilling spot, anyway. But Haze had never seen a kid in there and the chairs and tables were too small for him.

Haze plopped into one of the grown-up chairs, at a grown-up table, whipped out his Nintendo DS and cued up Madden's NFL. His mom said something about what room they were supposed to bed down in and disappeared downstairs.

A bit later he heard people coming down the hall. A guy was saying something softly, he couldn't hear, but he heard the girl, much louder—"I know, dad, I know." Then she said, "208, right," and, after more inaudibles from the dad, "Dad, I've got your cel—I'll just call you." Then the dad walked back away down the hall and the girl came in. She was a medium-height, medium-build white girl, on the pale side, with reddish brown slightly wild hair stuck up on her head with a pencil. Wearing black jeans and sandals and a big oversize white dress shirt with rolled-up sleeves. She turned and gave Haze a tiny little courtesy smile and kept walking over to the play area, where she slid down to the floor, back to Haze, leaning on a big orange rectangle. She unzipped her backpack and pulled out a book and a notebook and a pen. Then she pulled out a little jar and set it carefully on the floor. She opened the jar, then took the back off of her pen and dipped it on the jar. She tapped the pen lightly on the side and put it back together, then sealed the jar. She started writing or drawing something on the pad.

Haze went back to his game. After a couple of blown plays the girl was talking to him. "Huh?" he said.

"My name's Miranda, what's yours?" She had turned to face him and was looking right at him. She had these greenish eyes that just tried to pry right into you. Haze doubted he'd ever seen anybody look right in somebody's eyes that way unless it was some serious deal, definitely never somebody you just met.

"Um, I'm Haze"

"Haze?" she repeated.

"Yeah."

"Like purple haze?"

"Yeah," he smiled, "like purple haze."

Haze thought she looked like some kind of elf, like she should be wearing one of those Santa outfits, like one of his helpers. It was her hair and eyes that made her look like that.

"Miranda?" he repeated.

She nodded and said "nice to meet you" and turned back around.

He went back to his game but she turned around again and asked "What do you think about that rumble?"

"What?" He wasn't sure what she meant. "Outside? From the storm?"

She nodded, "Hm-mm."

"It's wind. Big wind," he said. "Depends on how close it hit you."

Miranda squinted and said, "It makes it sound like another planet."

10

Erik and his mom arrived at Lake Forest around six pm, the same time his dad reported for duty at the 3rd district police station in the city. The streets were totally deserted on the drive over. Gusts and squalls had begun, but nothing major. They avoided the interstate but noticed, when crossing it on an overpass, that the traffic had eased up a lot from the day before. Whoever was going had gone—everybody remaining, which seemed to be very few, had elected to roll the dice and stay. In an hour or so they'd close the bridges out of town and the city would be shut off from the outside world until the storm passed. Might be a fun prospect for people old enough to legally party, but that wasn't Erik. He would be stuck with mom in some hospital. Erik had watched his share of football, but he'd never seen a Bud Light commercial in a hospital.

Erik hadn't been to this particular hospital before—his mom had only been at Lake Forest a couple of months—so he was taken aback when they installed him in the pediatric wing. He found the room assigned to him especially creepy. Not the gurney or reclinable chair, rather the images of grinning Care Bears floating into the clouds grasping balloons. Too much. So he strolled down the hall to the lounge. They had the TV on with the usual wall-to-wall coverage of an empty city with no storm yet for an excuse. There was a black guy sitting at the table and a white girl on the floor in the toddler zone. They both seemed about his age. The black guy was wearing a red New York Yankees cap and a matching red New York Yankees jersey with white pinstripes, open over an XXL white t-shirt. Erik couldn't understand why they would change the colors on the Yankees gear to something different than the official team's. Red? Why? Like Cincinnati? What was wrong with the regulation white and navy? Why would any true fan do something like that? Ashleigh had pink LSU and Saints gear, but Erik figured that was just a girl thing. He saw the black guy had a Nintendo DS with Madden loaded up. "That Madden '04?" he asked.

"Uh-huh," he said, without looking up.

"Like it?"

"It's alright."

"Who you got throwing?"

"McNabb."

Erik laughed. "Hope he's more consistent for you than he is for the Eagles."

The black guy didn't say anything. Not very polite, but whatever. Erik pulled up a chair and drummed his fingers on the table and stared at the TV screen, wondering how he was going to get through these interminable hours stuck in this stuffy building. He'd much rather go outside, wear a helmet or whatever, and see some action. He could take a video cam and be a stormchaser, sell his footage to WWL. Anything but locked in a closet for "his own safety." He was sick of hearing about "his own safety." He just wished he had something real to do, to actually help instead of being the object of help, which was the most boring thing imaginable.

11

Haze knew what the white boy's problem with McNabb was. He could tell from his accent that he was one of those white guys that didn't like black quarterbacks. Miranda turned around and introduced herself, same way she'd done with him. The white boy's name was Erik. He seemed just as thrown off by her style of talking to people as Haze had been. He said "nice to meet you" to her and turned toward Haze and extended his hand. "Erik," he said, and Haze said "Haze," and they shook, and then Erik seemed to want to do a snap at the end, but Haze wasn't expecting it so he didn't follow through. They all just looked at the TV for a while. Well, Haze and Erik did, but the girl was plugged into her ipod and scribbling on her pad.

Haze dug through his booksack trying to find the adapter for his Nintendo, but—and it made him want to cry and kick something at the same time—he'd left it at home. Indicator was already on red, too. He had no idea what he was going to bury himself in now—if he did it in the math book, would anybody believe it? Or would it be like reading a book upside down in the movies? "Lip Science" was even more of a drag than the math book was. He liked playing a horn, not reading about it. Looked like he was going to have to get sociable with the company that was available.

On the news they were telling people it was too late to leave. Now was the time to "hunker down," like they always said. Haze said, "How you think it gon' go?"

"I don't know," Erik said. "Down to a category 4. Probably brush us on the south. Bad for Plaquemines."

"It could be bad for us all." It was Miranda again. Apparently her ipod wasn't on that loud. She was turned around facing them again from her camp over in the kiddie zone. "But we wouldn't know it. And it's not our fault. Because we haven't had a big one like this so close our whole lives, right?" She nodded with her eyebrows raised, waiting for an answer.

"Naw, no," Haze and Erik said.

"So we don't know what to imagine," she went on. "We don't have the pictures in our imagination to go to, so it's unthinkable. I mean what a BAD STORM might be like."

"Could be like Betsy," Haze offered.

"I don't think it'll be that bad," Erik said. "I think the media and the government want to keep people shaking in their boots all the time about something. Or else they're scared people'll sue 'em later. They got to talk it up like it's the end of the world every time."

They all agreed on the subject of hype, but had different opinions about the reasons for it. Haze thought it was good for media and government to sound the alarm loudly, even if it might end up a false alarm. "'Else people ain't doing &*%$," he explained. "They be sitting around watching Jerry Springer while they house be floating down the river."

"What's really going on," Miranda opined, "is that people desperately want adventure—and it's too bad in our comfortable times we can't really have it. Bad stuff happened in the past and that makes the past full of drama. Not for us, though. We only wish."

Erik winced, like he hated what she said, but didn't know how to express it, or didn't want to offend the girl.

"Yeah," Haze said, "OK." He didn't know how to get involved in this conversation and he didn't really want to. He decided he'd just nod and smile and agree as much as he could—he'd be out of here by tomorrow night anyway.

He did like the adventure of a storm, though. So in a way

the girl had a great point. Matter of fact, he was antsy for it to get started. The TV hype had gone on long enough, and it never seemed like you got a real storm out of it. Just extra windy and not even much rain, that's the way he remembered all the ones from before. But this one had that rumble sound low and constant even when the weather didn't seem rough at all.

12

Miranda's eyes flew open even before she was totally awake. Something had banged into the window above her head. She was alone in the lounge. She brushed her hair back and picked up her stuff and moved away from the window, to the interior wall on the other side of the room. The two boys must have retired to their beds. That was fine with her. She couldn't think of anything to talk about with them. The low rumble had become a serious howl now, detailed up and down with low crunchy groans, wild rattling, and high whistles. You could also hear stuff crashing, and a persistent sound of bending or stretching metal. The window kept getting splashed and re-splashed with torrents of rain always coming from a different direction, like an avant-garde robot with paintbrushes was doing it. Then things starting slapping into the window and getting blown off again—a plastic bag, a soiled cloth, a chunk of shredded tire. She could almost feel the wind under and around her, like it was worming itself through the very pores of the concrete building. It also felt as if the building itself was straining, stretching, and there was a sound to match that, too.

Haze came in. Looking sleepy, and, Miranda was surprised to notice, possibly a little scared, too. "It's going now, huh?" he said.

"Yes," Miranda answered. "This must be it." The clock on the wall read 5:30. It would be light soon. That would be better. Hurricanes were creepier in the dark. But she already felt a let-down that it could never really be creepy enough. She was just too old. The simple things like storms didn't produce the thrill they once did.

13

Haze approached the window carefully. It was supposed to
be hurricane-proof glass—that's why it wasn't shuttered—but
he still worried about some giant object flying through it and
crushing his head. His curiosity beat out his fear, though. He
just had to see what was going on outside.

"Be careful over there," he heard Miranda say. The view
from the window was patchy because of irregular splashes of
heavy rain. But he saw the Beauty Mart across the street had
lost its sign. It had landed on the abandoned car a few feet
from his mom's. The parking-lot's security lights were still
on—so were the streetlamps. Next to the Beauty Mart, a gas
station canopy had toppled over, also smashing a car. Plastic
trashcans were airborne, flying along several feet up in the air
like kites, until slamming into a building. Then they rolled
along the side of the building and took off in the air again.
A gurney had rolled out of the hospital somehow and was
moving steadily across the parking lot, like it knew where it
wanted to go. Then it stopped and shifted slightly and began
an equally determined roll in a different direction. A huge industrial dumpster was also making its way across the parking
lot, just more slowly. The palms lining the front of the hospital
were bent almost all the way over. Then they would pop back
up again, briefly, before getting pushed back down. Behind
the Beauty Mart something very large was flapping around,
like a tarp or a circus or event tent. Haze squinted and leaned
closer into the window. Then he jumped back and even let out
a little shriek as something struck the window right in front
of his nose. He ducked as if it were coming right at him. Some

flat grainy square, about a foot long. It was joined by several others, but then they blew off again. Haze decided they were roofing tiles. Peering through the window again, he saw the big flapping thing behind the Beauty Mart was a corrugated tin roof, painted white. It lifted up high, as if ready to float off on the wind, then slapped back down again, like it was tied down with a bungee cord. But when it rose, stuff flew out from under it. Sheets or blankets or something, Haze couldn't tell. Looked like ghosts.

Then the streetlights went out and all Haze could see was an inch past the glass, just a fog of driving raindrops and crawling waves of wind, punctuated by roofing tiles slapping the glass.

"Streetlights out," Haze muttered.

"It'll be getting light soon," Miranda said.

"If they weren't no hurricane," countered Haze.

Haze's mom came in. "Stand back from that window, boy! You got a death wish?" She seemed only then to notice someone else was in the room—Miranda—and Haze knew she felt embarrassed to have spoken that way with strangers around. "How you doing, mama?" he asked. She said fine, that she was just checking in. There wasn't much to do down-stairs at the moment. If there was to be a flood of emergency patients, they wouldn't start flowing in until the winds died down. She had been on-line but they lost internet . They looked up at the TV and saw that cable was out, too. There was just a fuzzy jumpy image from the metal in the coaxial cable acting as an antenna. When they turned the volume up they just heard mostly loud static and an occasional intel-ligible word. Haze thought he heard an expert saying they "dodged the bullet."

Miranda said, "At least we still have power." And then, on the downbeat, the lights went out.

14

Erik faded out of his thin sleep when the hospital generator rumbled on. It wasn't any louder than the storm itself, but it signaled some kind of change in his environment. So he sat up, listened, and, when the lights in his room automatically turned on, including an array of beeps and blinkers, he knew what had happened. He looked at his cell phone: 6:00 am. He decided he might as well give up trying to sleep. The storm had been making a ruckus for at least a couple of hours, and, before that, the guy in the room next to his—the black guy named Haze—was stomping around his room for some reason and blowing into a duck call or a kazoo, sounded like.

He got up off the reclining chair and went to the sink and splashed some water on his face. He turned on the TV but it was only static—cable out. Then his mom came in and asked him how he'd slept. He said OK.

"My turn to try to sneak some winks now," she said. "Glad that generator works."

"Me too," Erik agreed. "Probably turn into an oven in here without it."

"Saint Peter would have some arrivals to process, too," she added.

Erik remembered then that there were actually real patients in the building. He asked his mom how many they had.

"Oh, just about twenty lying in."

That didn't seem like too many.

"But we got to be ready for more when the storm dies down."

"What would they be coming in for?" Erik wondered.

His mom thought for a second. "Concussions, lacer-ations, heart attacks from exertion." She had been an RN for about five years now—Erik remembered when she had finished nursing school, right around when his older brother Justin was having his big year in the pocket for Archbishop Leray. At the time Erik was giddy with anticipation for his turn to be like Justin. He found out nature doesn't work that way. Distributes different gifts to different brothers—the trick was in discovering what those gifts were, because, though nature left hints, they were pretty subtle and surrounded by false leads.

"Most hurricane injuries and deaths," his mother contin-ued, in that textbook tone she adopted when talking techni-cal, "happen during clean-up, like from live power lines in the street and people playing with chainsaws." She was settling into the bed and pulling a sheet over her. Erik reached over her and hugged her. She said, "Mmmm," as she squeezed him, then "see you in a few, lamb-chop."

She had called him "lamb-chop" routinely when he was a boy, but less and less over the past couple years. He replied with the term he remembered from the glory days of his early boyhood—"OK, mommy-chop." Then he left her to rest and headed out toward the lounge.

In the hall he called his dad on his cel.

"How y'all doing over there?" Erik asked.

"We OK," his dad said. "In a few hours we'll be on the backside of the eye and we'll go out on a patrol. Keep the knuckleheads in line. How y'all doing?"

"Fine," Erik said. "Lost power but the generator kicked in."

"We still got power over here but ready if it goes. Y'all got water over there?"

"I don't know. Haven't really looked. Does it flood over here?"

"They get street flooding in the big downpours. Might not be able to drive for a few."

"As long as I'm outta here by tonight I'm not complaining."

"That shouldn't be a biggie," his dad predicted. "This one's loud but she's not dropping much rain. You just gotta worry about the canal over there."

"The canal?"

"Y'all just a mile from the Industrial Canal. Looks like it's filling up good, too. That's the number one concern for the city. Overtopping."

"But like you said, hadn't been much rain."

"The rain ain't the problem."

"What is it then?"

"Storm surge, Sherlock!"

"Coming from the lake?"

"Yeah and from the Hurricane Highway, the Mississippi River Gulf Outlet them damn port people did on us."

"The Mister GO?" Erik asked, using the popular term. His dad had cursed this waterway from Erik's youngest days. Whenever they pushed out from Delacroix his dad almost wept at the sight of salt marshes where cypress swamps used to be, open water where salt marshes used to be. Erik had noticed the slow but steady replacement of trees and grass with brackish water even during his own short lifetime. His dad had blamed it all on the shipping channel called MR-GO. But Erik would have thought it would relieve pressure on the Industrial Canal, not add to it.

"All that storm surge gets shoved up the Mister Go until it belches into the Canal," his dad explained, "like something going in you the wrong way, if you know what I mean."

"Y'all got reports on that?"

"Oh yeah, it's full. Already lapping over a little bit. That's OK, but they also worried about it holding."

"What holding?" Erik pressed, "The levee?"

"The floodwall," his dad corrected. "We don't rate a real levee," he snickered.

His dad was often dark, cynical, yet always laughing about whatever problem he was analyzing, so Erik wasn't sure how much to be truly worried.

As if reading his thoughts over the phone, his dad added, "Don't worry, it'll hold. Event's halfway through already and storm surge comes first, so we prob'ly alright. Anyway, they got us prepped for security, not rescue."

"Well, be safe," Erik said.

"You got it, pardner," his dad assured, "And look out for your mama."

Erik said OK and they signed off. He envied his dad, getting set to ride out into the city and be the first to see what the storm did. If only he could figure out a way to sneak out and feel the wind on his face. He would even settle for an open window, but of course these windows couldn't do that. For their own safety, every entry and exit was sealed.

15

A few hours later the eye had passed. To the east, over the Bayou Sauvage marshes. Miranda was talking with her dad in their room.

"That was a pretty scary one, huh?" he said.

"I guess," she said. "It's not like we were in a hut on the beach or something."

"Yes," he said, "We're lucky to have what we have. Shelter, safety."

"I'm just worried about my tree."

"The one outside your window?" he asked. "On Constance Street?"

"Yeah," she affirmed. "And I'm worried about Jess."

"Your new friend?"

"I guess."

"Why?"

"She's kind of traumatized from Ivan wrecking her house in Pensacola last year."

"Well, at least she doesn't have to worry about a wrecked house this time."

"What about you, dad?"

"What?"

"Do you have any traumatizing memories?" In an effort to be less general, she added, "Like from storms?"

"Well, I suppose I was around your age when Betsy struck. It was quite an event. The president came down, serious flooding in the Ninth Ward. We were OK, though. Just a few days without power. Of course we didn't even have air-conditioning then, so…"

"I wonder if the constant air conditioning has like changed the species," Miranda said, "like made us all more boring."

"Hmm…" Her dad was still going over his hurricane memories. He rubbed his chin. "Then came Camille. A friend from college—well, an acquaintance—passed away over there. On the coast, during Camille."

"Were y'all close?"

"Well, not really. He was just in one of my classes. But I thought about it for a while."

"When are we getting out of here, dad?"

"No reason to think we won't be home by dinner," he guessed. "If we get an influx, I'm sure I'll be able to drop you home and come back, at any rate."

"I'm worried the tree might have crashed through my window."

"Well, Miranda, that's quite possible," he admitted. "That's an old sycamore. If it came down at the right angle it could do a lot more damage than just breaking your window. We might have to all camp on the first floor for a few weeks!"

"That would be quite an adventure!" she grinned.

"I'm afraid your mother wouldn't be so fond of such an adventure. Good thing the odds are that we're fine." He kissed her on the forehead and went off to check on patients.

Miranda wandered into the lounge down the hall. Haze and Erik had pulled up chairs to the window and were gazing outside as if watching a game.

"Wish we could get this thing open," Erik complained.

"Good thing there ain't no fire," Haze said.

Miranda walked up to the glass and stared out too. The trees were still tossing around but nothing like earlier. The happiest factor was that the street out front was dry. There was even a teaser of blue far off in the southern sky.

"Looks like that water cleared," Haze said. "They had

about a foot in the street this morning."

"Ain't much," Erik observed.

"Ain't no Betsy."

"Doesn't look like it."

Miranda cut in: "But that was just certain neighbor-hoods. With Betsy. Right? There could be other areas besides here that had worse damage. Where do you two live?"

Haze answered first: "Lower Nine."

Then Erik, "Chalmette."

"Mmm," Miranda considered. "I don't know about those places." Which wasn't true. She knew they were both the scenes of big floods in the past, one done on purpose in 1927.

Haze asked, "Where you from?"

"New Orleans," she said.

They stared at her blankly until she thought to add, "Up-town, by the park."

The boys both nodded, said "uh-huh," and Miranda was bothered that she once again couldn't figure out what people were trying to say. But, before she could think up an appro-priate response, she was rudely startled off her thoughts by a massive blast that shook the building. Erik and Haze both tipped back in their chairs and tumbled out of them, scram-bling to their feet and staring hard at the window, as if afraid it might come showering into them in thousands of driven shards.

They all gaped at each other. Erik managed a "What the *&%$?"

They heard footsteps beating their way toward them in the hall. The door flew open and Miranda's dad and Erik's mom hustled in, asking "Are you OK?"

Nobody answered that question, but Miranda said, "Dad, what *was* that?"

"Uh…" He was visibly exasperated, shaken. All he could say was, "A big explosion…some kind?"

Haze said, "Sound like a building falling over, right behind us. Or in front—" He crept back to the window and peered out.

Erik had a theory. "Maybe it was an oil drum over on the canal wharves, maybe they got a fire."

"I don't see no smoke," Haze reported from the window.

Haze's mom rushed in next, looking out of breath but immediately relieved to see him. Miranda's dad inspected the window frame, as if looking for cracks or seams between the frame and the wall. They all stared out the window some more, then turned back toward the door, as if expecting to see something new and illuminating there. That's when it opened and another man came in. He had khakis and a white shirt with a logo—the management company's—and a walkie-talkie on his belt. Miranda's dad appeared relieved to see him. "Tony," he said, "Tell me that didn't come from this building."

"No, no," he said, "The hospital's not the location."

Everyone kept staring at him, expecting more explanation, so he added, "Not sure what caused it, but our structure seems fine. No smoke alarms or anything. No shattered glass. I got men on the roof surveying the area, trying to locate the origin." Then, as if on cue, his walkie-talkie buzzed and he talked into it. "Yeah? I'm coming up." To the people in the kids' lounge he said, "We're alright, fine. Whatever it is, it's not affecting us, so no worries." Then he turned and squeezed out the door. Too hurriedly for "no worries," it seemed to Miranda.

"Guess I'm done napping now," Erik's mom joked, with an unburdening sigh. "I could use some breakfast, though."

This seemed to remind all present how hungry they were. Miranda hadn't thought to eat—besides a bag of chips and a diet coke—since arriving at the hospital the previous afternoon. The apples and bananas in the fruit dispenser already looked spotty, mushy.

"Alma and Mister Joe in the cafeteria," Haze's mom pointed out. They were the skeleton foodservice staff, so everyone made their way downstairs.

16

Alma and Mister Joe had anticipated losing power, so they'd
cleaned out the refrigerators and left nothing meant to be
cooked raw. It smelled to Haze like Lizardi Street always
did for less threatening storms, when everybody dragged
their grills out and served up their household inventories
for neighbors to sample. Alma and Mister Joe fixed breaded
pork-chops, ribs, sausages, red beans, boiled cabbage, green
beans, corn, macaroni with red gravy, and a big oily salad.
Everybody drank milk cartons, even if they preferred soda,
out of the civic responsibility to let nothing spoilable go to
waste. Haze struggled to eat at a reasonable pace. His mom
had often scolded him in the past for shoveling his food,
asking how he could possibly taste it if it spent so little time in
his mouth—but she was too busy shoveling this time to talk.
Haze had done some quick but thorough planning in line. His
first plate consisted of pork chops, red beans, and corn. His
second would be ribs, sausage with red beans, and cabbage.
Then he would have a salad course while he decided what
dishes deserved an encore. The others must also have been
occupied with their gustatory planning, because this was the
quietest eating party Haze had ever attended. Even the white
girl's doctor father was gnawing on a porkchop bone like the
wolfman.

Dessert was ice cream, in half-pints. They were encour-
aged to go through two or three apiece. Haze was reminded of
a nature show he saw that talked about reptiles in the desert
eating enough in one sitting to get them through weeks or
months. They also hibernated—and, since hunger and fatigue

and a panic about a loud noise had brought all these folks down to earth, as it were, hibernation was the next item on their agenda, too. They all lumbered upstairs to their rooms, still quiet as newts, for delayed and deserved shut-eye. Haze looked forward to a little nap, after which he assumed it would be time to head home. The winds had died down to the low rumble again. The palms outside bent slightly every few seconds, but stood almost straight for just as long intervals.

Haze noticed only one confusing detail before passing out in the reclining chair in his room—there was about a half a foot of water in the street, though it had been dry earlier. He mentioned it to his mom. "We can drive through that," she muttered, stretching out on the bed, "Don't need no SUV for no half a foot." Then they were both out.

17

Erik awoke to someone stroking his hair. At first he sensed it was Ashleigh and he reached his arm over her. Then he remembered they had broken up, that he was at a hospital riding out a hurricane, and that it must be his mom. He recoiled and opened his eyes.

"Don't worry," she laughed, "I ain't no boa constrictor!"

Erik sat up. He felt like he had overslept, like he had missed something important. He asked his mom what time it was.

"Almost five, sleepyhead."

"Wow," he said, "I must have been more tired than I thought."

He began gathering things from around the room. Socks from the floor—he put on fresh ones—the sweatshirt he'd worn the night before because the AC had been so chilly. Finally he rummaged around under a sheet on one of the beds and pulled out the magazine he'd brought, *Louisiana Sportsman*. He stuffed all this into his duffle, pulled his toothpaste and brush, and went to the sink to brush his teeth.

His mom had watched all this with a look that Erik couldn't figure out, like she was intending to say something. Finally, she did: "Look like you packing up. You going somewhere?"

He spat into the sink and said "Home, right?"

"Not yet, impatient one."

"Why not?"

"Gotta wait for the water to go down."

Erik went to the window and saw that there was, indeed,

a couple of feet of water in the street. "How'd that get there?" he asked.

"They had a hurricane."

"But the street was dry this afternoon."

"Probably had some overflow from the lake, or the canal. That's what they saying."

He whipped out his cel and dialed his dad's number. But it didn't go through. The message said the call couldn't be completed at this time. He tried again and got the same result. Now he really felt like he'd slept through something important.

"You mean we got to stay another night?"

"Yep." Then she shifted from her amused smirk to her stern lecture look. "You oughtta count your blessings, too. Be thankful that's the sum of your troubles."

"You're always saying other people have bigger problems, mom," he reminded her.

"Always speaking the truth," she said, "We only got fuel for that generator for two days. We got people upstairs gonna be more than inconvenienced if it runs out."

"Where is the generator?"

She thought for a moment. "I don't know, Erik."

"Is it on the roof?"

"No idea."

Erik wondered if it was protected from water. Then again, he assumed engineers considered flood threat when they put it in, that they wouldn't put it either right on the ground or even below ground.

"I gotta do a round," his mom announced. "You can come with me if you behave. Or you can stay here or whatever."

Erik stared at the blank TV screen for a second, then said, "I'll come with."

They took the elevator one floor up. The little neighborhood hospital only had four floors. They had moved all patients who could be moved to larger facilities over the past few days. The only remaining ones were deemed too risky to transport. The first two people his mom checked on were both very old and unconscious, with tubes coming out of their fingers, arms, faces. One guy had a tube going right in his stomach, some oatmeal-looking stuff going directly in there from a bag hanging from a pole. His mom spoke quietly with this other nurse, looked at some machine readings, wrote stuff down, and moved on.

Then they came to a conscious person, an old lady who sat fairly upright (supported by pillows) and chatted with Miranda and her dad.

"Miranda?" the old woman was saying. "What a lovely name. Shakespeare."

"Miss Beatrice?" Erik's mom cut in. "This here is my son, Erik."

The old lady named Beatrice said what a handsome young man he was, what beautiful children they had, etc. Then she told them to cherish every day, no, every minute, of their lives, because one day they were going to end up in ex- actly the same spot she was, struggling for a few more breaths but knowing the outside world was already, as far along as she was, gone forever.

Erik shared a glance with Miranda and it seemed like she shot him a little sarcastic eye-rolling smirk. But the lights were dim and he couldn't bring himself to believe she'd react to that poor old lady that way.

Back in the hall, Erik announced he was hungry. He wasn't really, but he would rather be in the cafeteria than on the floor with the old dying people.

Haze was down there, pushing some chilly, congealed macaroni around with his fork. Miranda ended up down there, too, and they all looked at their food more than they ate it. They didn't talk, either, even though it was the first time they'd all sat at the same table. Finally, Erik said, "Well, to-morrow it'll be back to the old grind as usual."

"I guess we won't have school," Miranda said, "not with people just getting back."

"Be in school Thursday," Haze conjectured. "If it be Friday, then they'll just knock off the whole week."

"God Bless Katrina!" Erik grinned.

They heard a curious sound then, a trickle, like someone taking a pee. They all looked in different directions to find the source. It was coming from the wall, close to the floor, next to them: water spewing in a neat arc out of the wall socket next to their table. Surveying the long wall of the cafeteria, they saw the other outlets also doing the same thing. All the outlets had become fountains, and the water first splashed, then slowly began to collect on the floor.

Then they heard a big pop, followed by the clang of iron on concrete, from outside. Erik rushed to the window in time to hear the same sound again and see what was causing it. Manhole covers flying up into the air atop geysers of water, then crashing back to the ground, all up and down Lake Forest Boulevard. The street outside was filling quickly. Inside, too, the pools of water began to meet and join together until an even layer covered the whole cafeteria floor.

"We… better move up," Erik stuttered. The handful of people scattered at the other tables all made the same suggestion, in the same tenuous voice, and everyone began moving to the door. They heard cursing from the kitchen and Mister Joe and Alma came running out, shouting for help to move food supplies up to a higher floor. The kids and others turned back and went into the kitchen. Everyone filled up tubs with canned and boxed foods and the caravan proceeded. By the time they got to the stairs—just a couple of minutes later—they were splashing through several inches of water.

The closest available common room was the pediatrics

lounge, so that's where they all went. They deposited their trays of food on the counter and tables and then just stood around as if waiting for further instructions. The kids all put their backpacks on and patted their pockets.

18

Miranda's dad appeared at the door and motioned her into the hall. "Miranda," he said, "some unexpected things have happened, and we need to take some emergency measures."

"OK," she said, "like what?"

"The water is rising because there's been a catastrophic levee breach."

"Oh my God," Miranda exclaimed. "But what does that mean?"

"It means we have to evacuate the hospital."

"OK," she said. But she still didn't understand why her dad seemed so distraught. Clearly, more was coming.

"Lifeways is sending helicopters right now," he continued. "The problem is they don't really have many on hand. They have only one that's fully equipped medically, but we've asked them to send along a smaller passenger copter first, and that's en route right now."

The lights in the hall dimmed, then went totally out. Almost immediately, flashlight beams moved toward them from the opposite end of the hall, illuminating their faces in a haphazard strobe. "You have your flashlight in your backpack?"

"Yes," Miranda said, and unzipped the pack and groped for the flashlight. She felt it and pulled it out, zipping the pack back up and replacing it on her shoulder.

"Miranda." Her dad gripped her biceps. "I have to go."

"Go?" Miranda cried. "Go where?" She was embarrassed at the tremble in her voice.

"You have to go, too."

Before she could feel relieved, he made it clear that they

weren't going together. "I need to get to the third floor to ready the patients. You need to get to the roof and board the helicopter that's landing…it might already be up there. It will take you to Sinai. And I will follow soon."

"Who's going with me?"

"We've decided to send you kids ahead first. But Miranda—" she knew he was looking into her eyes, though she couldn't really see his, "I am following very shortly behind you. Get to Sinai and find your mom and I'll see you soon."

"But dad…" She was trying to find a way to say she wanted to stay with him, no matter the difficulty, but he didn't give her the time.

"I need you to be strong for this, honey." Then very slowly: "I will see you very soon." He hugged her fiercely and turned to greet the security guy, Tony. He patted Tony on the shoulder and said, "She's ready to roll," and, to Miranda, "Tony will take you up and get you boarded." She trained the flashlight on her dad's face as he turned. He winked and hurried off down the hall. She kept the flashlight on his back until he disappeared into the stairwell.

There was now a crunch of people around her. Tony was saying it was time to go so the little group followed him up the concrete stairwell. It was dark, but most everyone had flashlights. Maybe they should have decided to use only one, to save the juice in the others, but no one made the suggestion, so the crazy strobe of dancing beams continued lurching upward.

19

Haze was the first one onto the roof. He saw the chopper.
And saw a man walking away from it with two gas cans. They
seemed heavy. He thought it was unusual that they would
refuel the helicopter on a hospital roof, but he wasn't about
to bring up things he obviously knew nothing about. His
plan was to lay low and do what he was told. His long-term
plan was to lose this crowd at Sinai Hospital and get back to
his neighborhood—on foot if need be. His mom could try to
keep him, but she couldn't watch him every second. He was
done with hospitals, had no desire to try out two in the same
day.

The others came up behind him and the security guy
waved them all toward the helicopter. Looked like it was just
going to be the three kids. His mom had said something like
that but she also admitted she wasn't too sure what was going
on. She just knew their car was now sitting—floating?—in
three feet of water, so they'd better take whatever transpor-
tation was offered, when it was offered. So here was Haze,
boarding a helicopter with two white kids bound for a neighborhood he didn't know well enough to get around in.

They all climbed aboard through a rear passenger door.
There was a separate door for the pilot, also open, but he
didn't seem to be in. There were four passenger seats, in pairs
facing each other. Haze and the girl sat facing the rear and the
white boy took one facing front. They put their bags on their
laps like they were on the bus. The seat belts were like regular car seat belts. Then they waited. Nobody said anything.
The security guy, who stood just outside, cursed and asked

where the pilot was. Haze peered out the door and saw a guy come out of the rooftop exit sort of half-running. He had the relieved look of a guy who'd just taken a leak. The pilot, he guessed, but he didn't wear a uniform.

He got in and closed his door. Then the security guy told him "see you in a few," since the pilot was supposed to come right back after dropping them at Sinai.

The engine started up with a roar, first kind of a shaky racket but then more of a smooth loud whir. It got quieter when the security guy slammed the passenger door shut. The pilot craned around slightly and asked if everybody was ready. The white boy reached over and clicked the door lock. Then they all said "yeah," but Haze was sure it was only because they didn't know what else to say.

It was a strange feeling lifting off, like suddenly it was air instead of the ground under them, and then the machine lurched, then zipped forward, and they were flying. The kids let out a collective sigh, then all looked out of their separate windows. It was weirdly dark out there. Like they were over open water or some wilderness. No lights. Like there was no city there. Haze could dimly make out the tops of houses but he couldn't see the streets between them. The helicopter banked and Haze's window tilted upward. He saw patches of clear sky all lit up with stars. Haze had never recalled so many stars bunched so close together. They had all been few and far between before. It was like the clouds were bunching them together into little pockets. And the clear parts, though just slivers, were clearer than he could ever recall a sky being, like the hurricane had scrubbed off some kind of stains or tarnish.

The helicopter evened out and once again it seemed like they were over open water. But why would they be going over the lake to get uptown? Haze began to get suspicious, like they were getting taken to some secret place for some secret reason. But before he could panic about it, the chopper began to lurch and sputter. It would drop suddenly then struggle upward. Haze looked at the others and they looked just as terrified as he was sure he looked. He saw the white boy was straining forward, trying to see something in the cockpit. The pilot cursed up a storm and started slamming the dashboard with his fist. The white boy, Erik, said "Y'all got gas in this sucker?"

"Full when I left for Lake Forest," the pilot shouted.

Then it got totally quiet. Like someone turned off the motor. They were just floating, gliding on the air. Falling— that's what they were doing. Then they started gently spinning, slowly at first, then faster, like the Tilt-a-Whirl ride at City Park.

Nobody said anything. Probably a whole minute went by. All that could be heard was the loud breathing of the pilot. Then there was a bump and an abrupt stop to the spinning . Haze saw water splashing up against the window, but they were still moving forward, like they were cruising along in a motor boat. Then they slammed, hard, into something solid. Haze's legs flew up, then his head snapped forward and he bit into his tongue. He saw the white boy flip forward and back like a rag doll. He felt the sting in his tongue, heard shattering glass and crunching metal, and then felt a hand on his—the white girl's. The space they were in collapsed and the kids' knees were suddenly all bunched up together. And then they were stopped, still.

20

Erik's first main concern—after he was sure he was alive—was
his bones. Like were any or all of them broken. He didn't feel
any pain, but he knew that test was inconclusive. Last year
he'd taken a spill on his dirtbike and broken his collarbone,
but he'd had no idea it was broken until he tried to pick up
the bike and his arm just didn't work, just wouldn't bear any
weight—no pain, though (yet). The problem now was that the
cabin of the chopper had scrunched together so much that
they were like kids who got petrified playing Twister. They
were strapped into their seats, but the seats were in a different
configuration than when they first sat down. It was hard to
figure out where things were, like the seatbelt latches. Plus it
was dark. They had to get untangled somehow. The girl had
managed to get an arm twisted into her backpack, which
was now behind Erik's head. She wormed out a flashlight
and clicked it on. "Great idea," Erik said, and the girl seemed
to smile a little. The black guy had blood coming out of his
mouth. "Everybody OK?" Erik asked. The girl said "I think
so," and the black guy just seemed to shrug. Then he said,
"yeah," really softly, and not like he meant it.

No sound from up front. "Hey," Erik raised his voice,
"you OK up there?"

Nothing. Though his seat belt was still fastened, Erik
realized it had a lot of slack. It was because the back of the
seat had broken off from the bottom. He grasped the top of
the door—which had been forced out of its frame and into the
cabin, jutting right over the girl's head—and pulled himself
up and out of the seat. His arms, collarbones, etc, seemed to

be in decent working order. His legs, too, as he deduced after folding them into a crouch on the seat. Now the white girl had room to pull her legs up, too, which she did after simply unclicking her seatbelt. Now Erik and Miranda both crouched on their seats in the tight space under the crushed roof and inward jutting passenger door.

The black guy sighed, unclicked his seatbelt, gingerly removed it from his lap, and suddenly heaved himself full force against the other door, which swung out, came completely loose, and clattered onto what sounded like concrete. Then he climbed out and stood and stretched.

Miranda crawled out after him.

Erik tugged at his duffle bag, which was crumpled and snagged in the wreckage of what used to be the vacant passenger seat. He yanked at it violently, then paused for a rational assessment—without even cursing. He gave up on trying to dislodge the whole bag. Instead, he unzipped it and pulled out his flashlight and his sportsman knife. He shined the flashlight up front but all he could see was one bloody arm sticking at a gruesome angle out of a very tight space between dashboard and pilot seat. He followed the other kids out of the wreck.

They were on an overpass surrounded by water. There was no rain but it was very humid. Off in the distance they could see the skyline, which helped orient them. The central cluster of the downtown business district had lights still, but nowhere else. Off to the south—the west bank—were some lights, too, very far off. Erik could see the flames of the west bank Shell refinery, but nothing in the direction of the Texaco facility in Chalmette. The overpass had a few cars parked on the shoulders, to get them out of flood reach, but not as many as he'd seen in other neighborhoods on the drive to the hospital. They were in an industrial area, and the cars were probably from people who wanted to leave them close to work. The rooftops above the floodline were corrugated tin, warehouses. A couple of multistory cinderblock structures also rose up out of the flood. There didn't seem to be any people in them.

The kids all looked out over the scene (what they could see of it in the dark), then crossed to the opposite railing and took in a similarly desolate vista in that direction. Miranda and Eric scanned the faces of the empty buildings with their flashlight beams, but didn't see anything useful. Then they all walked up and over the overpass, toward the city, where it sloped back down into the dark still water. Here, as behind, the quiet water stretched to the edge of visibility. After standing there for a few seconds, they walked back toward the helicopter.

They all stayed several paces apart, as if happy to have space after the claustrophobic hospital and crawdad-hole confines of the wrecked chopper. No one seemed to know what to do.

Erik felt like he should have an answer. But he didn't.

21

Miranda wished she were alone. She was more stunned than scared. If only she were alone, she thought, she could process all this better and figure out how she felt about it. As she reviewed the events of the past few minutes, and tried to figure out the next step, two notions arose and toppled, almost on top of each other: one, she should just walk home. No—they were surrounded by water which appeared too deep to wade through (and God knew what was in it). Two: just wait, abide, patiently. This idea didn't seem so bad either—obviously they would be missed and sought. Fine—except these boys were here. Not only would she have to try to be nice and talk with them, they might not even be safe. She didn't know them from Adam. Also she could sense the tension between them—guy stuff, like they were going to end up in a fight. She couldn't avoid a dark prospect deep down that one would kill the other and the survivor would rape her.

The black one, Haze, had been gripping something tightly in his hand during the whole helicopter ride and crash. Whatever it was, he still held onto it. Now he put it to his mouth and blew into it. He turned from the others and began walking back to the city side of the overpass. He hopped up onto a car hood, his back to them, and kept buzzing into it. Different notes, but not fine differences. She realized it must be a mouthpiece for a brass instrument.

The white boy, Erik, said, "Hey, what is that thing?" He had walked up alongside Haze, a few feet away. Miranda followed, at a distance of a few more feet.

"You talking to me?" Haze said.

Erik just rolled his eyes and blew air through his nostrils.

"A 7-C, " Haze said.

"A 7-C what?"

"It's a mouthpiece, man," Haze answered, "for a trumpet." He added, "Or a cornet."

"Can that thing help us get out of here?" Erik asked, a little harshly.

"Help *me* get outta here," he muttered.

"What," Erik said, "it's a mini jetpack?"

Miranda stepped closer and cut in: "I think he means spiritually." She hadn't wanted to get involved but found that she couldn't help it. She always ended up talking even when she'd resolved not to.

"*Spiritually*?" Erik repeated.

"Yeah," Haze said, "Spiritually." And he closed his eyes and blew softly and serenely into it—pausing briefly to shake some blood out—and it sounded to Miranda almost like real music.

"Well," Erik said, in a quieter tone, "I was trying to figure a way out of this in a, you know, non-spiritual sense."

Miranda said, "We're bound to get rescued if we just wait."

Erik grimaced like the idea repulsed him.

Miranda wandered back over to the helicopter. The blades were standing up perpendicular to the ground like a big narrow X, or a St. Andrew's cross. The pilot's head was pushed into the crumpled windshield. His face pointed down, couldn't be seen. His right arm stuck out straight, pointing up and away from his shoulder. The whole rest of him was below the shoulder socket. Like he was crouching and curling into a fetal position except this one arm that froze while frantically waving at something. The windshield below the head was soaked deep crimson, and blood dripped at a steady pace from the seam between the windshield and frame.

She heard Erik behind her. "No need to look closer," he said softly, "He's…"

"Yeah," Miranda said. Then turned again in the other direction, back toward where Haze blew his red blues into a mouthpiece without a horn. She was doing a delicate balancing act in her head. On the one hand, trying not to panic. On the other, trying to feel the magnitude of the situation. Here she was, stranded. Just crashed out of the sky and there, a few paces behind her, was the only adult around, smashed, crushed, bloody, *dead*—she could think the word if she couldn't say it. Things like this just didn't happen to her, so she was having some trouble acknowledging the reality of her predicament. Or was it really a predicament? The crash was serious, but she survived. These boys might be annoying but she doubted they were really dangerous. Probably the adventure was over and she was now essentially just waiting for a ride. She remembered her cellphone and returned to the helicopter to get it. Erik was still standing there observing the wreckage.

"Any chance this thing could blow up?" she asked.

"No," he said.

"Because it would have when we crashed already?"

"'Cause there's no gas in it—that's WHY we crashed."

Miranda didn't like Erik's exasperated tone. She leaned into the chopper and stretched her arm and pulled out her backpack. She pulled out her cel and dialed—but got what she expected: "call cannot be completed at this time." As she turned away, Erik climbed in after her and came out with his phone. He punched on the keys but apparently got the same result. They walked back toward Haze and saw he had pocketed his mouthpiece and was trying his phone, too. His silence indicated the same lack of success.

"So what's the plan, guys?" Erik asked.

"I ain't got no plan," Haze said.

When Erik looked at Miranda she just shook her head.

"Just sit here and play Gilligan's Island, huh?" Erik laughed.

"They'll come for us," Miranda said, "somebody will."

"When," Erik asked, "when we're skeletons?"

Miranda frowned. "That kind of hyperbole is funny, but not useful."

"What would be useful would be a *&%^ boat!" Erik said. He tried the door of the car they stood next to, then moved down to the next, tried it, and then the next. There were only three left to try, parked on the other side, so he darted over and tried them all. "If we had a coat hanger we could get this one open," he said.

"But why?" Miranda asked. Did he forget they were surrounded by high water?

"Seats might float," he said.

"You're going to tear out somebody's car seat?" Miranda asked. "Isn't that kind of extreme?" She looked at Haze, who seemed to nod, and maybe smirk a little, but she wished he'd speak up and say something.

Erik just kicked the car in response. He turned his flashlight on again and scanned the nearest buildings, then moved to the opposite railing again and did the same. "That one there's just a few yards off," he said, pointing to a flat-topped brick building to the south. "We could swim that easy," he said.

It looked more like at least a hundred yards to Miranda. But anyway, there was no way she was going in that water. She said so. Erik sighed and they both looked at Haze.

"I ain't going in there either," he said.

"Anyway," Miranda said, "why would we be better off over there?"

"'Less they got a boat on the roof," Haze said.

Erik squeezed his lips together in consternation. "They

might have a land-line," he offered. "We could call for help."

"But help's coming anyway!" Miranda protested.

"What makes you so sure?" Erik asked.

"They're going to notice when we don't show up at Sinai."

Haze had an agitated look on his face, as if he were about to say something, but they all fell silent, because they heard a distant engine. Sounded like a helicopter, drawing closer. From the direction of the hospital.

"Y'all see it?" Haze asked, jumping onto the roof of a car.

"Is that it?" Miranda asked. She saw the lights off toward the lake, moving through the air at a rapid clip in the direction of the city. There were two. She turned on her flashlight and waved it in the direction of the choppers. The boys did it, too.

"They're pretty far off," Erik said.

He was right. But along the surface they noticed other lights, other waving flashlights, about a mile to the north of the kids' location. They flashed on in flurries as the helicopters flew over, and then stopped after they passed, like they were doing the wave.

"Looks like we not the only ones," Haze observed.

They continued listening as the rumble of the choppers receded.

"Hell with this," Erik said, kicking off his sneakers and tying them together with the laces.

"What are you doing?" Miranda asked.

"It's the principle of it," Erik argued. "Not being a sitting duck. Doing something."

"But what?" Miranda pressed. "What are you doing?"

He looped the sneakers around his neck and tucked them under his shirt, against his chest. Then he pulled them out and reversed them, so they were tucked against his back. "Going swimming," he said. He scouted around the edge of the overpass, walked down it toward the city, and then turned to face Miranda and Haze with a wild grin. He saluted, hung over the side, and dropped. They heard the splash and hurried over to where he'd jumped. He surfaced and shouted, "Yeah, it's deep." After going under and re-surfacing again, he added "Prob'ly eight feet." He took a deep breath and turned and splashed off in the direction of the building he'd pointed out before.

They watched him until they couldn't see him anymore. And listened until they couldn't hear the splashing. Miranda cast a sidelong glance at Haze and felt a sudden shudder of fear.

22

Haze couldn't help but notice, after Erik swam off, how
Miranda edged away from him and stayed away. He figured
she had some little girl crush on the guy. He didn't know—he
didn't get Nickelodeon. He climbed back up on his perch
from before, the hood of a Camry, and tossed his mouthpiece lightly in his hand. He wanted to play it, but it stung the
cut on his tongue and made it bleed more so he didn't. He
assumed his mother was in one of those choppers that just
passed. Probably they would land at Sinai hospital, figure out
the kids never got there, and send out the cavalry. It would
be hours at the earliest. Another thought tugged at him, too:
what if Sinai hospital was also surrounded by water? What if
the whole city was under? Was there any hope at all for his
own house? He knew there was no point in worrying over this
stuff, but it was hard not to. Worrying was like that: you did
it even when there was no point, even when you didn't want
to. Then again, hope was the same way, just sort of happened.
Maybe, he consoled himself, whatever levee that obviously
broke just filled up the area around where they were. After
all, they'd heard that blast—sounded pretty close. There were
quite a few canals in between New Orleans East and everywhere else. Maybe it was just around here that took the hit
this time. He could tell from how his thoughts swam around
that he was tired. He knew it would be wise to sleep, so he
closed his eyes and leaned back on the windshield and gave it
a try.

It might have worked. He couldn't be sure. But when he
opened his eyes again he saw some graying in the sky back in

the direction of the hospital. He hopped down and strolled toward the helicopter, trying not to look at or think about the pilot. It was still dark enough that you'd have to get up really close to see the gore—Haze wasn't interested. Miranda was sitting on the ground leaning against a car and writing something in a notebook. She had her flashlight on the ground pointed at it so she could see.

"Looks like morning," Haze said.

The girl jumped in terror at the sound of his voice.

"Uh, sorry," Haze said, "I didn't mean to…"

The girl shut her notebook and capped her pen and put it all back in her pack. "Yeah," she said, standing up. "They'll be coming for us soon."

They heard the distant hum of helicopters again. This time from the direction of the city. They turned and walked to the railing closest to the sound. In the waxing light they saw the distant silhouettes buzzing toward them. Lots of them. A long line flying in formation, like an attack. They got closer and then fanned out. One end of the line turned off to the left and another to the right. Behind this first row, another approached. As they got closer they recognized them as the red Coast Guard choppers. Haze pumped his fist in joy and relief, but a second later it dawned on him that, out of this whole army of helicopters, none was intended for them. They just flew right over them as if they weren't there. The idea of jumping up and down seemed ridiculous. Like wasting your last dollar on a lottery ticket.

As it got lighter, they could see further, and then they saw one batch of rescue choppers slow down and hover, still probably a mile off. It was where they'd seen the flurry of flashlights the night before. They saw a chopper hover and a man repel down on a cable to the roof of a house. They noticed then that the roof had at least a dozen folks on it. They attached a couple of them somehow to the cable and the cable drew back up toward the helicopter.

In three out of four directions—but nowhere very close to them—they saw hovering choppers doing the same thing. Rescuing people—from their houses. So there was definitely a rescue operation in play. But for them? Would they ever think to stop on some lonely overpass that nobody was supposed to live around?

Miranda seemed to be thinking the same thing. She shook her head dismally. "Wow," she said.

"Looks like a big disaster," Haze said.

"Yeah," Miranda agreed. "Like in a movie."

"Wish we had some popcorn then."

"Yeah, and some skittles."

"Some AC," Haze added, squinting in the direction of the sun, which was now over the horizon. The sky was cloudless. It already felt like at least eighty-five degrees, at—Haze checked his cel-phone—7 am. He saw at the edges of Miranda's hair, already, the beads of sweat forming.

"Yeah," she said, "Or maybe just some shade?" She checked the clock on her cel, too, then turned it off. He pulled his out and did the same. They saw the chopper closest to them pull up one last fare, this time joined by the guy who did all the fastening, and pull away. It turned back toward the city, fully loaded. It was followed by another, then another, though by now, in the clear light, Haze and Miranda could see rooftop after rooftop holding angry left-behinds, waving fists at the departing choppers. How many hours (days?) would it take them to lift all these people off to safety? What if the water rose even higher?

"Maybe we *should* try to swim somewhere," Miranda groaned.

Haze couldn't bear to tell her his secret—that he had never learned to swim—so he tried to come up quickly with another answer.

"If we had a boat…" is all he could offer. "'Cause if we swim," he continued, "where we swimming to?" He shook his head. "You see where this water ends?"

Miranda looked in one direction, then another, turned slowly, methodically, in a complete circle. Then said, softly, "No."

<h1 align="center">23</h1>

Eric was especially careful not to open his eyes underwater. After he jumped, in, tried to touch bottom, and said "see ya" to Miranda and Haze, he just stroked steadily in the direction of the two-story building he'd sighted from the overpass. He kept his head down and his breath in, getting bearings only when he brought his head up to gulp air. At some point he must have drifted off track. He paused, treaded water, and looked around. The sky seemed to be brightening. He saw the building he was aiming for, just a bit off to the left of his trajectory. He corrected and stroked hard, but not wildly. Then he bumped into something solid, some barely submerged flat surface. He climbed up onto it, thankful for a chance to rest. He quickly determined he was on top of a 24 or 26 foot delivery truck. He paced the length of it and examined his destination, now within a hundred feet. As it got lighter he could make out block letters just above the waterline: *Trinity Yachts*. "Score!" he shouted.

But the sound of his voice piercing the stillness startled him. He cupped his hands around his mouth and this time shouted "hey!" in the direction of the Trinity Yachts building. Again his voice just kind of thudded and died in the still air. He secured his shoes again around his neck (they were totally soaked) and dove back in, more resolutely than before, swimming a beeline for the pale yellow cinderblock structure. There was an iron stairwell coming out of the water. It led to a landing by a second-floor entrance, a very secure looking metal door. Having reached it, his next task was to figure out how to get inside. His rubber-coated Rayovac flashlight was supposed to be waterproof. He slid the switch and was re-lieved to affirm that it was. There was a large window next to the landing he stood on. He sat on the railing, gripping it with his right hand, and leaned back and trained the light through the window with his left.

Just a standard office. File cabinets, desks. A phone. That was a reason to try to get in. As he vainly looked for some object on the little landing to smash in the window with, he heard the distant rumbling of engines, drawing nearer. He soon recognized the sound as helicopters—more than one—flying in his direction. They were coming from the other side of the building, so he couldn't see them until they were di-rectly overhead. They flew over and the sound receded again. Then another line came and continued toward the lake. So the rescue effort had begun—which meant that it was needed. Looking into the water he noticed the colors of the rainbow undulating in the barely lapping current—oil. Gas. Lord knew what else. Then he saw, like an answer to a prayer, a random cinderblock a few steps below the landing, just under the surface of the water. He figured it was probably used to prop open the heavy metal door on days of moderate weather. He reached down and picked it up. His task now was to decide how to hurl it through the window with enough force to actually bust it. He had just one try, since a miss would send it splashing into the water and sinking to the bottom. He hoist-ed it, tested out a couple of angles. It was like a perimeter shot in basketball—only, fortunately, the window was a lot bigger than the basket. It was a wide picture window, one large pane. He grunted and tossed it. It hit the window squarely in the middle, as he had intended. It didn't shatter, but it cracked, and the cinderblock scraped past the ledge and splashed into the water. Examining the crack, Erik judged he could kick the window in if he could get up onto the ledge and get a good enough hand-hold to balance there and kick with adequate force. He slipped into his soaked sneakers, stood carefully on the railing and edged onto the ledge. He felt terror at falling but reminded himself that he had just been in that exact same water, so what was there to fear? It was just that, now he was starting to dry off, he really didn't want to get back into that toxic stew—ever.

Luckily the window didn't need much prodding. The long shards bent in, piece by piece, enough for him to eventually swing his whole body from the upper ledge of the roof into the office, where he was careful to land on his feet. There wasn't even that much shattered glass. He pulled his flashlight from his jeans pocket—though it was getting lighter outside, it was still dark in the room—and quickly located the phone he'd seen before. He sat in the old swivel chair and picked up the receiver.

It had a dial tone. "OK," he muttered. The first number he punched was his dad's precinct. It rang. And rang some more. No answer. Which was exceedingly odd, since there was somebody on duty whose only job was to pick up that phone, 24/7. He hung up and dialed again. Same result. He hung up, thought. Then he dialed his house, but it didn't surprise him that there was no answer there. He hadn't expected anyone to be there, he just wanted to see if the answering machine picked up. It didn't, which just told him they didn't have power—no surprise there.

Then he dialed Ashleigh's cellphone. She picked up.

"How's the beach?" he asked.

"Omigod Erik!" she shrieked. "Where are you?"

"Trinity Yachts," he answered.

"Are you OK?" she asked, apparently deciding not to ask what and where the hell Trinity Yachts was.

"I'm a little wet," he said.

"Did you get flooded?"

"Yeah." He couldn't think of anything else to say. He

began to wonder why he had called her. What could she do? She was in a different place. Worse than that, she was from a different time. It was like calling up Abe Lincoln for advice on how to power a rocket.

"What's going on Erik, are you at the hospital still?"

"No," he said, "we evacuated when the water started coming up."

"They say on the news the water's coming up all over the city. They got levees springing holes all over the place."

"Hm" is all he could muster, like he was supposed to say, "Gosh, well I'll be!" He just didn't know what to say to somebody telling him the whole city was going under. "What about the Quarter?" he asked.

"They got reporters on Canal Street, and it looks sorta dry, just like a foot maybe."

He realized that Ashleigh couldn't really do anything for him but he tried to figure out some way to salvage his decision, make the call useful somehow. But how? Tell her to tell her dad to tell somebody to come for him in a boat at some building he didn't even know the address of? That is, after they were done rescuing everybody else?

"Ashleigh, I gotta go," he said. "I gotta do some stuff."

"I been trying to call you but your phone don't work."

"Yeah I'm calling you from a land-line here."

"You gonna stay at that number?"

He thought about the prospect. Scanned the little office. Cozy enough, but it would turn into an oven within an hour or so. "No," he said.

"Where you going? Are you with your mom?"

"No," he said. Then he figured out how she could help. "Ashleigh, if you hear from my mom, tell her I'm fine and I'm headed up to Sinai Hospital to meet her. And tell everyone. I'm going to Sinai. Tell everyone I'm doing fine. OK?"

"Why, you mean she's up there? Where are you?"

"Trinity Yachts," he said. "I gotta go." He hung up before she could say 'I love you' because he just didn't want to hear it. Seemed fake. Or not relevant. The phone rang a second after he cradled the receiver, but he let it ring while he rummaged around the office in the growing light. He opened a mini-fridge and saw a few soft-drinks, a Tupperware container, and a convenience-store tuna sandwich. He opened a coke—it was still somewhat cold—and guzzled half of it in one draught. He opened the sandwich and devoured it in a few bites. The Tupperware container had cantaloupe chunks but they were already a bit too slimy for him to risk. He knew that whatever difficulties he faced now would become a different order of urgent altogether if he ended up with food poisoning. Perusing the cabinet above the counter by the mini fridge, he found a half-full tin of Charles Chips and a bag of Famous Amos cookies—unopened! Also a couple of microwave chili servings.

But he kept imagining how Miranda and Haze would respond if he managed to get back to them with these things. He realized then what his plan needed to be. To get back to them. That would have to be the first step—everything else could be decided later. He remembered a scene in a western that always impressed him, an outlaw trying to keep his band together, saying if people can't stick with their team they're no better than animals. That girl and that boy, unforeseen as it was, were now his team, and he'd be lower than catfish dung if he just split and didn't bother to try to help them out.

But how? "Maybe there's a yacht around here," he muttered to the empty office. Again, the sound of his voice creeped him out. In the cabinet under the counter was a box of garbage bags. He pulled one out, put the others inside it, then stuffed it with the snacks and sodas. He flung it on his back like Santa Claus and exited the office by the hall door, ready to make lemonade with whatever lemons his path might turn up for him.

He quickly saw he could have avoided the ordeal of breaking the window had he only swum around to the other side—these windows had already been blown out by the storm. Outside, just a few feet from the office building, was a sloped tin roof that came to a stop inches above the waterline. Next to this structure was a tangle of masts and rigging—yes, there *had* been plenty of boats here. Erik deduced that he was on an inlet that emptied into the Industrial Canal. The long shed probably covered the facility where yachts were made, repaired, stored, something. Anyway, there they were, but they hadn't been moored with long enough ropes, so they were swamped, listing toward the winches where they'd been too tightly secured. Erik used his flashlight to punch out enough stray glass from the window to climb up into it and jump down to the tin roof next door.

He walked along the edge looking out for some salvageable boat. The problem was, even if one of these could be found in mint condition, it wouldn't be much use to him. He didn't need a yacht, he needed a dinghy. A pirogue with a pole. Further out he saw some boats that had come unmoored, including a seventy-foot luxury vessel that was just nonchalantly floating out there, waiting to be powered up. He couldn't tell if it was floating over where the canal had been or over where dry land had been. Probably it would shoal on an old truck or something—or the floodwall itself—before getting anywhere. It dawned on Erik that there was probably, somewhere on the premises, a simple rowboat for ferrying personnel and customers around. He thought he saw the hull of just such a boat sticking up between a 28 foot sloop crammed up onto a 60 foot yacht which had smashed into the far end of the warehouse roof. He trotted over, as fast as he could manage on the slippery and malleable corrugated tin.

Yes—sticking almost straight into the air was a humble little aluminum 12 foot bass fisher—oars at the ready in the oarlocks. He dropped his bag of goodies and tried to figure out how best to get the skiff free. The bow of the 60 foot yacht was totally out of the water, rising a few feet above his head, at about a hundred-forty-five degree angle over the warehouse roof. Walking around it, he saw the sailboat's bow was propped on the starboard bow of the yacht—there was plenty of space between the sailboat's hull and the deck of the yacht, but who knew when it would tumble down and crush whatever dared to board that deck? The little aluminum flatboat was propped against the yacht's starboard side, the same side supporting the sailboat, but it seemed, on closer inspection, that the sailboat itself was not touching the skiff at all. All Erik had to do—it appeared—was get up onto the yacht and tip the skiff over.

He circled back around to the port side of the sixty-footer. From this side, all but the front ten feet or so seemed to be afloat. He saw also that there was another vessel up under the big yacht. Could they be stacked up underwater? Bubbles popped up on the surface, like from air pockets in a sunken ship. The image of a trapped person down there flashed in his head—it was female—but he quickly choked it off. Now was not the time for counter-productive imagining of sick stuff. If there were someone sucking up their last breaths, Erik would never know it, because there was no way he was diving down into that oil spill and opening his eyes.

He stepped gingerly onto a mast that stretched out along the sloping roof, level with the bottom of the yacht's hull and running alongside it, like a floating catwalk. The vessel it was attached to was under the yacht's stern, totally on its side. Erik decided he'd try to stay as dry as possible, but without much hope. The mast seemed stable enough to tightrope on for now, so he continued, even after it sank to a foot or so beneath the waterline and some ominous creaking set in. He was looking for the best spot to scramble up onto the yacht. Happily, the sailboat whose mast supported him wasn't so much under the yacht as floating on its side behind it, so he was able to climb up onto the mildly bobbing sailboat's side, and from there scurry up the ladder on the stern of the big pleasure boat— her name was "Gumbo Trinity." He fought the urge to explore the boat and crept slowly up the starboard side, toward the little rowboat. There was a great sudden groan. He almost fell overboard as the yacht lurched and rolled backward, filling the air with the sound of scraping, bending tin, and crushing fiberglass. Then the re-settlement seemed to be over for the moment. The "Gumbo Trinity" had slid completely off the warehouse roof and found water again. Almost all of her, anyway: now the bow was cradled in a crevasse of ripped and crumpled tin rather than sitting neatly on top of an intact roof. Her bow had dropped about six feet and now she was almost level again. She'd battered up a few lesser vessels behind and under her to make room.

Erik stood up slowly and peered over the side. The skiff was free! The 28 foot sloop that had been propped up against the "Gumbo Trinity" was now at a more awkward angle, dangling from a tangle of tackle binding the two boats together. But the skiff sat at the ready, its bottom wet in about a half-foot of water lapping over the warehouse roofline. Erik hung over the side of the yacht and dropped into the aluminum 12-footer. He really didn't want to get out of it again. He wanted to lie in it and wrap his arms around the benches. He pulled an oar out of one of the oarlocks. Yes, he'd be able to hook his bag with the oar and drag it over. He did it, stood for a second, and remembered what his mom told him once about praying. "Pray when you feel like it—I mean it. And don't pray when you want something, pray to thank God after you get it." So he did. It wasn't eloquent—he just knelt on one knee, closed his eyes and said, "Thank you Jesus, thank you

Jesus." Then, using one oar as a pole (he'd pulled the other one in), he pushed off from the stalwart tin roof, pushed away from the "Gumbo Trinity," over the barely submerged sailboat behind it, and was finally able to sit and row. He backed up a yard or two and saw his way out of the boatyard, away from the canal, around the offices (and, he guessed, an underwater showroom), until he was rowing over dry land. As he dipped and raised the oars, creaking aluminum and the plash of paddles in water were the only sounds to be heard besides the constant ebbing and flowing drone of far-off helicopters. That and his own breathing, which gradually got deeper and more rhythmic.

Something was missing. Birds. No sea gulls, even. It was the only time in his life he'd been on a waterfront—whatever kind of strange waterfront this was—and heard not a single caw.

24

Miranda tried to write down a description of her situation, and her feelings about where she was, but couldn't find the right words. "Stuck on an overpass surrounded by water…" That was as far as she got. It was because she didn't know the end of the story. She didn't know what happened next. And if she just made something up, then she might be disappointed if things went differently. She felt better in one sense, though. She wasn't scared of Haze anymore. He seemed really polite and nice, and she liked how he played his mouthpiece. She figured a boy that into music couldn't really be mean or dangerous. Now he'd put the mouthpiece away again and just sat on the hood of the Camry staring into space while she sat inside, on the passenger seat. She'd opened all the doors to try to air it out, and, though it was still stifling, at least it was out of the now blazing sun. She opened the glove compartment and rummaged through it. A couple of old cassette tapes, insurance stuff, title, and a couple of ball-point pens. She took the pens and stashed them in her backpack. She swung out of the car and asked Haze how long he'd been playing trumpet.

"Few years," he said. "I started in 6th grade. You play?"

"I used to do choir," she said, "but it got kind of boring. I guess I didn't like the people that much."

"You play in a band you got to get along with your band-mates."

"I'm not sure I'm that good at getting along with people," she admitted.

"Why not?" Haze asked. "They boring?"

"Kind of," she said.

After a pause, Haze said, "That water look like it going down?"

That was an idea she hadn't thought of. But it was a relief to consider. Probably the water would, eventually, go down, and, even if no one came to get them, they could walk home. Eventually—but when was that? Her throat started to feel dry. How long could someone go without water? To drink?

"How long has it been since we ate?" she asked.

Haze had hopped down from the car and begun strolling down the overpass to the water's edge. "Last night," he said.

She followed him. "So basically we've just missed breakfast."

"And a midnight snack," he added. He looked perturbed when he got to the waterline. He shook his head and walked back in the other direction, toward the helicopter. She didn't follow him in that direction because she didn't want to get near the wreck and the dead pilot's body in the daylight. She felt like she had to conserve her strength and seeing a mangled body in too much light would sap too much of it. Haze came back quickly. "Why is this water rising?"

"It's rising?" she said. Indeed, the front end of the lowest car on the bridge was now nudging the water, when there had been a few feet of dry concrete between car and waterline earlier in the morning. Haze walked back to the top of the overpass and climbed onto a white SUV. He waved his arms in a wide circle at the nearest zooming rescue chopper, but didn't continue the effort for more than a second. He jumped down and stared at the ground, nodding. "We might have to go in that water," he said. He looked scared.

She was scared of the water, too. It was thick and dark, you couldn't see an inch below the surface. And the swaying rainbows in it meant gasoline and probably other harmful chemicals. It would be like swimming in poison. "Can you swim?" she asked.

He looked at her sharply. "A little," he said. "Be better if we could find something that floats."

"Maybe in the helicopter," she suggested. "But…"

He seemed to read her mind. "You don't wanna go messing around the dead man." He nodded. "Me neither. What if he start to, y'know, like decompose?"

"It's getting hot. That'll make it go faster. The putrefaction."

"The what?"

"That's what they call it—putrefaction."

"You ever seen a dead animal? Like first, and then later?"

"Not later."

"They had a dog over on the corner by my house. First he was just dead, y'know, lying there." He spoke softly. Their backs were to the helicopter, as if they didn't want to offend the pilot's corpse with their conversation. "Then he like, next couple'a days, he blew up like a balloon, with his legs sticking out, but like somebody blew him up tight, as far as his skin could go. Then, later, it was worms and flies all in him." He paused, nodded at the ground, looked up. "Then it was just like skin and bones. Then just bones."

"Did anybody ever move him?"

"Yeah, we did. After he was just bones we took him under the house and used to play games with him, like we was in some kind of secret club and he was our leader. We got other kids to come see him. Had him on this old piece of rug under there and we would go under there and light candles. Try to do spells."

"Is he still under your house?"

"Prob'ly. We kind of forgot about him. I guess he still there."

"That's quite a story," Miranda said, and wondered if she would have played with the dead thing so carelessly. She imagined probably not. Not without hand sanitizer, anyway.

"So we oughtta go look in the helicopter for life jackets?" Haze asked.

"I guess," Miranda concurred. "The seats might float, like in an airplane."

They turned back toward the helicopter and started walking, slowly but steadily. She felt like taking his hand but didn't. She had no idea how he'd interpret it. She had been down that road once with Eli, back in that parallel universe that used to be called Miranda Maitre's life.

"We oughtta pray for him," Haze said.

"The pilot?"

"Yeah," he said. "We feeling bad about it 'cause he's just smashed up dead and we gon' keep feeling bad about it 'till we pray over him. You know, send him back home, kinda."

"OK," she said. She was surprised to feel that the idea was a relief to her. It never would have occurred to her, but now that Haze mentioned it, it seemed so much like the natural and right thing to do—even elegant. Now she didn't feel as squeamish as she had before about approaching the body. First she had been curious about it, then freaked out, but now she had kind of a neutral feeling, which was her favorite way to feel. Calm, contained.

They got up to within a few feet of the wreck—still the pilot's face wasn't visible, really just a tangle of matted hair and now hardened blood—and now Miranda did take Haze's hand, since she supposed people often did it when they prayed. He nodded at her as if suggesting that she be the one to say something.

She began with a favorite poem. "This world is not conclusion. A species stands beyond—Invisible, as music—But positive, as sound." She paused to let those words sink in and begin their effect. Then she continued in a more typically churchy vein: "Dear God, we ask that you take to your bosom another of your imperfect children, who tried…probably…"

she groped for words, "to do right by others…and enjoy his modest store of happiness. We know very little. We didn't know a thing about this man except that he died, in some sense, for us. He knew not the hour of his end, as neither do we, yet we pray that his life was thrilling to him and valuable to others." She nodded—almost done. "May he now know peace and rest. *Requiem aeternam dona eis, Domine.* Amen."

"Amen," Haze muttered, with a slight tremble in his voice.

She opened her eyes and realized some tears had welled up. They were still holding hands. She lifted hers up, gave a final little squeeze, and nodded at him and let go. Then they walked around to the open passenger door to see if they could pry loose the seat cushions. "Should I pray for us, too?" she joked.

"I been doing that," Haze said with a smile. As they tugged at the seat cushions and Miranda marveled at how they were able to smile and joke even in their bleak predicament, they heard a shout.

"Ahoy!"

They scrambled out from under the bent chopper, and saw a boat approaching the overpass from the other side. There was a man rowing. His torso was bare but he had a t-shirt tied around his head and draping down like a Bedouin head scarf. "Ahoy," he shouted again.

Miranda and Haze hurried down to meet him as the skiff attained the overpass. It was Erik. "Thought y'all might need a lift," he announced. He stood up and jumped out and pulled the front of the boat up onto the concrete. He reached into a big garbage bag and pulled out a couple of soda cans. "Thirsty?" he inquired. "Hungry?" He pulled out a big round tin—potato chips—and a bag of chocolate chip cookies.

Miranda gulped down some Mountain Dew and couldn't suppress a belch. "Oh," she said, "excuse me."

Haze chuckled modestly.

Erik said, "Excuse ME," and let out a bigger one.

After they'd gone through all the chips—they just all dove in with their hands, in rapid succession—and half the cookies, Haze mumbled, through a half-full mouth, "We should save some."

Once again, though the idea hadn't occurred to Miranda, it seemed wise.

"OK," Erik agreed, as he rolled the top of the sack and placed it carefully back in the bag in the boat. "Also got these," he said, and showed two containers of microwave chili.

"Just need the microwave," Haze said.

"Or we eat it cold, like polar bears," Erik said.

Miranda said, "They wouldn't last long around here." She was already soaked through with sweat, and the boys seemed to be, too. Erik looked badly sunburned already. His skin, in fact, seemed already to be peeling.

"You're getting burned," Miranda pointed out.

Erik looked at Haze in a conspiratorial way and then turned to Miranda and dead-panned, "Uh-huh."

"Shouldn't you put your shirt back on?" she pressed.

Erik touched his fingertips gingerly to his shoulder and chest and said, "I took it off 'cause I couldn't stand how it was chafing and rubbing on me."

Miranda got into the boat and sat on the forward of the two benches. Erik sat on the rear one. Haze still stood to the side. "So?" Miranda said, "Where to now?"

"I got that covered," Erik said.

"Back to Lake Forest?" Miranda asked.

"No sense in that," Erik laughed. "Gotta head back toward the city."

Haze said, "They got the Industrial Canal between here and the city."

"A boat's mighty useful for crossing a canal," Erik observed.

Haze looked up at the helicopters buzzing back and

forth. "Maybe if we get to that neighborhood over there," he pointed toward the lake, at the cluster of rooftops the choppers had been going back and forth to all morning, "where they picking people up."

"No point in trading a bridge for a roof," Erik argued. "Especially if you got a boat."

Miranda began to sense again that uneasy, unsafe feeling she'd felt earlier. It wasn't Erik. It was both of them together, like harmless chemicals that combust when mixed.

"I'm sure we can come to a sensible agreement," she said. "Haze is right that we could get picked up over there, and it's not that far, but Erik's got a good point too about us having this boat."

"Us, huh?" Erik laughed, derisively. "Naw, naw," he said, shaking his head. "This is the way it is—what we need here is a clear chain of command. If we all argue about what we're supposed to do when…Hell, let's have a committee and Miranda here can take notes in her little book!"

Nobody said anything for a few seconds.

"Whatever," Erik said, "the boat's going," he turned his head and jabbed an index finger at the city skyline, "—thataway! So who's coming?"

Miranda was already sitting in the boat and, though she didn't like his tone, she much preferred his idea of heading toward the city and, hopefully, high ground, rather than just ending up on a roof with other desperate people she didn't know. Haze shook his head and sheepishly climbed in the boat and sat, cross-legged in the bottom between the two benches.

They rowed down a lane formed by lightposts and utility poles on either side, many of which leaned into the street, wires dangling in the water. Intersections were identifiable where another lane of posts and poles would bisect theirs. They headed roughly in the direction of the skyline. Eventually they came to a commercial strip, identifiable from the tall signposts on either side. Most were empty rectangular frames because their signs had been blown out. But a couple survived. A Radio Shack, a Popeyes. A Firestone tire place. It felt good to be moving along in the boat. Much better than waiting around. "Want me to row for a while?" Miranda asked.

"No," Erik said, "I got some more in me."

Miranda dug into her backpack and pulled out a pair of pajama shorts. "I just need to get something on my head," she explained, "the sun's baking my brain." She wore the shorts like a hat, the elastic band just over her ears.

They saw what looked like columns of smoke ahead, in different spots. "A fire in all this?" Miranda wondered aloud.

"Hope the fire department got boats," Haze said.

As they got closer they saw flames, too. About a half-block away, down a side street. It was a roaring bonfire, but they couldn't see anything that might be fueling it. It wasn't coming from a house, it was just right out in the middle of the thoroughfare. Tongues of thick flame, making black smoke, coming right out of the water. Fire on water, literally.

"Is it oil?" Miranda asked.

"Could be a busted gas line," Erik guessed. "City's gonna have to cut the gas."

They witnessed the same thing again just a few blocks later.

No one spoke for a long time. Seemed like hours. Miranda just tried to stay in that space she'd found after praying for the pilot, far from the edge of panic, not looking too far into the future, just trying to witness what was in front of her—like she enjoyed doing at home in her straight-back chair, even though the circumstances couldn't be further apart. *I taste a liquor never brewed—*

Eventually the rooftops of homes began to appear around them. The ones closest to the street had apparently already been cleared. They had jagged holes in the roofs where people had managed somehow to hatchet or claw out from the attics below. The rescue was ongoing not much more than a block away. As a rescue chopper hovered over a house not fifty yards from them, they felt the wake caused by the whipping rotors rock the boat under them. Miranda peered out from under her makeshift head wrap and saw three little terrified black children being hoisted up toward the chopper in a basket. One of them seemed to catch her eye, a little boy, as full of wonder at seeing her there in a boat on the boulevard as she was to see him rising into the sky.

25

Haze thought about just leaping out of the boat and making for one of the rooftops where people were getting rescued. He was somewhat afraid of drowning. But he was more afraid of getting pulled out of the soup by Erik and then owing him. He didn't like Erik's attitude at all. Haze wasn't really used to people like this. He'd had plenty of white teachers. And got along fine with white people at the grocery store, movies, parades, etc. But he'd never really had to get along with them for a longer period of time, especially where it wasn't clear what everybody's job was. He finally got to a point where the girl Miranda was showing him respect, but Erik didn't seem interested in respecting a black man. Miranda loved God, that was something. But Erik didn't seem like the loving type.

Getting rescued by a coast guard or a fireman was different—that was their job, you knew they wouldn't throw it in your face.

On the other hand, this ride was headed downtown and as soon as his sneakers hit some dry pavement he was on his own. For now, he was happy to be crouching down low in the boat facing forward, like everybody was, so nobody had to look at each other. And none of that foolish chit-chat.

As the afternoon wore on, the sun got more brutal. Like the weather got tired of mixing it up and decided to go with long numbers instead: first driving wind and rain—enough to put the city under—then totally still and cloudless with a merciless sun to make you curse the day you cursed the rain. Miranda turned and said, "Maybe we should take a break, get out of the sun?"

Haze thought Erik would be his usual slave-driver self and tell the girl to shut up, but then again maybe the girl could sway him better than he could. Erik said, "Yeah, I'm getting kinda wore out."

But there was no point in stopping if they couldn't find shade. Trees now lined the street, more residential than industrial, but the trees weren't tall, weren't old, and the branches hung so close over the water that it would be cramped to try to get up under them. The rooftops around them were empty now, so they assumed the Coast Guard had already hit the area. Directly ahead of them on the left was a place where the choppers had probably been worked hard: a three-story school building. Draped from the third floor was a big sheet with the word "Help" sprayed across it, but the roof seemed empty. The sheet barely budged in the breeze, even though it was three floors off the ground.

"Can you see any windows open over there?" Erik asked.

"Yeah," Haze said, "they got a few." The windows were the old kind where the bottom and top panels both pivot out and then next to each other, instead of just sliding the bottom one up. Most of them were opened, as if someone had done it to get some air moving inside. Looked deserted now, though. And as they drew closer, the dusty silence only got deeper. They got close enough to peer through the windows into the shady recesses of the big classrooms. Something about it unsettled Haze, though. "This place creeping me out," he said.

"That's 'cause it's a school," quipped Erik.
They rowed up alongside. The boat was about three feet below the second floor windows. They all stood at the same time and the boat rocked, almost tripping Haze overboard. He grabbed onto a windowsill to catch his balance and then hoisted himself up and into the classroom.

It looked like a social studies class. Had a big stand-up globe next to the teacher's desk, in front of the blackboard on the wall opposite the bank of windows. Thank God for those windows, too. 39 had a new "climate-controlled" building. Lots of rooms had no windows at all and the few windows they had didn't open. Must be an oven now.

The teacher had written "Our Goals for the Year" on the blackboard in fancy handwriting. Under this you could see where less smooth lettering had been erased—she must have had students go up and try to write their goals. Above the blackboard was a row of pictures—Reverend Doctor King, Mary McCleod Bethune, and some others Haze didn't recognize. On the other walls were posters with the usual finger-wagging messages. "Respect," in big letters, with a picture of a boy talking to his grandpa. "Discipline," with a picture of some football players all lined up neatly, ready to run drills or learn a play or something.

Miranda climbed in next, followed by Erik. They all paced around the room, around the islands of desks pushed together for group work. Erik peered into the cloakroom. "They been having a party in here," he said. Haze went over and saw a pile of crushed beer cans just inside the cloakroom door.

"Think they used to have computers in here?" Miranda asked. She was at the other end of the room, standing in front of a row of four carols with wires and cables sticking out of wall sockets.

"Wait," Erik said, "listen!"

Haze, too, heard movement above, plodding feet, sliding chairs or desks.

"Should we go up and see?" whispered Miranda.

Haze was sitting at a desk groping through some kid's stuff. All new—fresh box of pencils, a glue stick, a little tablet, a brand new book about Rondé and Tiki Barber. And the kid's id: Torrance Willis Dugue. The school was Charles Drew Learning Academy. Haze thought it used to be called Judah

Benjamin.

When nobody answered Miranda's question, Haze looked up and saw they were both looking at him. They obviously wanted him to go see what was up on the third floor. "Alright, alright," he said.

"I have to, uh…tinkle," Miranda announced. Girls. Always ready with the pretty word. His mom used to say she had to "tap some dew off the lily."

"Well it's a school," Haze said, "You know they got a bathroom."

Miranda just stood there and looked at the open door to the hallway.

"Let me check it out first," offered Erik.

"Naw, naw," Haze cut in, "I'll do it, I'll check it. Y'all just…" He raised and lowered his hands in a 'sit-down' gesture. He was going to say "y'all just chill" but he felt self-conscious about talking the way they probably thought all black people talked. He was also annoyed to notice that he, too, spoke in hushed tones, like they had succeeded in spooking him, too.

He stepped quietly out into the hall. He passed another open classroom. It was probably a lot like the last one on the first day of school, but somebody had the desks all pushed to the side and put a mattress in the middle of the floor. Broken bottles, too, and the morning barroom smell of old spilt booze. But the smell wafting down the hall was worse—he knew Miranda wouldn't want to go "tinkle" in there. He peered into the half open door but didn't actually go in. The restroom floor was covered in old soiled toilet paper, diapers, too, and it was slick with some sticky liquid. He saw, too, along the walls, that people had just defecated in whatever free spot they could find. He backed away and returned to the social studies classroom. Erik was leaning back in the teacher's chair with his feet up on the desk. Miranda was sitting cross-legged on top of a kid's desk.

"You don't wanna go in there," he told Miranda.

She nodded. "OK."

Haze scanned the room for a solution. "Here," he said. He strode over to an open hutch with books and supplies on it and pulled a bunch of worksheets out of a plastic bin. "Here," he said handing her the bin. "Take it back in the cloakroom. They already got a buncha spilt beer in there. Pee pretty much the same thing."

"OK," Miranda said, taking the bin and heading for the cloakroom.

Erik nodded. "Good," he said. "We can all use it."

"Good thing I found a big one," Haze said.

Erik smiled, at least a little bit.

Haze was already thinking ahead to the hairier matter of BM. Another class's cloakroom would have to be designated for that. That is, if they stayed long enough and ate enough for that to become an issue.

More chair sliding and a flurry of murmurs upstairs reminded Haze of his next task. He wasn't sure why he was afraid. Maybe it was because they weren't all just trotting up-stairs to say hi to the neighbors? Obviously Miranda and Erik thought it wiser to send up a spy first. And he, like some black lieutenant on *Star Trek*, got the job. Well, better him than them, they were right about that. One thing was for sure: it wouldn't be white people up there, not in this neighborhood.

He headed out to the hall and up the stairs. He paused on the third floor landing and listened. Couldn't hear anything. So he nudged the hall door open as slowly as he could, stuck his head out, and saw that the hall seemed empty—of peo-ple. But it was clear that people had been here. It was littered with old food wrappers and cans and bottles. Also garbage bags with clothes spilling out and a couple of mattresses that looked like they'd been dragged around in that dirty water. He padded toward the end of the hall. The voices got clearer as he approached. Two, maybe three men, in some kind of heated discussion. He couldn't tell if it was friendly or an argument. He ducked into the adjacent classroom to eavesdrop. This room had a mattress on the floor, too. Looked like somebody had bled on it.

"Man, we shoulda gone on that helicopter," he heard a voice say.

"With all this stuff? They wouldn't even let people bring they clothes."

"What we gonna do with this stuff? How we gon' get it outta here?"

"We gotta wait and see. Don't you know the Lord will provide?"

They all laughed at that.

"What if that girl snitch?"

"She ain't gon' snitch."

"What if she do? Po-lice ain't coming. When's the last time you seen a po-lice? They done turned tail and run."

"That's why, we get us a boat, or maybe if that water go down, we got us a jackpot."

"But where we gon' pass this stuff if they ain't got no city left?"

"No city!" the man snorted. "Gotta country."

They stopped talking. Haze wanted to make his exit—he had heard enough. But he wanted them to start talking again so they'd be less likely to hear his footsteps.

"I got to go take care a'business," one of them said. A chair pushed back. Haze assumed from his tone that he meant go to the bathroom. But where? Haze pressed himself in the corner behind the door. The footsteps came out of the next room and right into the one where Haze hid. Could he be invisible?

No. The man walked right in and saw him. He wasn't

much older than Haze, but he was big. And he had an automatic pistol sticking out of the front of his pants. "Whatchu doing here?" he glared.

"I…thought I could get rescued," Haze stammered.

"Say, T., Zig-Zag, we got us a surprise in here!"

The two others came crowding through the door and looked him over.

One was his age or younger, with dreds, too, but a real shorty, shorter than Erik. The other guy was older, probably the leader. One of the few things he remembered about his dad was a conversation where his dad told him to size up a room that way. To notice who looked like what and who might be a threat and who not to worry about. He didn't see guns poking out of these other guys, but that didn't mean they didn't have them.

"Whatchu doing up in here?" the older one barked.

"I saw y'all had a sign said, 'help' and I thought they would come rescue… and I wanted to get rescued, too."

"You did?" the older one asked. "How'd you get here?"

He hadn't thought it through that far. "I swum."

The boss poked at him roughly. He jumped and the others laughed. "How come you ain't wet?"

"I come in a boat."

"Man, he just making stuff up!" laughed the one with the gun.

"You come in a boat," the leader said, "where it at?"

"They dropped me off here…to get rescued." Haze figured his best strategy now would be to act really scared—it came easily.

"Who dropped you off in a boat?" the boss said, getting up close to him.

"Aquaman?" taunted the little one.

"These white people," Haze improvised.

"White people?"

"These white people got me off my roof and they said I could get rescued here."

The men seemed to think this idea over. The lower-downs looked at the leader. He said, "Why you hiding up in here if you tryna get rescued?"

The little one broke into a grin at this, like he recognized something in the way the boss talked that was familiar and promised fun. "I say we put him back in the water!" the little one said.

"Yeah," the boss said, "you said you could swim."

"Be getting dark out there," the one with the gun chimed in—they were all playing along now. "Snakes be coming out in the dark."

"Think he could outswim a poison snake?" the little one asked.

Haze was at a total loss on what to do. But getting thrown in the water was better than leading them to those poor white kids downstairs. He continued to act scared, and it continued to be an easy act to pull off. But if only he could get them to throw him out the window in the other room—the one directly over where Erik and Miranda were—they would definitely hear him splashing in. Then maybe Erik would get the chance to save his poor black helpless ghetto ass after all. But then again, he might be a clueless boy scout about it and just get him and Miranda discovered. On the other hand, Haze wasn't sure he was ready to drown for those Barbie dolls, either.

"Naw," he cried, "wait a minute!"

"What?" the boss said.

"I...I got another plan."

"Another plan?" the boss grinned. "What plan you got?"

"Them white people dropped me off," he stammered. "Maybe they still around."

The men seemed to lose some of their hilarity and get

more focused, businesslike.

"Where they at?" asked the boss, softly.

"They downstairs."

"Ain't nobody else up in here," the chubby one said. "He lying!"

"I ain't lying!" Haze yelled. "Everybody ALWAYS telling me I'm lying! I ain't now, I ain't, ya heard me?!" He stomped the floor for emphasis with each "ain't!" He tried to get some tears going in his eyes, and that worked out pretty easily too.

"Whoa, now, OK," the lead guy said, "settle down." His sudden wild shouting seemed to put the others on edge, but the boss made eye contact with them and nodded slowly. "We gon' go down and look—if they ain't nobody down there, we gon' be mad."

"If they was somebody down there," the shorty said, "crazy face here just let 'em know we was here with all his hollering. He prob'ly working with 'em"

"Man, I look like the po-lice to you? What I care about white people?" Haze said. "They already know y'all up in here anyway."

"Green gon' stay up here with the snitch," the older one said, "Me and Zig-zag gon' snoop around." Green was the big one with the gun. The others crept off. Haze's guard just stared at him with a big mean grin. Haze had hoped they would all go down with him and he'd be able to think of something on the way.

"Man, stop looking at me, bitch!" Haze yelled frantically, like a picked-on kid at school, and kicked a desk over. He was banking on the hope that Green wouldn't kill him without getting told.

"Who you calling bitch?" Green glared.

"Everybody always looking at me!" Haze shouted. It was getting darker, harder to see, but he thought he could make out a mild look of pity on Green's face, which meant he was possibly buying the crazy act. But then he re-thought the wisdom of that approach. In a normal world, they would just let the crazy guy go—but here? Why wouldn't they just kill some crazy kid rather than putting up with him, even if he was harmless, powerless?

Haze took a few steps in a random direction—not toward the door—to see what his captor would do.

"Hey, hey, you goin' for a walk?" Green sneered, fingering the butt of the gun in his waistband. "Git yo' ass back where you was and don't jump 'less you told, y'hear me?"

Haze obeyed, but talked on the way. "Man, why'd they give you a gat? Big ol' cement truck like you gotta wave that little stick around. Not man enough to handle one nigga twice as small as you."

"Oh, you wanna talk about handle, huh? You want the gun? I'll *give* you the gun!"

It must have been still light enough to see the sudden glint in Haze's eye, because the big tough apparently figured out Haze was playing games with him. "What you putting on anyway? Acting crazy, now you acting all foxy like you think you in a movie. This ain't no movie, chump! This yo' last living breath, that's what this is!" He stared hard at Haze, but Haze just tried to look stony-faced. Even if it was his last breath, there was no point in thinking about it—better to think there might still be a way out, even if there wasn't.

"I'll still give you the gun, though," Green added, "Just you gotta get it from over here." He backed up, pulled out the gun, and laid it on a desk to his left—about three yards from Haze. Then he stepped in front of the desk and smiled. "You getting it?" he asked.

Haze took one step toward him. Green said, "alright," and waved him forward. Then Haze darted in the opposite direction—to the window—and leaped out of it.

He hit the water and went under. He splashed his arms

wildly and this somehow got his head above the surface. Whatever he was doing seemed to be keeping him afloat so he kept doing it. He was able to breathe and also turn and look around—but he was wearing out fast. His arms had to beat so fast they were losing steam after just a few seconds. He was first thrilled to see the boat—then devastated. The white kids hadn't gotten out! He thought "hell with them, I can row that thing" but knew he wouldn't be able to just leave them. He managed to reach a hand up and grab a windowsill. He knew it would be the room next to the one where they'd originally come in—the one with the boat under the window. He pulled himself up and peered inside. It was empty, so he hoisted himself up and through the window. He heard voices from the next room—white ones and black ones, so he knew his friends had been caught.

He carefully stepped around the old broken liquor bot-tles, and over the old mattress, toward the door. But again, like before, he couldn't come up with a plan. The only dif-ference was that now he was wet, sopping and dripping and heavier and slower. As he neared the door he heard footsteps and a voice coming his way, so he stepped to the side of the door and instinctively gripped the legs of a school desk stacked on top of another one.

Miranda came stumbling in, as if pushed, and the boss man came in behind her. The boss man growled, "We gon' get to know each other."

When they were both past the doorway, Haze hoisted the desk and crashed it into the back of the lead thug's head. He went down, along with a mess of thin paperbacks and colored pencils that had come out of the desk. He started to get up and Haze brought it down again. Then he got a better grip and brought it down two more times, aiming for the neck more than the head. He heard a scuffle next door, too, and Green appeared in the door with his gun drawn. He pointed it at Haze, but twisted suddenly, as if trying to get something off his back.

Miranda was standing there. Haze darted over as Green grunted again and dropped the gun and fell to his knees, still grabbing at his side. Miranda picked up the gun. Green had a broken bottle sticking out of his lower back—that's what he was trying to reach. Haze said, "Gimme the gun!"

Miranda stared at him, blankly. Then she tossed the gun, but not to Haze. She winged it, like a frisbee, through the nearest window. Haze heard it splash in the water.

They both ran to the other room where Erik was on the floor with the shorty. The shorty was on his back and Erik was straddling him and choking him. Miranda shouted, "C'mon" and hurried to the window and jumped out, into the boat. Haze was right behind her, followed by Erik. Miranda was at the oars, and the boat was already far enough out that Erik had to leap pretty far to land in it. The force of his thud almost tipped it over. Haze peered at the receding school windows. It was dark now, fully night, but he saw nothing even in the shape of a face.

26

Erik was racing on adrenalin more than he thought possible. Shaking. He hoped the others didn't notice. He thought about offering to row but Miranda seemed quite committed to the job. She wasn't steady enough, dipped the oars too deep, brought them up too fast, but the boat did keep moving away from the school, so, form or not, she was basically functional. He wanted to ask if she was all right, too, but it seemed almost like a pointless question. She probably wasn't super all right, but apparently as all right as could be expected. He knew there hadn't been enough time for anything to really happen in that other room before he heard the commotion and the guy with the gun ran out and he jumped on the other guy. He had to say something, though. It just seemed like people should be talking. "What happened back there?" he asked. Because that seemed like a less difficult question than the more urgent one, which was, where were they going?

"I don't know, man," Haze said, "I'm still trying to puzzle that one out."

Miranda sighed loudly. "Things were almost really bad but then we got away," she said, in an abrasively loud voice. "We should be happy."

Erik said, "Whoopee, I'm happy."

"You don't need to get sarcastic about it," Miranda countered.

"I'm not sarcastic. I just don't see how it's time to be happy yet."

He heard Haze grunt. He couldn't see his face—Miranda was between them. But he assumed he had some stuck-up smirk. Like he thought Erik had just blown some big play but he wasn't going to poison the team by saying anything.

"Hey Haze," he called, "How did those guys end up coming down there and where were you?"

No answer. But Haze had his own question: "Where we going?"

Miranda pulled in the oars and threw down the handles in front of her. After an exasperated silence, she said, "I guess you're right. I have no idea where I'm rowing. Let's just float, how about that? I have no idea where the %#$@ we are."

It was the first time Erik had heard the girl swear. Maybe she wasn't so prim after all. Then he tried to think about where they were and realized he didn't know either.

Miranda scrubbed at her wrist with the hem of her shirt. "I think that's blood on it," she said.

"So…" Erik ventured the question one more time: "What happened in there?" He knew there wasn't really time for the worst to happen, so he figured the question was safe. But he still didn't get an immediate answer. And the silence was deep, not only in the boat, but everywhere. Not like a city but not like the country either. There were no cars, no radios, no people shouting next door. But also no cicadas, no frogs, no birds. The helicopters had disappeared, too. The sky was the only thing like the country—it was like out over the marshes, studded with stars you never saw even close to the city. Every now and then, at a far off distance, gunfire erupted, in concentrated bursts, then stopped. They just reclined in the boat and let it twist in slow circles between the empty rooftops.

"Haze was in there," Miranda said. "He hit the guy with a desk."

"Then Miranda took out the guy with the gun," Haze added.

Erik was incredulous. "*Took out* the guy with a gun?"

"Yeah," Haze answered. And then, as if he, too, was

curious, "What did you do to him?"

Miranda exhaled quickly. "Stabbed him. With a broken bottle."

Erik whistled. "Way to go, tombraider—nice."

"I don't think of it as nice."

"I hope you don't feel bad about taking the bastard out! These people need to be taken out."

"I didn't *take* anybody *out*," she retorted. "Doesn't that term mean kill somebody? Well, I didn't kill anybody, OK?"

Haze spoke, so softly Erik could barely hear him—"Kept him from killing me."

After a pause, Miranda said, "Maybe. *If* he would have hit you, *if* he got you in like the head or the heart or something—*if* the gun was even loaded!"

Erik couldn't believe what he was hearing. "Are you supposed to think about all that while somebody's aiming a gun at you? All that thinking'll just end up getting *you* killed instead of *them*."

"This isn't a political argument. OK? This isn't forensics. And it doesn't matter because I didn't kill anybody and you know what? I really don't want to talk about it with you guys anyway."

"OK," Erik said.

The boat continued to swirl in slow wide eddies, but, miraculously, it also seemed to move in a fairly steady direction down the street, so there was some imperceptible current after all. Erik shifted his legs to keep them from falling asleep and ended up nudging the garbage bag from the yacht factory with his foot. It gave him something uncontroversial to say: "Who's hungry?"

Haze said, "We all past hungry, we on starving by now."

"Oh yeah," Miranda recalled, "There's food in there, huh?"

Erik emptied the bag into the floor of the boat. Half a bag

of cookies, two individual servings of chili, a diet coke and a
sprite. "Here," he said, "y'all take these." He handed a chili to
Miranda and tossed the other one to Haze. He heard them
peeling the tops off. After some slurping sounds, he heard
Haze say, through a full mouth, "you got something?"

"Yeah, I got one," he lied. He hunched over so they might
think he was eating even though he wasn't. "And we got cookies for dessert."

"Is that all?" Miranda asked.

"Yep," Erik confirmed, passing the drinks. "The last
supper."

27

The brain is wider than the sky. Miranda had never had reason to doubt Emily on that. She had lived by that equation. But here, tonight, reclining in the bed of this drifting boat, the sky seemed wider than the brain. So many days, so many long afternoons, she meandered in endless recesses of her mind, endless nooks and crannies always giving way to other submerged spaces. Yet here, on this bright night, the cellar door of her brain seemed firmly shut. It wasn't locked. She saw it there, waiting to be opened, but it didn't seem like the right time. The sky, not the brain, the warm brown oily water, not a sea of subconscious symbols waiting to be deciphered, hogged her attention. She didn't even want to take that mental door leading to the past, since that, too, was stored in the brain. She was pleased to realize that the mental navigation skills she'd picked up from exploring her brain were just as useful for keeping it *incognito*. She had thought of Emily earlier, too, when Haze wanted to say a prayer over the helicopter pilot. But as soon as she'd opened that door, a pale hand appeared in it and gently waved her away. She wondered even now if Dickinson's words belonged here. She wasn't sure. She wasn 't sure either way—maybe they did, maybe they didn't.

After sucking back her tepid chunky chili, and mopping out all the residue she could with fingers and tongue, she noticed how filthy her hands were. With stuff way older than the chili. She rinsed and rubbed her hands in the water but stopped when she heard Erik's remark that the water was probably dirtier than whatever was on her hands before. She dried her hands on her jeans but left a hand dangling over the side of the boat, trailing in the water. She tried to doze even though she really wasn't comfortable. She didn't want to lie lengthways in the boat, because there wasn't really room for that between the seats, and it would selfishly eat up too much space. She didn't want to be some princessy entitled girl who expected these boys to accommodate her comfort at the expense of their own. So she lay across the width of it, legs crossed portside, head propped and one hand dangling behind her starboard. Boy to the left, boy to the right. But she no longer feared them. They were in the same boat, as it were, and the boys seemed to be honoring the implications of that, too, even though they didn't appear to get along well with each other.

She sat up when her hand brushed against something stiff and furry, like a slice of wet carpet, in the water. It was a dog. Blown up like a balloon, legs sticking straight out. Light brown fur like a yellow lab or golden retriever. More white on the distended belly, and the pink of the skin toward the hind legs. Drifting around in circles like the boat.

"Dead dog," Haze pointed out.

"Yeah," Miranda said. She wondered if Haze remembered the dog he'd told her about earlier, that had become a kind of god, and how a rotting animal in water compared to one on the ground. It would sink eventually, and end up on the ground anyway. It was still under them, after all, with sidewalks, plots of grass, bushes, fire hydrants, just like before.

"See them houses over there?" Haze jerked his chin toward some rooftops to the left of the wide road they drifted in the middle of. "We should row over there and camp out on one of those roofs, huh?"

Miranda glanced toward Erik, since he seemed to want the last word on things, and then instantly upbraided herself for kowtowing to the alpha dog. He was hunched over snoring, anyway. Good for him. If she wanted to sleep, she realized, Haze's idea was best—as long as they could find a relatively flat roof.

"Yeah," she nodded. "OK."

Haze rose a little, stepped over her—saying "excuse me"—and repositioned himself on the middle seat, taking the oars. He dipped one, then the other. The boat veered to the left, then the right, but didn't really move forward at all. Miranda remembered learning to row at Camp Istrouma, in Utica, Mississippi. She glanced toward Erik again, and, satisfied that he still slept as soundly as could be expected, sat up and coached Haze quietly. "Put them in at the same time if you want to go straight, like this—" she put her balled fists to her chest—"dip, just below the surface,"—then she pushed her fists evenly forward—"then lift them out of the water…" She repeated the motions a couple of times and he got the hang of it. "If you do one side at a time it turns the boat in the direction…" She thought about it, mimed the motion, "…in the direction of the side you're rowing on."

Haze got the hang pretty quickly.

"Then it's like riding a bike," she added.

They steered into a suburban residential lane. All one-story ranch houses. Which meant, now, rows of rooftops. On closer inspection, she noticed most had rough holes hacked out from below. There was a mattress on one—which would have been inviting if it hadn't reminded her of the horrible mattresses at that grisly school. Other rooftops had clothes strewn on them, sheets. The quiet was suddenly pierced by wild barking and they saw, on the far side of the street they floated over, a trio of scraggly dogs running the length of the roofline, yelping at them frantically. Thankfully, none jumped into the water and swam at them. Erik perked up a bit, mumbled "dogs," and collapsed back into his makeshift slouch.

"That one?" Haze asked, nodding at a rare roof with

nothing on it, and no hole either.

"Sure," Miranda agreed.

They pulled up alongside. Miranda got out and stood and stretched. Haze took the rope at the bow and tied it around the house's gutter pipe. He stumbled a few paces and collapsed onto the roof, flat on his back, arms and legs splayed out wide. Erik, without saying a word, settled into the bed of the boat, lengthwise, head under the middle seat, feet propped on the front one.

All she could remember about falling asleep was how delicious the taste of it was.

She woke up to some sound close by, like someone or something moving. The dogs a few houses down had stopped their barking long ago. Now they slept, at different ends of their roof, like they didn't know each other. Haze had curled onto his side. Erik was in the same position she'd last seen him in, down in the boat. She heard a rustle again, from the house next door. The stars had faded and gray appeared in the east. It was her first sense of orientation in a while.

She stood up slowly and turned and looked behind her. She could see the shape of the city's skyline but, unlike the night before, looking from the overpass they'd crashed on, the downtown skyscrapers were dark. She supposed that meant things were getting worse rather than better. Had the water reached downtown? The Quarter? If the Quarter was under, the city was gone. Forever. After three-hundred years, toast. Maybe it was always meant to happen. Her new friend—if that's what she was—Jess, the girl from Pensacola, had said lots of people felt New Orleans deserved it. But Miranda still didn't know what she'd meant by that. Why? What had New Orleans done to Pensacola?

The rustling next door resumed. Miranda turned to her left and saw something pop its head out of a hole in the roof, and then drop back down again.

A dog? Nutria?

Erik and Haze still slept. Despite the widening gray in the east, it was actually darker now than it had been earlier, under the starlight.

The head reappeared again. This time followed by a body. It was a person, crawling up and perching on the edge of the opening, feet dangling down into the attic. It appeared to be a girl. She threw a fleeting glance Miranda's way, and then stared straight ahead again. Asian girl, looked like. But you couldn't tell from her hair because it was bright punkrock neon red, a bit longer than a bob, down to about the middle of her neck on one side.

"Good morning!" Miranda called.

The girl threw another glance her way, but then dropped back into her hole without saying anything.

"Good morning," Haze said, sitting up and blinking. "Yeah, it's morning all right," he acknowledged with some reluctance.

Miranda heard a thud from the boat, followed by an oath, as Erik slid forward to get his head out from under the seat so he could sit up. His eyes looked glassy as he cast them around. His skin was red and peeling. It looked a degree or two more severe than bad sunburn. "We parked, huh?" he asked.

"How does your skin feel?" Miranda asked.

"Like somebody went at it with a cheese grater." He held a hand close to his forearm but didn 't actually touch it. He ran a finger within a half inch of it, but didn't make contact.

"There's a girl over there," Miranda said, pointing at the roof next door. "Hey, where did you go?" she called.

"You musta seen a ghost," Haze speculated. "They must got plenty of 'em now."

"In that house there?" Erik asked.

Then the head appeared again, and the girl hoisted herself up and out and sat, knees together and arms folded, but continued to look straight ahead rather than at them.

Haze, Miranda and Erik all looked at each other. Haze reached into his pocket and came out with his mouthpiece. First he just blew soundless air into it, then slow, low long tones. Though it didn't seem to be his aim, it got the girl next door's attention. She looked over to figure out what the sound was, then looked ahead again.

Erik stared at her and smacked his dry mouth. To Haze and Miranda he said, "We gotta find some water." Then he shouted to the other girl—who seemed about their age—"You got any water over there?"

She looked up, almost met his gaze, appeared to think for a minute (which didn't make sense to Miranda), and shook her head.

Erik shrugged. "Well," he said, "we ready to move on?"

Haze buzzed an affirmative sounding fanfare on his mouthpiece and stood and ambled down to the boat.

Erik took his shirt off.

"You should probably leave that on," Miranda said.

"I can't take it. It's all stiff and…scrapey."

"Hey," Miranda called to the girl next door, "do you have an extra shirt over there?"

The girl glanced over and shook her head.

"You don't have a shirt in your house?" Miranda pressed. "Is that your house?"

"Prob'ly," Haze interjected, "she got no shirt in her attic. All the clothes in the house need to go in the dryer."

That made enough sense to make her feel bad that she asked.

"They might have a shirt over there," Haze said, gesturing at a roof across the street with an open suitcase with clothes spilling out.

"Do you want to come with us?" Miranda asked the girl.

The girl looked at the tops of her feet. Then tossed Miranda another furtive glance, looked back at her feet, and started nodding. After a few nods she said "OK."

"OK, then," Erik said, oars at the ready. Haze took a spot on the back bench, so Miranda sat on the front one. They paddled over to the new girl's house and she stood up tentatively and walked down her roof to the boat. She had flip-flops, pink polyester workout shorts and one of those vintage rock-and-roll tank-tops from Old Navy. Led Zeppelin. Miranda wondered if she knew the band or just wore the shirt. Eli had been a big classic rock head so Miranda knew Led Zep and knew that the image of the flying man on the shirt was from *Song Remains the Same.*

"You wanna bring anything?" Erik asked, when the girl had reached the boat.

She looked confused by the question.

"Is this your house?" Miranda asked.

After a pause, the girl nodded.

"You want to bring anything?" Haze repeated.

"No," the girl laughed politely, "no."

She got in behind Miranda, in front of Erik, and sat in the bottom. The boat rocked and bumped against her roof.

"What's your name?" Miranda asked.

"Vy," she replied, smiling politely.

"Vy?" Miranda repeated, "like the letter?" and held up two fingers in a 'V' shape.

"Hm-mm, yeah," she said.

"Means 'life' in French."

Vy had no response for that.

"I'm Miranda, and that's Erik, and that's Haze."

She nodded and made a lackluster effort to smile at each of them.

Erik rowed across the street and boarded the roof with the suitcase. After some rifling, he returned with a big soft floppy white T. He put it on and saw that it had a big Fat Albert face on the front. Haze openly laughed but Erik just got back in the boat and took up the oars again.

Erik steered the boat in the direction of the skyline, through an alley between two houses. Miranda heard, once again, the escalating rumble of approaching helicopters. She turned to face Vy, "Did they come through here?" She thought they must have, since every roof but Vy's obviously used to have people but didn't anymore.

But Vy just looked confused. "The helicopters, the rescue," Miranda explained, "Did they come through here?"

"Oh," Vy nodded, "yeah."

"Why didn't you go with them?" Erik asked.

She just shrugged and shook her head.

"Maybe she afraid a'heights," Haze quipped from the back.

Their way between two houses was blocked. Some kind of debris, a white plastic bag, with garbage spilling out. Closer up, they saw it was one of those cheap tourist rain ponchos they hawk in the Quarter after it starts pouring. Poking out of it was a body, a human one, floating face down with big puffy blanched legs sticking out under the poncho, swollen feet bursting out of house slippers.

Erik twisted around to see what the obstruction was. "O-Kaayyy," he sighed, and began backing the boat out.

"Yeah," Haze said, after rising slightly to see what was up, "let's go the other way."

Miranda turned to look at Vy again, to see if she had seen it, too.

"He's been there since yesterday," she said. "I don't know him."

It was not Death, for I stood up, And all the Dead, lie down—

28

Haze figured the new girl was Vietnamese. They had a couple of them at 39. He asked her where she went to school and she said Reed. That settled it—all they had at Reed was black and Vietnamese and she wasn't black. He used to think they were all Chinese, running the corner groceries and nail salons and the handful at his school. "Chinese" is the word everybody used, anyway. But then a teacher explained that they weren't Chinese, but from Vietnam, and came over after the war they had over there. He never really talked to one before, besides at the counter at the grocery. They didn't join the band or play sports or go to dances. Just kind of kept to themselves.

The sun was well up and the helicopters streaking the sky again by the time they caught sight of the Industrial Canal. Haze wasn't really sure what the plan was, but he hoped the flooding would all be on this side of the Canal so they could just walk over a bridge and hit dry land again finally.

The tallest bridge over the Canal was called the "High-Rise." It pitched up steeply a hundred feet over the waterway to allow passage for sea-going vessels without needing a drawbridge. The view from the top was like the view from a ten story building. It was so steep, it looked to Haze, when he was a kid, like the road came to an abrupt end at the top, high above the canal.

They could see now, from a distance, that the summit of the bridge had been converted into a helicopter terminal. Several choppers hovered near, and after one lifted off, another quickly came down in its spot. They couldn't see the western slope of the bridge but the eastern slope, facing them, was crowded with people.

"Where they taking them?" Haze asked. But none of his boatmates had an answer. As they drew nearer, they could see individuals crowded close to the water's edge. At this point they were rowing through the wide lake that had formed over Interstate 10. Erik stopped rowing about fifty yards out and they all surveyed the scene. There was a light chop in the water from helicopters circling close overhead and from other boats, as well.

Two airboats passed a couple of yards in front of them. They were loaded with people who looked like they'd spent a night or two on the roof. But when they reached their destination—the foot of the High-Rise bridge—they didn't seem happy about it. "This where you taking us?" they heard one of them yell. The airboat crews—who looked like average guys, not in uniform, anyway—had to all but throw their passengers off the boats. They pushed off quickly, as other people waded off the bridge after them, begging to be taken away. "We been here two days! Get us offa here!"

Erik backpaddled a few feet as they all silently watched and wondered. Haze's dream of leaving the boat behind and walking over this bridge to dry land obviously wasn't going to happen. If the other side of the Canal were dry, all these people would have walked over it a long time ago. Haze squinted up to the top of the bridge and noticed that, while each helicopter deposited a few people, they all left empty. Scanning further down, he saw a line of guys in Army uniforms pushing people back from the landing pad. Each push got a little more aggressive.

Erik caught Haze's eye and said, "Ain't no way I'm going anywhere near there."

"Me neither," Haze said. But then he wondered why Erik directed this comment to him rather than to the others up front. That's when he noticed everyone on the bridge was black. Every last one. Not a single white face he could see. Except the airboaters and the soldiers. So was Erik rubbing it in or what? What was he supposed to say? Was he supposed to want to go join that hopeless pitiful mistreated mob because that was where black people belonged? He couldn't even bear to look at the scene anymore, so he shifted around to face away from it. He thought about blowing into his mouthpiece but he felt too self-conscious.

He gazed over to the north side of the six-lane interstate. Gentilly Road and Chef Menteur Highway were over there, places where they used to go shopping. He saw the top of an army truck rumble by between some low buildings in the near distance. He turned back to the others and then the significance of what he'd just seen struck him: a truck. Not a boat. "Hey y'all, look," he exclaimed. The other heads turned in time to see another Army truck rumble by slowly, not that far away, maybe two or three hundred yards.

Miranda said, "OK—what are we looking at?"

But Erik said, "That truck, right?"

Haze nodded. "Maybe Chef Highway dry."

Erik looked to the chaotic overpass, then back to the north. "Don't have too many other options." He turned the boat and began paddling to the north side of Interstate 10. Miranda said, "Why are we going over there?"

Erik said, "You rather go to the bridge over the river hell, I'll drop you off."

"But I thought we wanted to get to the other side of the Canal, to the rest of the city, so why are we going in this direction?"

Vy spoke up. "My uncle has a gas station."

It didn't take long for them to see that as an important fact.

"It got a food mart?" Haze asked.

She nodded. "Yeah."

"Over there?" Miranda asked, pointing forward.

"On Chef Menteur, by the Canal."

Haze's first motivation had been to feel some dry sidewalk under his shoes. But the idea of a cold drink and a bag of corn chips plus the dry sidewalk was more ecstasy than he could imagine.

29

Erik felt the twelve-foot fence along the interstate scrape the bottom of the boat as they passed over it. Though he had never noticed before, the land, he now guessed, must rise fairly sharply between the expressway and Chef Highway. As they paddled once again down a residential street, they saw the rise in the land reflected by what appeared to be a drop in the waterline relative to the buildings. At the start of the first block, the water was actually over the roofline. By the end, it lapped at the tops of first-floor windows. By the end of the second block, it was at the bottom of people's windows. Over the next block it receded even further until Haze jumped out and exclaimed, "Thank you Jesus, I'm standing on land!"

The water came to just below his knee. At this point the boat started to shoal on various unseen objects in the road so Erik jumped out, too, and pulled the boat behind him. (The girls didn't seem to want to wade—they remained seated).

He heard Vy say, "It's right up there." Straight ahead was a Chevron station. He picked up his pace and saw the front end of an NOPD squad car and picked it up even more. But when he turned back to wave the others forward he noticed Haze was hanging back and eying the squad car suspiciously. Erik dropped the rope he'd been pulling the boat with and jogged up to the gas station.

He rounded the corner and saw an NOPD officer approaching the food mart. He almost shouted at him but noticed he had his weapon drawn. "Police officer!" the cop shouted. "Come out where I can see you!"

Erik stood stock still and wondered where the cop's

partner was. He didn't want to inject himself into the operation and become a hindrance, but he didn't want to turn
around and run either. The squad car was idling, door open,
with nobody else in it. They were standing in about a foot of
water.

A few young men spilled out of the food mart door,
hands halfway up or not at all, and immediately scattered in
different directions. "That's right, move along," the officer said.
But he kept his weapon up and at the ready. A couple of little
kids ran out next. The officer lowered his weapon slightly and
stepped forward a couple of paces. Then another man came
ambling out of the smashed-up door at a leisurely pace. He
seemed unperturbed by the cop's presence. He had a big bag
of chips and kept eating out of it as he walked out.

"OK, now, move along."

"Ain't nobody in there for me to pay for these chips," the
man said.

And Erik realized he had seen this man before. He was
really just a kid, probably younger than Erik. He was large,
though, about six-feet and on the chubby side, with close
shaved hair and an almost babyish face. A second later he realized where he'd seen him: at the abandoned schoolhouse. It
was the guy they called "Green." He had the same over-sized
white t-shirt, but it was browned and stiffened on one side by
dried blood.

"Step away from the door," the officer commanded.

Erik noticed that the other looters waited a few yards off
and watched.

"Why, whatchu gon' do?" Green challenged.

"Step away from the door."

Green put his hand in the bag of chips again, but this
time came out with a gun.

"Hey!" Erik called.

Startled, the cop turned. Green fired.

The cop continued turning, but more stiffly, and dropped

his gun. His other hand went to his neck, which was bubbling with blood. It kept bubbling out, like a broken water mane, quickly soaking the front of his shirt. Then he collapsed into the ashy gray water.

Erik sprinted toward Green but tripped—no, someone had grabbed his leg. Green heard the splash and turned around to see Haze grappling with Erik.

"Get offa me!" Erik hissed, elbowing Haze, who was now trying to pull him up and back.

"We didn't see nothing," Haze said.

Green's boyish face spread into an ostentatious grin. "Y'all again?!" He turned back to the other looters—the few who hadn't fled after the shooting. "Y'all not gonna believe this."

Haze was inching backward with Erik, who kept struggling to break free of his grip.

"Where y'all going?" Green yelled. "I ain't done wichya'll yet. Y'all ain't dead yet," he chuckled.

"I'm not done with you either, punk," Erik shouted.

Green and two guys behind him laughed at this. "Let'im go, my black brother, let'im go," Green entreated. "Why you taking up wit' whitey anyway?"

The conversation was interrupted by a low-flying helicopter that got close enough to perforate the water with M-16 fire. Erik and Haze stumbled and ran away from the line of fire, and Green and his crew ran in the other direction. The helicopter circled back quickly and Erik waved his hands and called to it, "Officer down! Officer down!" but they answered with another round peppered right at his feet. They got close enough for Erik to see the gunner, who sat with his legs dangling out of the open hatch. He wore jeans and a t-shirt and sneakers. There was no official insignia on the chopper, either. As it rounded its turn, the gunner made eye contact with Erik and mouthed what seemed like, "Get the *%&$ out!"

30

"We got to get outta here, man!" Haze argued. But Erik glared at him, brushed his hand off his shoulder, pushed him roughly to the side and walked back toward the boat.

"Don't be getting mad at me!" Haze called. The girls were back at the boat, but Haze knew they'd seen the whole thing, too, because they'd walked up and peered around the corner together. Haze caught up with Erik and put his hand on his shoulder again. Erik brushed it off again and said "Don't touch me, man!" and pushed him. Haze pushed him back. Then Erik took a swing. Haze dodged it, but when Erik swung again he blocked and chipped him one on the chin, just a light tap. But too much for Erik: he dove right into Haze, knocking him back into the dirty gutter water and then straddling him, trying to land punches.

Haze heard Miranda say "Hey! Hey! Get off of him!"

Haze managed to twist around and throw him off, but he couldn't back down now. He danced in the shallow water, dukes up, "C'mon, now, you want it? C'mon." Erik got up and they circled a couple of times, eyes locked on each others' faces and fists.

"You have got to me kidding me!" Miranda said. "What IS this? Y'all think this is some reality TV show? We don't have time for this."

"Yeah," Vy agreed. "I don't want to stay here. We should go somewhere."

Haze wanted to stop, too, he knew how ridiculous this fighting stuff was, but those girls didn't really understand that he had to do it if pushed as far as he'd been pushed. It was the only way this white boy would respect him.

Miranda stepped in between them, grabbing each one's shirt at the collar. "STOP!" she shouted, glaring first at Erik, then at Haze. She let go of Haze when he lowered his fists, and placed the flat of her palm on his chest. "Stop," she repeated, softly this time, and looking right into Haze's eyes. He noticed how tired and wrinkled her face looked, and how sunken it looked under her eyes.

Erik had dropped his fists, too. They just stood there. Erik looking at down at the water over their feet, with its pervasive oil-slick rainbow, and Haze finding that he couldn't stop looking at Miranda. She looked at him, too. Her brow tightened into a quizzical expression, then she moved her hand and said, "OK, now shake and make up."

"Don't push it," Erik said, getting into the boat and gripping the oars.

"No," Miranda said.

"No what?" Erik said.

"You can't be the one who rows all the time."

"Why not?"

"It's like…," she looked flustered, "symbolic. If you have the oars all the time it makes the rest of us feel like…"

"Like he the boss," Haze said. Then he corrected: "Like he think he the boss."

Erik grimaced. "Who found the *$%&ing boat?"

Miranda thought for a moment. "Thank you for finding the boat. Thank you for coming back and getting us. And for that food you got, too. Now let us help you. Just rest and let one of us row for awhile."

"OK, OK," Erik conceded.

"I'll row," Haze offered.

Erik looked like he was going to pipe up but Miranda caught his eye first and he kept his mouth shut. Then he said, "Too shallow to row here. Gotta pull till we hit deeper water."

"I'll pull then," Haze said.

So Haze pulled. He was surprised how light it was, how easy to pull, with three people in it. He figured that was one good thing about water. Better than wheels, really. When it got about knee-deep he got in and rowed. That, too, was easier than it seemed when he first tried it the night before. He could hit a good steady rhythm and it felt like something that was good for you.

When they got back to the interstate, Vy asked where they were going.

"It's about crossing the Canal right?" Haze said. "Getting to the city?"

"Yeah," Erik and Miranda said in unison.

Haze almost asked where he should cross, but he realized he could figure that out just as well as any of the others. He rowed across the interstate back to the southern side, where they'd started their day, then pivoted to the right.

"Are you worried about your uncle?" Miranda asked Vy. They were both sitting in front of him. Miranda had turned on her bench to face backward and Vy sat in the bottom facing forward. "My uncle?"

"Yes," Miranda explained, "you said he owned that Chevron station?"

"I don't think he was there," she said.

The other good thing about rowing was that he could be doing something but also think at the same time. He was hungry, hot, and sweaty. But, when he thought about it, he realized he wasn't scared. He was scared by the gas station, and back at that school. But not rowing around. He'd gotten comfortable with it. But he had trouble deciding what to think about. Ever since they got out of that gas station scrape, and he got that troubled boy Erik off of him, he was looking forward to putting together sounds in his head, that is, *composing*. Or was it arranging? It was something he did with sounds in his head since he didn't have a horn and didn't want to be bugging people blowing into his mouthpiece all the time. The choppers got him started on it. One of them coming from one direction at one speed, another one a little faster or slower from a different direction. Another one hovering nearby. Put them together and hear them all doing their thing at the same time. And recreate it different ways. The splashing of the oars in the water fit in, too. And the changing rhythm of the rocking boat, like steady and still on a backstreet or choppy over a wide boulevard. He supposed what he was doing was "making lemonade out of lemons." That's something Ms. Williams, the social worker from 39, told him. "You got to make lemonade out of lemons, Rodney. It's what black people have always done."

And that was the other, less fun thing he had to think about. Black. And Erik. Black and Erik. What was Erik's problem with black? And did he have a responsibility to confront this boy or could he blow it off?

He knew what he didn't want to think about: getting shot in the neck and bleeding to death in that stinky street water. People got killed all the time. Sure, it could be you. No point in thinking about it.

31

Miranda was proud that she got the boys under control. She'd never had people—especially boys—listen to her that way and heed her suggestions. Maybe they just needed to blow off a little steam. Of course, she couldn't be sure they wouldn't go at it again. Boy management required constant vigilance.

It was something to focus on, which she needed, to keep scenes from welling up out of her recent memory. She replayed the sight of that poor cop turning around and the gurgling out of his neck and the dazed look in his eyes, like he was recognizing the kids looking at him and trying to remember their names—before he fell. But it was pretty much like remembering a scene from a movie. Which is how she wanted to keep it. She supposed she could write about the whole thing. But it wasn't really her kind of story. She looked at her backpack, knowing her notebook and pen were in there, but couldn't visualize pulling them out and writing even the date, or her name. Actually, she didn't even know the date. Was it September yet?

Haze had brought the boat right up to the Industrial Canal floodwall. Whatever purpose it had once served, it didn't have much of one now. A thin strip of concrete threading through the water, like a token, decorative fence dividing people's lawns. As they grabbed hold of the wall and looked over, she saw that the water separated by it wasn't exactly the same. The proper Industrial Canal water seemed more like natural water meant for boats. It was choppier, seemed deeper. It was a shipping canal, a much bigger affair than an average drainage canal. Miranda had never really sized it up before, only quick glances driving over the High-Rise on the way to Florida. It seemed really more like a river or a bay than a canal. It was a far wider expanse than the new river over I-10.

Miranda, Haze and Vy all gripped the floodwall and gazed over the Canal, waiting for someone to organize the process of getting themselves and the boat over the wall and into the next body of water, to navigate the crossing. Erik seemed done with leadership. He sat forlornly on the back bench, staring into the middle distance, avoiding the faces of his comrades.

"Well," Miranda said, "we ready to cross over?"

"Ready," Haze said.

Vy nodded.

Erik kept silent. Just kept staring at nothing.

"I think he feels bad," Vy said.

Then Erik looked at her. "Yeah," he said. "I do feel bad."

"Well let's get over this channel and see what's on the other side," Miranda said. "I think we'll all feel better to get on the good side of the canal. Maybe all this disaster is confined to the godforsaken East. "

Her words fell a thousand feet into pitch black silence and she knew, again, that her foot was agile enough to kick up into her mouth. But, by now, the others knew her well enough to say something about it.

"My house is on this side of the Canal," Haze pointed out.

"Mine, too," added Erik.

"Oh, well," Miranda scrambled, "I didn't mean 'godforsaken,' that's harsh. Maybe just…flood-prone?"

"Me and Haze are on the river side of the MR-GO," Erik said. "Maybe the flooding's just on the lakeside."

"Yeah," Miranda nodded. "Could be." But she knew their hopes were ill founded.

Maybe Vy was better off. She knew her house was ruined and that was that. Probably Miranda's home uptown was the only one in the bunch that had a chance. As far as she knew, her part of town had never flooded before. She remembered the significant events from her Louisiana History class—Betsy, 1927, 1979. Then again, they had seen enough the past couple of days to know that nothing on this scale had ever happened to the city before. The Big One, indeed. Was it possible the whole city was under? That's what everybody said the Big One would bring. So if her house was dry, was this, then, *not* The Big One?

She looked at Vy and wondered about the girl's family. Did they leave her home alone? Where were they?

Nobody was talking or moving so she turned her mind to more practical matters: inertia would just make everything worse. "OK," she said. "Let's all climb up onto this wall and sit on it and drag the boat across."

Haze nodded. "Roger, skipper."

"Yeah," Erik said, "Let's do it."

Vy hopped neatly up onto the wall and scooched over to allow room for the others. Then Miranda did the same.

Haze pulled the oars out the oarlocks and slid them under the benches. Erik stepped gingerly around him to the front, grabbed the rope tied to the towring and hopped up. Haze climbed up and flipped a leg over, straddling the floodwall. Finally Erik jumped up next to Haze. "Here," he said to Haze, "grip my arm." Haze did so and Erik leaned down far with his other arm and managed to pivot the boat around to a perpendicular angle with the floodwall. He had the mooring rope wrapped twice around his forearm. He managed to hoist the boat high enough to get the bow propped onto the floodwall. "Good thing it's aluminum," he breathed. He straightened up and let go of Haze's grip and said, "Haze, can you get around me?"

Haze said "uh-huh" and stood up carefully and, with a light touch on Erik's shoulders for balance, stepped around him and seated himself on the other side of the rope and tow-ring. Working together, they pulled the vessel up pretty easily and slid it all the way over, jumping into it as soon as it settled into the Canal. Then the girls hopped in and Miranda asked whose turn it was to row. They all looked at Vy.

"You want to row, Vy?" Miranda asked.

"No."

Miranda looked out over the Canal again. "I don't want to do it either," she said.

"It's you, baby," Erik said, looking at Haze.

"OK," Haze said, and took up his place on the middle bench.

It seemed to be slow going at first. Haze seemed to be working pretty hard but not getting very far. "Don't try to cut straight across," Erik said. "You working too hard. Go ahead and drift with it a bit. We'll probably end up over there." He pointed to a couple of cranes across the Canal a bit further south.

As they approached the middle of the Canal they got stuck on something. To the right and left, poles that looked a lot like masts jutted out of the water.
"Sunken vessel," Erik said. "We probably up on the pilot-house."

Haze pulled an oar out and pushed off of the submerged surface to gain some leeway, then steered around it.

They were slowed down again as they drifted past the opening of the Mississippi River Gulf outlet. It spilled into a wide turning basin and injected a current that pushed them back toward the lake. "Don't fight it," Erik said. "Let it push us back, then go around it."

"I know what to do, "Haze said. And apparently he did. He back paddled, with the grain of the current, and then struck for the flat, glassy waters bordering the eddies sent in by the MR-GO. He located the shortest stretch of northward flowing current and cut straight across it, hard to the west.

But this tack bore its own pitfalls. Almost directly in their path was a breach in the western floodwall. The concrete panel straight ahead of them leaned outward from the canal, and water eked through on one side and freely flowed on the other—where, for a hundred feet or so, they could see no floodwalls at all. As if they had been flattened and were now totally submerged. But the water formed rapids as it poured over into the railyard bordering the canal on the western side—so something had massed up in the breach, almost filling it, which caused the current to strain and quicken in its course out of the channel.

"Looks like that's the spot to go over," Erik said.

"I gotcha," said Haze. The boat was already caught up into the stream leading over the side, so Haze had only to right the course occasionally with a light dip of this or that oar.

They had gotten so used to the constant whirr of helicopters overhead that they hadn't noticed one hovering almost directly over them. A loudspeaker came from it: "Clear the area," it blared, angrily, "no watercraft authorized for canal. Clear the area."

Miranda looked up and saw that this chopper was much larger than the ones she'd seen so far and that it was dragging along a huge canvas bag on a cable.

The loudspeaker crackled again: "Get the *&%^ out of the way, you idiots!"

They heard a light snap, and then, to Miranda's horror, they saw the giant canvas load drop from the cable. A second later it impacted the water a scant twenty feet from them, settling in the canal breach they had been striving for. They heard a sharp whizzing sound and saw something cut through the water like an invisible knife, threading right at them in a line of thin spray—the cable that had attached the load to the helicopter. Miranda felt sharp heat inches from her face and Haze jumped as the cable sliced the paddle off the starboard oar. The paddle flew into the air as the wake caused by the splashdown rolled toward them. When it hit the hull of their rowboat, the little dinghy seemed to go airborne and stay there for a second. Then it curved downward and dove, falling faster than Miranda, so that Miranda was in the air still when the bow hit the water. Her tush came down and struck the bench hard enough to bruise her tailbone, then her body, totally beyond her control, pitched forward into the canal.

She choked on some salty water before she thought to hold her breath. She kept her eyes open even though they stung and she couldn't really see anything. She scissored her legs wildly, but when she tried to come up, her head struck the underside of the boat. She groped blindly along the bottom of the hull until she felt a hand and grasped it. She came up on the side, gasping, to see Haze's face turn from terror to a beam of relief as he hoisted her up back into the boat.

"Jesus Christ," Erik said, "are you OK?"

"Yeah, she alright," Haze said, squeezing both her hands and staring into her face. Somehow his saying it made it so, even though she was still coughing and spluttering. She tried to smile back at him—she felt very much like smiling—but she wasn't sure if her face complied.

She fell onto her back, bumping her head on the rim (but that didn't bother her either). Then she sat up, in the space between the middle and rear benches. "OK," she said. Now that she was coming to terms with something that should have terrified her, and realizing she was no longer terrified, she wondered what, besides her soaked clothes, was different. Because she felt oddly changed. Something about the fear, adrenaline. Or the water?

She saw Vy's head peering over Haze's shoulder, and saw Erik directly above her, nodding and smiling, too. "We can't make it without you, boss," Erik said, "we need you."

"Who made her the boss?" Haze grinned.

"OK, OK," she said, wiping some of the wet off her face, and slicking back her hair, "your *team member* thinks it's time to get out of this canal before we all get dunked."

"Yes sir, team member," Haze replied, gripping the oars dramatically (though one was reduced to a stub, without a paddle, by the snapping cable).

Miranda's backpack had gone over when she did. She saw it bobbing a few yards off. Haze saw it, too. "Wanna go get it?" he asked.

"No. I don't need it." It had her pen, inkwell, journal. But she had no use for them now. What she needed was what was inside her. Backtracking for mementoes of a bygone time, no matter how recent, seemed foolish, immature, weak, out of touch with reality. There was no time or energy for doodling in their current impasse. Maybe another time. Maybe—she couldn't even bring herself to think 'probably'.

The wake from the sandbag drop had pushed them back almost to the middle of the canal. Another helicopter approached with another sandbag, but now, at least, they were further from the impact. Also, most of this sandbag landed on top of the last. They could feel the concussion in the air, but there was very little splash or wake.

"Can that really work?" Erik wondered aloud. "Seems nig—."

Miranda saw Haze snap a derisive glance back, while Erik bit his lip.

"You mean it seems jerry-rigged," Haze suggested.

"Yeah," Erik agreed.

"Yeah," Haze said.

"Speaking of making do," interjected Miranda, "how are you going to row this thing with just one oar?"

"Gotta do it like a canoe," Erik suggested. "Take the one

and switch from side to side with it."

That's what Haze did, though it appeared awkward, since he had to lean a lot and even slide over on the bench a little for every dip of the paddle. It was slower going, but it basically worked. In little lurches, they kept moving forward.

32

Vy Tran had never been this long on a boat before. Her Grandfather often went fishing with her brother and cousins, but she had never wanted to go. Maybe she remembered too sensitively her grandmother's stories of leaving Vietnam on a boat—actually a bunch of inner-tubes lashed together. Her grandmother, her *Ba*, had always been adamant about it: she would never get in a boat, or anything that floated on water, again.

How strange that the water came to her.

Vy wanted to be courteous and talk with her new friends—they certainly seemed nice enough. But it also seemed that she should remain silent in honor of her *Ba*, whom she still felt guilty about leaving behind. But she couldn't have asked these kids to take her with them. Who knows when they'd find a place to bury her? They would have recommended throwing her overboard, with a cheap prayer or two, so she could bloat up and float around with the others, mixed with the dead dogs and garbage. No, the attic where she breathed her last was better than that. At least it was dry.

The first inkling she had that big, irreparable things were going to happen was on Sunday afternoon on the drive over to *Ba*'s. Not the absence of traffic or the distant rumbling winds, but the giant thunderhead slowly making its way across the sky, that everybody else shrugged off. It looked like something that would have to be paid in souls. One half of the sky was clear, the other taken up by this towering deep indigo mass, like an alien spaceship, birds darting out of the way in front of it. So silent, though. And no lightning or thunder or punishing winds yet. It just quietly ate up the clear sky until it was gone. And then what had looked like a steep mountain bordering a flat clear valley just became an indiscriminate gray. By that time, she knew, all the hardships had already been written—just waiting to be fulfilled. Deep in the heart of the cloud mountain was the list that had *Ba*'s name on it.

Vy hadn't spent much time in the part of the city where they were going, the famous part that all the tourists came to see. Her family lived in the east, and on the westbank. She thought if she could get to the Interstate (an unflooded part), she could walk over the Mississippi River bridge and get to her own house. The only reason they'd spent the night at her grandparents' was that their westbank neighborhood was more prone to flooding than, they thought, her grandmother's area was. Her mother and two younger brothers had gone to Houston but her *Ba* hadn't wanted to endure the traffic. So she and her father and older brother had joined her.

She still had no idea where her father and brother ended up, since they left in knee deep water to get a boat from her uncle's a few blocks away.

Maybe they waited for her back home in Marrero, on the westbank. The big maybe—the world was going to do what it wanted, maybe this and maybe that. What was to-day? Wednesday? Thursday? Some schoolday. Maybe she was supposed to be sitting in her biology class at Ehret, worrying about the stuff they said they were going to make her cut open—dead worms, pigs, cats. Or dodging giant sandbags falling out of the sky into the Industrial Canal, where she tossed around in a little dinghy with three kids she'd never met before. Nobody knew what was written in the clouds.

"Check that out," Erik said. She turned with the others and saw a giant barge wedged into a breach in the canal wall, on the opposite side from the one they tried to plug with sandbags.

"That thing keeping the water out?" Haze asked.

"No," Erik said.

He was right. As they rowed more parallel with it they could see that there was enough water under it that it was actually floating still, gently bobbing, half in the canal and half out, as the canal placidly emptied into a broad lake punctuated by treetops and a few buildings. Not that many houses, though. At least, Vy thought, not that many people had lived here—whatever the neighborhood was called.

33

Erik knew the neighborhood, if only from driving through. It was the Lower Ninth Ward. He looked at the back of Haze's head but couldn't tell if he was taking it in or not. But he wondered what had happened to all the houses that had lined the Canal. He could see only a few scattered rooftops where there had been densely packed blocks. He wondered if his bearings were confused until he recognized a couple of landmarks—a steeple, some big public building, school, whatever. They were things he'd noticed whizzing by on the north side of St. Claude Avenue on his drive to and from Archbishop Leray. But it was confusing because these landmarks had been surrounded by other houses that now appeared not to be there. A stand of tall trees in the midst of the wide watery expanse provided a clue: roofs and walls and doors and windowframes, and mattresses, and couches…and a car, had piled up against them, like tree debris on the cutting bank of a river after flood stage. But it was houses. Whatever had happened here must have gone differently than the flood where they were, which had been slow, creeping, and quiet. It would have taken a mighty current to wash all those houses off their foundations and sweep them along until they smashed up against the nearest obstacle. And he knew it was 99 percent certain they had people in them when the sudden deluge struck. People probably even now stuck to the walls, had to be.

Haze's people? Hopefully they lived closer to the river, probably it wasn't so bad there. And what about his own people? If the Lower Nine was under, hope for Chalmette seemed that much more elusive. There was no levee in between. Just the Jackson Barracks, home of the National Guard. Surely the Guard wouldn't put its barracks in the middle of a flood zone—maybe the land hiked up imperceptibly along with the home values somewhere between the urban ghetto of the Lower Nine and the suburb of Chalmette. Grounds for hope, however flimsy.

Haze wasn't paddling much, and seemed to be letting the boat drift in the direction of the barge breach they were all staring at. So Erik said, "We're not crossing over to this side, trying to get to the city side."

"I know," Haze protested. "Just taking a look."

"Do you recognize this neighborhood?" Miranda asked.

"No," Haze said.

The canal was wide and calm at this point, so it was easy for him to turn fairly sharply to the right—with one oar, turning was easier than going straight. The straight shot to the opposite shore was more laborious, but Haze kept at it, body moving in a nice steady rhythm, until the job was done.

Haze was a nice guy. But it was hard to tell what was going on his his head. He had that blank face that didn't show anything. Could be planning to stab you in the back at the first chance—or not. Erik's dad had sent him mixed messages on how to deal with people you'd never met before. In some moods he'd said don't trust anyone but yourself. Other times he'd said you pretty much had to trust people until they gave you a reason not to. And, honestly, Haze had not given him a reason not to. So maybe he was one of the good ones.

He learned fast. Had gotten a pretty good hang on rowing. A few minutes later they were bumping the floodwall on the western side, the side where the skyline loomed a few miles away. In the burning sunlight they could see black patches on top of the Superdome, as if some of the roof had been sheared off or collapsed. Immediately over the floodwall they were disappointed—not shocked—to see the same brown water with the oily sheen over the top, stretching down the sidestreets in all directions. But at least this side of the canal, the Upper Ninth Ward, had the same street layout and houses it had before the storm. There were a few stripped roofs, and the ubiquitous dangling wires and cables from the dead powerlines above, but other than that, if you kept your eye a good eight feet or so above where the ground used to be, the view looked pretty much the same as last week. It had become Venice, though, a city of canals instead of streets.

Also, the water on this side appeared to be less deep. Maybe just six, or even five feet, instead of eight or twelve. And more of the houses had second stories, and, because they were older, more were built the old fashioned way, raised a few feet off the ground. If you had a boat, you could just live on the second floor and get around fine—until the water rotted out the submerged frame, sucked the mortar out from the bricks in the pilings, and the whole structure collapsed. But that would probably take weeks, if not longer.

They all got out and sat on the floodwall while Haze and Erik pulled the boat over and lowered it in on the other side. The floodwall here on the western shore rose a few feet higher out of the flood than the scant foot or so where they had come from. Erik dropped back into the bass fisher and offered to row.

"Fine with me," Haze said.

They all got back in, Haze behind him like before, which had made Erik nervous at first, but not so much anymore. They were all too bushed to spring anything on each other now. The sun was starting to slant, making shade from tall trees and houses in the narrow backstreet canals.

At first he rowed directly away from the Industrial Canal, just to put some distance between them. He knew he had to cut to the left after a few blocks to approach the river, where the highest ground and—hopefully—the heart of the old city was still to be found. A wide avenue, a row of live oaks down the middle, offered a nice straight shot riverbound, so Erik lazily curved to the left and drifted while he selected a felled oak branch which could stand in as a paddle. It proved more difficult for Erik than it had been for Haze to propel the wide flat skiff like a canoe—his body and arms just didn't have the required extension. So he found a longish, more or less straight limb with a tight bunching of smaller branches and leaves at one end. He pulled the bare end through the oarlock and it functioned almost like a regular paddle. He straight-ened up and pushed the boat along at a comfortable steady pace. A sign confirmed what he had hoped: it was Poland Avenue, which ended up crossing St. Claude right before the drawbridge that led to Chalmette.

Poland Avenue proved to be a smooth, easily navigable stream, despite the occasional obstacle of houses washed off their pilings into the middle of the thoroughfare. They sat at angles like foundered ships and had to be rowed around. Erik looked through an open window of one of them and saw a neatly kept bedroom. Because of the angle, the furniture had slid down the floor and collected at one end of the room, but the bed was still made, and the family pictures, along with a Jesus portrait, still hung on the wall. A darker square under the pictures showed where the dresser had stood for years.

It was so quiet on the avenue as to be almost peaceful. There were breezes, however weak, and shade. No one talk-ed. And the helicopters, though they could still be heard, were apparently far off in the distance. Just the dip of oar and branch and the sound of parting water.

His thoughts turned from Haze to Vy. He had never seen a Vietnamese club girl. Well, he had, at those places Ashleigh used to drag him to. But not many and he'd never talked to one. She didn't seem to have an accent. Probably born here, he surmised, a regular American girl. She was quiet but she didn't seem shy. Her face looked like a girl just planning on where to go shopping or where to go out or something, not sad or tragic. Just like thinking about normal things. Pretty, too.

They passed a few houses that seemed to be inhabited. Balconies and raised porches had coolers, faintly smoking grills, couches with sheets on them, and mattresses dragged from inside. A few had boats lashed to the railings. And they passed people, too, old folks mostly, scantily clad and fanning themselves, who waved as if it were just an average summer evening on the Poland Avenue Canal residential development.

Just as he started to envy the people in the houses—because they had dry sleeping arrangements with roofs actually over them instead of under them—a breeze brought the sound of windchimes down the avenue. It was the bamboo kind. They had one in their yard, too. Deep, flutey sounds. As they drew closer, they heard also the small tinkly metal ones. They came from a house on the right, from a wide balcony on a two-story townhome. It had lots of plants on it and wicker furniture…and cats, lots of them. Erik counted seven before he saw a woman, too, who rose from a hammock and leaned over the railing to greet them. An older black woman with long gray dreadlocks that looked almost like matted hay. Erik waved back, as did the others, as they had done to the other nice old folks along the avenue. The house was painted like a Jamaican vacation cottage, bright yellow, green, and red. As they drew within a few feet the woman's eyes widened, as if in recognition, and she said, "Oh Lord, Rodney? Is that you?"

34

Though he never liked being called "Rodney," Haze was happy to see Ms. Williams. Of all the folks at 39, even more than Mr. Brice, she was the one he would have picked to run into at a time like this. She was a counselor, after all, and, man, did he need some counseling. She was also a really nice lady who made them all very comfortable. They moored their boat and climbed up onto the balcony and walked inside the first regular house they'd been in since they'd left their own. It was eerie: the bottom floor was flooded out but the top was totally unaffected. From the inside, you couldn't tell anything had happened. No AC, TV, or even fans, but it was surprisingly cool in there. "High ceilings and transoms," Ms. Williams informed them.

"Transoms?" Haze asked.

Miranda pointed at a little rectangular window over a doorframe—each door had one.

"Yes," Ms. Williams confirmed.

Haze's house had them, too. He hoped the fish liked them.

She offered them water right after all of them collapsed on the soft couch and easy chairs in the living room, which opened through wide double doors onto the balcony. "Rodney, would you help me?" she asked.

"Yeah, Rodney," Erik chuckled.

Ms. Williams gave Erik one of the those smiling squinting teacher stares to wipe the grin off his face, then Haze went with her back to the kitchen. The house smelled of incense—Song of Sudan—but he didn't see it burning anywhere. The cats followed them into the kitchen mewing. "Only three of these are mine," she said. "Going to have a public health emergency dealing with their potty needs," she complained. "I'd like to shoo them all to the back porch at night, but the bad ones are out there."

Haze looked through the screen door and saw several tough-looking toms scoping him out. "At least they not people," he said.

Ms. Williams gave him a quizzical expression. "People seem to be making out pretty well, considering."

"Don't seem like that to me," Haze countered.

"Well," she sighed, taking a stack of Mardi Gras cups out of a cabinet, "I have to wonder where you've been, child. I hope you'll tell me."

"Yeah, I'll tell you."

She gave him another curious expression and it dawned on him that she might think he was acting rude. "Yes, ma'am," he corrected.

She grinned. "Hm," she clucked.

He was fine with telling her everything, but he just didn't know when to do it. He didn't want to spill it all in front of the others.

She had a few big five-gallon water jugs from a delivery service. "Could you lift another one of these on for me?" she requested, pointing to a dispenser in the corner. Haze took the empty one off, peeled off the top of a new one and upended it onto the dispenser. He was momentarily mesmerized by the great belching bubbles in the whirlpooling water as it filled the ceramic dispenser. It sounded luxurious when cup after cup was filled from the rushing spigot. They each carried two cups back into the living room. These were all downed in a second so they went back, re-filled, and returned.

Just as thoughts turned to food, they heard a shout from outside.

"Mama C! You there, mama? Got some for you!"

They followed Ms. Williams out to the wide balcony and saw a shirtless man with a nappy 'fro and beard in one of those old-fashioned wooden canoes—a pirogue. The middle of the boat was littered with cans—full ones. "You got guests, mama?" he inquired.

"Yes," Ms. Williams said, "unexpected but welcome. Whatchu got in there?"

"I reckon enough. For tonight." He rummaged in the cans. "Winn Dixie on Almonaster pretty much cleaned out," he reported. "But they got little groceries all over ain't much been picked over yet. Here, you want some yams?" He held up a can.

Ms. Williams took it and a few more—peaches in syrup, a couple of cans of petit pois, *Blue Runner* red beans, and a couple of bags of plaintain chips. "You went by the Cubans, huh?"

"Yes, ma'am," he said.

"They over there?"

"No, they not around."

"You want some water?"

"No, I'm alright, mama. I filled up the bathtub."

"You still drinking that city water?"

"Ain't killed me yet," he said, shoving off, "I'll check on you tomorrow."

"OK, then," she called, waving.

"I filled up my sinks and bathtub, too," she told them as they filed back inside, each ardently cradling a can. "But I use them just for washing. Maybe y'all want to wash up a little bit, but y'all prob'ly want supper first."

"Was that your son?" Miranda asked. Haze was embarrassed by the question. The guy didn't look anything like her and was too old to be her son anyway.

"No, child," she said. "They call me Mama C in the neighborhood."

"Why?" Miranda pressed.

"Not sure. Just always have. I've always been active in the community."

"What's the C stand for?"

"My first name's Calinda," Ms. Williams said. Haze couldn't tell if she was irritated or OK with Miranda's interrogation. It just didn't seem respectful to ask her all those questions.

"Whew," Ms. Williams said, "Let me get a fan on." She reached behind a chair and clipped a small rotating fan onto the window sill.

"You got a fan?" Haze asked, incredulous.

"Got a few," she answered, "Run on batteries. I save them for the evening since it's no point blowing the hot air around during the day."

Haze followed her back into the kitchen where they opened the cans and put a bit of each onto paper plates and took them out to the others. After prolonged silent chomping, Ms. Williams said "It's nice in the evening to lay in the bath with a fan on you. Really cools you down. Y'all could take turns. I got a bathtub with water that hasn't been used at all yet."

Miranda was the only one who nodded vigorously. But Ms. Williams said, "Of course y'all will have to take turns. Rodney can go first and then y'all can decide who's next."

Following her into the kitchen with the empty plates, which were placed out on the back porch for the strays to have at, he asked why she decreed he should be first in the bathtub. "Because I know you, honey," she answered.

"Miranda could have my turn," he said.

"Is that the white girl?"

Haze nodded. "Yes ma'am."

"You like her?"

Wow, Haze thought, this woman was just as bad as Miranda. "I like her like a friend," Haze retorted. "I'm supposed to like her some other way?"

"You not supposed to like her any way," was her answer. "So that means how you like her is totally up to you."

"Guess you right about that." Haze didn't know how he felt about Miranda. That is, he didn't recognize how he felt about her. The closest thing was how he'd felt about characters in movies from time to time. Or magazine covers, even. Jennifer Anniston, for example, even though he would be way too embarrassed to ever tell that to anyone. In other words, the way he felt about Miranda was like what a kid in the line at the grocery store would think about some celebrity in *People* magazine. But he knew her so he supposed she could be called a friend. Even though when this ordeal was over there was a less than zero percent chance he'd ever see her again.

"Say, Ms. Williams," Haze ventured, "I could ask you a personal question?"

"You can ask. I might not answer."

"You got white friends?"

She pursed her lips. "I think so. I mean I know I *have* had white friends. A couple I was pretty tight with, too. I don't know about now, though."

"Why not?" Haze pressed. "They do you wrong?"

"No. It's just…the way our society is, it takes effort. Back when I was closer to your age, people made that effort more, white people, too. Now folks just want to be comfortable, so maybe they hang around their own people more."

Haze nodded.

"But that doesn't mean black and white CAN'T be friends," Ms. Williams explained. "I got white *allies*. And I know we need that. More than friends. But my point is, there's not much point in thinking about it, either way. Except to understand history and how things got the way they are."

"You mean all the things white people did to us?"

"Yes, Rodney, but…" She shook her head and frowned,

trying to find words. "Even that *us* sounds so strange right now because…I'm not sure we—I mean black people—are even an *us* anymore. And I don't think we can blame white people for that."

Haze didn't understand and it must have shown on his face because Ms. Williams shook her head again and said, "I'm not being very clear." It also seemed to Haze that her eyes were tearing up. The whole topic was obviously upsetting her. "I'm afraid we failed," she said, voice cracking. "We got to a certain point and then…I just thought things would have turned out better."

Haze wondered how, like if things were better, how would they be? It seemed to him that, minus the storm and the immediate crisis of the past few days, things were OK, or had been.

"We stopped caring for our own," she continued. "When the white folks was holding us down, we took care of our own. As soon as they gave up the fight, we did, too. Not for ourselves, but for us as a community. Started acting like white folks, all about making good for ourselves, leaving the community behind. Ever heard a white man talk about holding out a hand for his white brothers? Besides a klansman? They got us as soon as they told us we could be regular Americans. We reached for the pie and kicked our brothers and sisters out the way. Just like they do. And getting mad at your white friends ain't doing nothing for that situation."

"I'm not mad at them." Haze considered. "I just don't know what they thinking about *me*."

"They might like you."

This was a possibility that hadn't really occurred to him. But he liked the idea.

35

Miranda never thought she'd get naked and get in someone else's dirty bathwater before. But the same went for stabbing someone with a broken bottle, witnessing cop killings, and embarking on a rustic urban survival cruise. If one of the others had preceded her in the bath she would have felt ickier. But Haze was different. He seemed familiar and at the same time strange enough to be interesting. He seemed somehow solid, reliable, strong and…ethical. Like Denzel Washington playing an inner-city teacher or a starship captain. And there was something captivating about his face. The high cheekbones and forehead, almond shaped eyes. His skin was so UN-teen. Smooth, clear, not blemished by acne or redness or pockmarks. He was tall, too. She assumed most women would classify him as attractive, but, honestly, she had never found something particularly physically attractive in any men before, not even movie-star heart-throbs, even though she had to fake it back when she tried to have girlfriends a few years ago, before she gave up on that experiment.

But Haze filled her with a warm curiosity. She wanted to have a sincere, private conversation with him, ask him about everything. Nothing he had gone through would shock her because she already felt, on a gut level she hadn't known was there, safe, comfortable, even content around him just from the way he was.

But she also knew that the moment—lying in cool water with the little fan brushing her slowly from head to foot and back again—was having its influence. In other words, the psychic impact she was attributing to Haze could have very little to do with him and more to do with cool bath, fan, flickering candle. In order to gauge her immediate feelings, she had always compared them to past feelings in similar circumstances. If the subject was boys, that meant Eli. But she was having trouble remembering the her that existed a week ago. Sure, she remembered all the stuff she and Eli had done, including his physical overtures which, after a couple of make-out sessions, had just turned her off to seeing him at all. But she couldn't remember the quality of her feelings that well. Especially when she tried to match them up to Haze. If the subject was romance, she used to imagine herself in the antebellum period, and in the Civil War, doing things like saving her horses from stables set alight by marauding yankees. For obvious reasons, it was hard to fit Haze into these scenarios. Then again, whenever she had tried to insert men at all, the fantasy got hazy and eventually faded away. Lying in the tub, hearing the indistinct murmurs of Haze and Ms. Williams in the adjoining room, she found that her formerly elaborate daydreaming couldn't really get off the ground. And when she tried to clear her mind and just feel the texture of the moment, she found she couldn't do that either. It seemed all she wanted to do was get out of the tub and jump back into the experience that she had thought—until she got into the tub—she wanted so much to escape.

She got out and dried off and took a moment to marvel at how, for the first time in her life she could remember, she wanted company more than solitude. And kids her own age!

The bathroom was in a hall connecting the kitchen to this other room that Ms. Williams called her "chapel room." It had a few chairs facing a big chest of drawers topped by a crowded assortment of candles, statues of varying sizes and styles, old flowers and herbs in waterless vases, and pictures in frames. Some of the stuff was Catholic, like saint cards and a couple of little saint statues, but there were also some

African carvings, including a big mask on the wall. The pictures seemed to be family members, going back to some very old-looking photos, formal portraits of stiff frowners in hats. But there were also some prints, of slaves, that Miranda had seen re-produced in history books. On the wall behind the chest were some abstract designs in chalk, patterns roughly in the shape of crosses and exes, sprouting curlicues and bounded by constellations of dots. Ms. Williams and Haze seemed to be having a deep conversation, so Miranda just kept moving through to the front room, where they'd put down cushions from couches and chairs to make pallets for each of them. Candles lit up this room, too. The fan was turned off since no one was in there.

Miranda went on out to the porch in search of Erik and Vy. They were out there but didn't seem to be talking. There, too, candles flickered in the light evening breeze.

"The only thing bad about that bath," Miranda said as she sank into a wicker chair, "was putting back on these horrible clothes." She had traded her stiff jeans for a pair of cotton shorts—intended for sleeping, but used most recently as a hat—but put on the same old bra and one of her dad's dress shirts she'd had on for…days? She had to do calculations to figure out how long it had been. When she came up with the answer she shared it with the others: "Can you guys believe it's only been three days since the storm?"

They didn't say anything so she elaborated: "So that means that four or five days ago, it was just the way our lives used to be, like our regular lives. I just find that impossible to believe, but it's true."

Erik looked up from the ground, at Vy, and then at Miranda. "That's depressing," he said. "I don't want to talk about before, the way things used to be."

"But how can you talk about after? I mean, who knows?"

"It doesn't matter," he said. "After's all there is."

Vy perked up a bit. Raised her eyebrows and nodded. Looked like she was preparing to say something but didn't.

"No before, no after," Miranda observed, "doesn't leave much to talk about."

"Can talk about now," Erik offered.

But that seemed more like a philosophical conundrum to Miranda than a possibility. Did he mean talk about their surroundings? "Yeah," she said, taking in the candles and the winding oak branches rising out of the water and stretching down the avenue in both directions. "It's a weirdly beautiful night."

Vy nodded again.

"But the weirdest thing," she added, "is how unimaginable this whole experience was just a few days ago." She immediately realized she had brought up the past again, so she admitted it. "Wow," she sighed, "it is hard to not talk about before." She realized, too, that Erik probably made that recommendation because of something with Vy. Miranda knew that her parents, and Erik's and Haze's, were presumably safe. But that somehow didn't seem likely with Vy.

"Let's talk about tomorrow," Erik said. "Like the plan."

Miranda sighed. "It's comfortable here. So hospitable. Peaceful."

"We gotta move on," Erik countered. "Can't just sit around here."

Miranda yawned. "I'm just too tired to think right now." What she realized but couldn't say was that this present was not really all that unbearable to her. As long as they stumbled on food and water, and met nice people instead of killers, it was an interesting lifestyle, somewhat like traveling.

She went in and saw that Ms. Williams had come into the living room, too. Haze sat on one of the cushions on the floor. Miranda took the one next to him. "Hi," he said, but inched a bit away from her.

Ms. Williams sat on a rocker in the corner. Erik and Vy came in and lay on the other two pallets. Ms. Williams told them they could stay as long as they wanted. That she would send a message with the man who'd come earlier, so their people could come and get them, though—who knew?—it could take a while.

"Naw," Erik said, "We gotta move on."

"Yes," Ms. Williams noted, "Rodney said the same thing."

Miranda was mildly surprised that Haze, too, had advocated moving on so soon. She had thought he might want to stay with her, since they seemed to know each other.

Haze had the next question, directed at Ms. Williams: "How long you gon' stay?"

She harumphed. "Where I'm gon' go?"

"You could come with us," Haze volunteered. "To higher ground."

"They ain't go no '*higher ground*' somewhere in this city. Might be ground with no water on it, but it ain't higher ground."

Miranda wasn't sure what she meant. "I think Haze means dry land," she interjected.

"Oh," said Ms. Williams, "I don't know if I like dry."

"I know why she wants to stay," Vy said, sitting up on her pallet.

They all looked at Vy. Miranda nodded encouragingly.

"It's…" Vy seemed to grope for words. "…what's here."

"I know what she means," Erik said.

"I don't," said Haze.

Miranda said, "I'm afraid I don't either."

Ms. Williams peered at Vy a second longer, then turned to Miranda and said, "I think your friend Vy does know what I mean, better than me, I think." She knitted her brow and offered Vy a sympathetic smile. "Although my sense of it might be less personal, more—," she considered, "—collective." She cast her eyes down and then lifted her head, though her eyes were closed. "My people have died here."

The announcement fell on the air in the room with a solemn, almost liturgical ring. They all just chewed on it in their own ways. Like Haze, this black person wasn't like the ones Miranda had met before—a few kids at her school and, honestly, janitors, Winn Dixie cashiers, etc. Ms. Williams was more like some movie character. Or was it the lighting? That influence of the moment that clouded rational apprehension? *Inebriate of Air—am I—And Debauchee of Dew-*. Or maybe just that she'd never been in this kind of situation with black people—that was probably it.

After a slow deep breath Ms. Williams continued, "Have y'all heard of San Malo?"

Sounded like a Mexican-American War battle to Miranda, but she wasn't sure, and, for once, didn't open her mouth anyway.

"These waters," Ms. Williams went on, "they come back to us every time a child turns grandmother age, to remind us of our earthly status. It ain't new—a flood. But for Juan San Malo these waters were his salvation, his freedom. He was a slave. At least was considered so for a while, until he made his own freedom, not by the rules of money and society, but by the greater forces of the spirit. Which one of y'all knows what a maroon was? What that means—maroon—back in slavery times?"

The other kids shook their heads—except Erik, who had a pillow over his face—and Miranda, who knew the answer. She almost raised her hand but stopped herself before the elbow went up. "Escaped slaves who formed independent communities in the swamps, sometimes aided by Indians, and lived off the land."

Ms. Williams beamed as Miranda almost blushed from the approbation.

"Rodney," Ms. Williams complained, "how come this girl knows that and not you?"

"I don't know," Haze said.

"Oh, don't fret," she said, "it's not you. It's what we were talking about back in the kitchen. Remember?"

Haze nodded thoughtfully.

Miranda blushed again, but this time in a bad way. She surmised he wouldn't take well to her knowing more about black history than he did. Not because he was black—because he was a boy. She remembered how Eli used to love to lecture her about classic rock, and she had to smile and go, "Oh yeah? Cool" over and over again. Then she remembered how totally unlike Eli this other boy was, in looks and everything, and had a hard time thinking of Haze as a boy at all. More like a man, yes—but a man in a movie, not like any actual one she had ever come across.

"Juan San Malo came from up around Des Allemands, what they used to call the German Coast, up the river in St. Charles Parish." Ms. Williams took a deep breath, as if trying to remember details. "Instead of butting his head against the Cabildo or the Calaboose, by leading a direct uprising against slavery, he just founded a new country right where he stood—in a puddle of water nobody thought you could live in. They called it Gaillardeland. It started right back of every back fence of every plantation along the river." She took a sip of water and continued. "Right outside that door," she pointed," was a *pasaje*, a secret route to one of a network of secret settlements where Creole slaves built cabins and lived off the bounty of the bayous. On the corner over there is Miro Street—Esteban Miro was the governor who went after the maroons in the 1780s and finally captured San Malo. But the funny thing about the villages San Malo founded is that they weren't totally isolated, but—until Miro went after them—just a normal part of life here. The maroons came to town and traded in the markets, visited the plantations where they had friends and kin, spent the night if it got too late. Back then, before the Americans, things were a lot more fluid. You had a lot of free blacks in New Orleans so nobody could be sure just from your skin color if you were slave or free. As a matter of fact, the first people Miro sent after San Malo were free black militia. Then they tried to pay slaves to go find him, but they found out that the slaves were just taking their money and lying about where San Malo's villages were. For a while it didn't seem worth it to go after the maroons, who were pretty much minding their own business. But there kept being more of them. A lot of the slaves went back and forth—to Gaillardeland and back to New Orleans—but the work on the plantations basically got done and San Malo never said anything about wanting anything but to be left alone."

She paused and rocked, as if waiting for someone to ask, "And then what happened?" When no one asked she continued anyway. "But the bigwigs at the Cabildo started worrying about the example that was being set, and about the audacity. Just looking the other way while a regular percentage of slaves quit and went off to a free community just a few miles away from the Big House started to seem like a risky course of action. And maybe San Malo had other plans besides just offering an alternative lifestyle to bondage—what if he woke up one morning and wanted revenge? There were at least a hundred maroons out there already and they all had guns. And the bigger the communities got, the more comfortable and attractive they started to look to slaves still on the plantation. So they started sending out expeditions to find him.

"But the *pasajes* were like a labyrinth, and every settlement was tucked away behind thick cypresses, brush, and waist-high water full of snakes and gators. The maroons didn't fear the swamp water—that was their strength. Also, even if an expedition did get close, they made so much racket hacking through the brush and slapping at the mosquitoes that the maroons were long gone by the time this or that cabin was discovered. And San Malo himself moved around a lot. In Des Allemands one day, Congo Square the next. Drinking at a tavern in the city on Tuesday, out at Chef Menteur by Wednesday. The Spanish figured out soon enough that pretty much every slave in the city knew him, had just seen him the night before, and knew exactly where the misty capitals of Gaillardeland were located. A whole lot of them had been out there, in fact. They just didn't keep as tight a leash on the slaves in the Spanish days as they did later, after the Americans came.

"Finally, they found a rat. A slave busted for stealing a chicken. To get out of his lashes and for two-hundred pesos on top, he guided a couple of pirogues of Spanish grenadiers and paid slaves to root out San Malo. It was the slaves that caught him. Like always, the maroons heard the party coming at them from a mile away and took off on foot over a marsh, wading through chest-deep water. One of the slaves, who'd been with San Malo before, knew the direction they would take. He scurried up an oak and unloaded buckshot at some rustling marsh grasses. San Malo must have been praying to the wrong god, because he took a hit in the leg. He rose as best as he could and identified himself. The ruckus of everybody in the search party trying to claim they got him allowed the maroons with him to get away. San Malo they brought in, put him in the *calabozo*, the jail behind the Cabildo.

"Miro had wanted him to get a fair trial, but he was in Pensacola doing an Indian Treaty. They had this guy Reggio who wanted to hurry up and hang San Malo, mainly because the wound in his leg where he got shot had gotten infected and he wasn't expected to live out the week anyway. They tortured him to get him to name accomplices, but he never did. Even on the gallows where they hanged him in front of the

Cabildo, he proclaimed the innocence of himself and all the maroons from the crimes they wanted to put on them. They left his body hanging there for the buzzards to feed on as an example, but the example backfired. They wanted the slaves to quake in fear at what might happen to them if they ran off to the swamps. But instead they made a maroon hero.

"San Malo was born in Louisiana. He didn't want to go 'back' to Africa even if he could. And he didn't want to flee somewhere else. He wanted to be free *and* home. Before America declared independence, San Malo declared independence for enslaved Creoles of color. And then, lo and behold, the free blacks thought he acted kind of heroically, too, and they started to wonder if, given the treatment San Malo got, they could expect much better—even if they were technically free. Even the white people started singing songs about him. Because he didn't sell out his people, or his country. And he was a master of the bayous."

She stopped talking and sat there nodding, protruding her lower lip in thought, and rocking. Miranda thought the story was at the same time deliciously romantic but also more hopeless than Ms. Williams made it out to be. It's not like slavery was ended anytime soon after that. The whole scene she found herself in reminded her of this Disney movie, *Song of the South*, that her parents had brought back from Japan (since it was considered racist in the U.S.), where the old slave Uncle Remus spun tales by firelight. She realized then why both Haze and Ms. Williams seemed more like movie characters than real. It was only in movies that she had seen white and black spend so much quality time together. Yet both her parents talked lovingly of old black ladies that were a big part of their families growing up. They had spent a whole day of a family vacation once driving around backroads in Mississippi looking for one of these ladies. Her mom was in tears at the end of the day because they couldn't find her.

What had happened? She knew, the Civil Rights Movement. But she didn't know if it was because black people didn't want to be around white people anymore, because of what they had done, or because white people didn't want black people around anymore if they couldn't still boss them.

"So now I hope y'all can see," Ms. Williams continued, "why I don't want to leave here. San Malo consecrated the very land we're sitting on now—and yes, the water, which is a part and parcel of that land—as the homeland of the Afro-Creole people, an independent nation. I ain't giving it up. Other people in the rest of America might see it differently, but the way I see it, staying put in the land your ancestors claimed is the way to stay spiritually intact. My own blood was shed on this spot. Hell no, I ain't going."

Miranda wanted to ask why Africa wasn't Ms. Williams' actual, more original homeland, with the ancestors and everything, but she thought her question might be taken the wrong way. Of course the ancestor game could be taken a bit far. Who really knew anything detailed about ancestors past a great-great-grandfather, maybe? She thought America was really only the true homeland of Native Americans. If you were going back two-hundred years or so, why not five-hundred or a thousand?

Apparently Vy was thinking the same thing. She asked, in that timid way that clashed so much with her hair, "Well, what about Africa—is that like a home, too?"

Ms. Williams seemed more amused than offended by the question—though Haze seemed to frown at it. "I suppose," she conceded, "but it's way more distant than even two hundred years ago here. It's a symbol, and some people all they got is symbols." Then her face darkened and her tone became more brusque. "Anyway, who do you think sold us over here in the first place?" She didn't wait for a hand to go up.

"Africans. It was other Africans sold us onto those ships just like that slave that sold out San Malo. And San Malo and them created a new language, culture, everything. I ain't African. I'm Creole. And it might be small, but this here is Gaillardeland, homeland of the free Afro-Creoles, land where my fathers died, like the American song says."

Miranda would never have thought someone could see an ancestor getting shot and hanged as a reason to love a place. But she was beginning to understand. At least she thought so.

"I think I know what she means," Vy said softly. She opened her mouth to add something but stopped. This time Ms. Williams pressed her. "Do you have a question?"

"Yeah." She sat up and put her arms around her knees and rocked a couple of times. "I mean," she said, "If your ancestor dies, are you supposed to stay by them even if you die, too?"

"Oh, no, child," Ms. Williams remonstrated. She seemed to sense that Vy was talking about something more tangible, recent. "I didn't say anything about living people dying. Juan San Malo shouldn't have died—and nobody should die for him. I'm talking about living for him—big difference. Do me a favor, all of y'all: don't die for anything. There's never a good enough reason for somebody—'specially y'all's age—to lay down their life. If a country asks you to die for it, think about what kinda country would ask such a thing."

Nobody had anything else to say. But Miranda could tell from Erik's uncomfortably shifting body, and how he dug into the pillow over his head, that she had said something that bothered him.

"Well, laying down to bed for the night," Ms. Williams said, rising slowly and stretching, "that sounds like a great idea."

The quiet room was filled with sighing and shuffling as

the kids got comfortable on their pallets, and as Ms. Williams padded around putting out the candles. She had a silver bell on a rod that she lowered over each flame to snuff it out, and she touched her other hand to her head and murmured something each time.

Miranda slept deeply and woke up only once during the night. She had dreamt that Haze was lying on the ground with his neck gurgling blood. But he was also smiling at her like he had when they pulled her out of the Industrial Canal, and making some cute joke. Something like, "What? My jugular? For black folks that ain't nothing."

36

Erik dreamt, too. Also of a cop bleeding to death on the street—but it was his dad. He couldn't get back to sleep after that, and didn't want to. The sky through the windows was already graying so he went out to the balcony. Something seemed different out there. He looked at the house next door and saw a perfect straight brown stripe wrapping around it about a foot above the water. That's when he realized: the water had gone down! Not a whole lot—about ten inches—but at least that meant it wasn't rising anymore. He wanted to rush in and wake the others with the news but he remembered where he was and that he didn't feel totally welcome. Ms. Williams seemed to him like one of those black ladies who wanted to make white people feel bad about crap that happened centuries before he was born. It didn't seem right for her to throw that stuff in his face.

Vy was stirring. She opened her eyes and saw him and jumped up suddenly and ran to his side. Then she took stock of her surroundings and pushed past him through the door and fell into a chair on the balcony. "We're still here," she said.

"Yeah," Erik said, "I'm with you…we should get moving."

"Yeah," Vy agreed. "I don't know why, though."

"To get somewhere, I guess." But Erik was well aware of how lame his answer sounded. He sat down across from her, on the wicker love seat against the wall. He knew no one had really talked to Vy about what she needed to do, and how that might be different than what the others needed. "We were all at Lake Forest Hospital," he said. "When they evacuated, our helicopter crashed. But our parents all were supposed to be going to Sinai Hospital, so that's where we're all going. We could probably walk there in half a day. If we could walk. And if we didn't have obstacles. So, that's where we're headed." He paused, waiting for her to say what she needed, where she needed to go. But she just sat there, so he kept talking—just to avoid sitting there not saying anything. "But I'd rather just go home. From here it's probably the same distance either way. Problem is, home might not be there. Or maybe it is. Just don't know."

"I need to go to the westbank," she said.

Erik thought about that. It wasn't where he was going. Also he wasn't sure how you could get there. On the other hand, they did have a boat, after all. You couldn't just take it down the Industrial Canal because of the lock system. And if you could just row it straight up to the river levee from here, New Orleans was over, probably the west bank, too. "You got family over there?"

"Marrero," she nodded. "I don't know if I have family there, but that's where our house is. My mom is in Houston. I don't know where my dad is."

"Did you know where he was before the storm?"

"Yeah."

"What was that house you were at? In the East?"

"My grandma's."

Erik knew from how she stared straight at the ground that the grandma was probably still in the house, and that she didn't want to talk about it. But he had to ask. "You want to talk about it?"

She shook her head. He wanted to hug her. First for her, then for him. Then he wanted to get her to the westbank. If they had a car they could drive over the bridge. Would he have to steal a car? Maybe Haze knew how to hot-wire one.

He couldn't stand sitting there in silence with her and he couldn't get up the guts to hug her, so he went back inside, feeling defeated and antsy at the same time.

Haze and Miranda were sitting up on their pallets. They were grinning at each other like they'd been telling jokes. But when they saw him come in, Haze stood up and got business-like. "We ready to go?"

"I guess," Erik said. "Not like we got packing to do."

Ms. Williams came in from her weird voodoo room and they said their goodbyes. She gave each of them a carrot for breakfast. They took a couple of cans of food, too—though Erik knew they had no way of opening the cans. Miranda was so bending over backwards gushing and thanking the lady that Erik didn't want to bust her groove by bringing up reality.

They all noticed when they dropped over the balcony railing into the boat how much lower the water was. Erik pointed out the stark brown ribbons wrapped around every house, about a foot over the water. "That was the old water line," he said. He sat on the middle bench and took up the oars—the oar, that is, and the oak branch. "I feel like rowing," he said. "I'm starting to like this old tub."

He felt well rested for the first time in days and he relished dipping oar and branch into the water, pushing them forward and lifting again, making the boat glide in a straight line at an even speed down the avenue, columns of oaks on his left, houses on the right. He chewed on the carrot in his mouth like it was a cigar. He felt less uncertain than the day before. He would proceed with the rest of them as close to the river as was needed to hit dry land (there had to be at least a sliver), and then up to Canal Street. Then he'd see about getting Vy to the westbank and leave Miranda and Haze to their own devices—it was starting to look like they wouldn't mind that at all, anyway.

They knew the water was getting lower as they floated southward because the houses seemed to get higher. By Ms. Williams', only second-floor balconies rose above the flood.

Then the tops of doors began to appear, then doorknobs, whole windows, until finally, the porches of homes with higher elevations sat serenely above the flood, most with extra chairs dragged out and an extra grill or two. Not many people were out, but it was early. At any rate, most homes now had dry first floors, except the rare ones in this older neighborhood built slab-on-grade. Mainly corner taverns and groceries—all with kicked—in doors and floating contents (garbage) spilling out with the lapping waters. Every structure had the same brown stripe, too. Like someone had painted it across the row of houses with a slanted ruler. "Everybody knows where the flood stage is now," Erik observed, pointing at the ubiquitous stripe. "That line says where sea level is."

"Looks like something from the toilet," Haze said. "Makes it look like we in a toilet."

"Yeah," Erik agreed, "and one that ain't flushing right."

But the long toilet ride was coming to an end. They could see in the distance flashing blue squad car lights. As they got closer, they could see what looked like a crowd of people in the heat haze, too, about five or six blocks ahead, maybe. And then the skiff scraped up onto a slight bump in the road. For a while now, Erik had been poling rather than rowing. Now that there was less than a foot of water, it seemed they had no other choice than to ditch the boat and wade through the muck. Luckily the neutral ground was higher and there were little rises in it with no water at all, and the rest had just puddle depth, a few inches. So they all got out onto the neutral ground. Erik dragged the boat up to the middle and flipped it over.

"Yuck," Miranda said as she looked down at the water around her feet.

"At least it's not up to your mouth," Erik said. His skin was bothering him again. That burn all over as if he'd been dipped in acid. Most of the time he could ignore it, but some-times it seemed to flare up. Now just putting his feet in the water reminded the rest of his body what the water had done to him when he was submerged in it. Had to be some chem-ical in it, Drano or something. He wasn't as worried as he'd been before because his legs, if not his arms, had progressed from burning to itching, which he took as a good sign.

It felt strange to walk again. Vy was wearing the least appropriate shoes—flip-flops. She stepped carefully onto whatever patch of sodden grass she could find, and climbed up onto the big roots of the live oaks. She was able almost al-ways to find dry or almost dry landings, until the streets, too, were free of water, about a block later. Then they all strode down the asphalt toward the action at the corner of Poland and St. Claude. Erik felt that thrill of re-entering civilization that he'd felt coming back from hunting and fishing trips. But this time the thrill was a scary one. The squad car up in the intersection, did it have live cops in it? Or dead ones on the road beside it? He saw plenty of people—black ones—but no uniform yet. "Wait, y'all," he said, and stopped. He could tell by how quickly the others stopped that they must have had the same doubts he did.

Haze was the first to say something. "Yeah, we should check that out." They stood around nodding until Miranda said, looking at Haze, "That should be you, right?"

Haze smiled slightly and said, "Yeah." He nodded and headed on, but he crossed to the other side of the street, where, because of the angle of the intersection, his approach would be less obvious.

"Haze," Miranda called. "Be careful."

He looked back and nodded and kept moving forward at a relaxed pace, but like he knew where he was going.

"I'm not sure we should let him go alone," Miranda said.

"Why?" Erik asked. "That's ALL black folks up there."

"Yeah, I guess. But I'm not sure that's a reason."

"Yeah," Erik said. He couldn't tell if Miranda was clueless about race relations or just an idealist. "Well, reality sucks. Whatever."

37

Vy wasn't sure what to think about the stuff Ms. Williams had said the night before. She knew lots of black people were really into Africa, from her school, where they had the kente cloth everywhere and a kwaanza pageant and where one of the teachers' first names was actually 'Africa'—spelled with a 'k,' though. A few kids wore Africa pendants around their necks, especially the ones with dredlocks, like Haze. She didn't entirely trust Haze because the kids at her school with the dreds were the ones that used to get on the Vietnamese kids' case a lot for supposedly getting special treatment. The Vietnamese kids were only about ten percent and they were a tight group. When she got the red streaks in her hair the first time, they raised a stink because they wouldn't let the black kids dye their hair different colors. It was supposedly against the dress code. It was true, too—they did let the Vietnamese students off easy for things, but that was because they just didn't want to deal with them.

She was surprised because Ms. Williams looked like the kind of black lady that would say she wanted to go back to Africa, and she didn't, she wanted to stay. Even after how the white people had treated them so bad for so long. But her grandmother had a similar attitude. It was all about America and how great it was, never about how great Vietnam was and how it would be better if she could be re-united with it or something. Her dad offered to pay for a trip back for her, just to visit, and she said no way. And then at her house a few days ago, she didn't even want to leave with a hurricane coming. Said how they had built so much here, it was home now, her garden and all her neighbors. She said the water would go down and the neighbors would all come back and dry out and re-plant and go on. It was America so there was no need to leave because it was a democracy. After she passed, when the helicopters came through, Vy stayed, still waiting for the water to go down so she could get her *Ba* to a chair in the garden and just prop her up in her chair out there, just for a minute. But the water didn't go down fast at all. Was there a day later. And Vy realized the cucumbers and cilantro and tomatoes, mirlitons and lemon grass, would be depressingly dead after having their sunlight choked off for so long by that dark water. So what was the point? Sure, she loved her garden, but now she and it were both dead. At least America was still around, that's what she would say.

But the black people Vy knew acted like they were all mad at America. At least that's what her dad told her. It crossed her mind a couple of times that her uncle might have been in his gas station up on Chef Highway. Like the cop, lying on the ground dead. Shot in the neck or the face or some other terrible spot. But she knew there was no point in picturing things like that. And that's what Erik said on the balcony last night, too. Whatever bad things happen to you, after they're over, there's no point in wasting your brain on them because there's nothing you can do about it and thinking about bad things in the past would just hold you back from prospering in the future.

An Vy knew for sure there was at least some hope for the future, something that would make her grandmother happy to know: the whole city was not under, because she stood right now on a bone dry sidewalk. If could get across the bridge, she could walk to Marerro. And, she noticed, walking would work better than driving, even if she had a car. The streets were strewn with tree branches, some on the large side, and other debris from ripped-off roofs and blown-out walls.

A few yards in front of them was a downed utility pole spanning the whole width of the avenue, its wires tangled all in the trees and in the other twisted and leaning poles. You would need a tank to get down this street. At least, Erik said, the power lines were most likely dead.

Vy could tell Miranda was worried about Haze. It had been a few minutes and he hadn't come back. "Maybe we should go check on him," she said.

"What's the point of sending him to re-con if we have to go check on him?" Erik asked.

Miranda bit her lip. She looked angry. "Well I'm going, Captain Courageous. At least a little closer."

"Did you forget what happened at the school?" Erik demanded. "Or what they did to that cop?"

Miranda twisted up her face. "Who's they?"

Erik got red. "The *&%^ing brothers, that's who! Wake up, Miranda. They're the ones turning this city into a hellhole!"

"Whoa, whoa!" Miranda shook her pointed finger. But it wasn't pointed right in Erik's face. She was a couple of feet away. "The cop we saw get shot was black!" She seemed to be crying a little.

"I only notice the blue," Erik said.

"Well, notice the black next time, too! At least when it's doing you a favor." She looked back toward the intersection. "I'm going. See you around."

"Hey!" Erik called. "You know I'm not going to let you sashay over there alone!"

"If you had a gun you could kill me."

"I'm just trying to protect you!"

"At what price? If I buy your racist worldview?"

"What?" Erik stared in disbelief. "You're calling me a racist now?"

Vy felt like it was now her turn to be the peacemaker, to

get them to stop turning on each other. "Guys," she said. They looked at her and she tried to come up with something to say. "Didn't you say we weren't supposed to argue?"

Erik and Miranda appeared to ponder the question, but neither said anything. "Let's all just go over there together," Vy suggested. "What can they do to all three of us?"

Miranda said, "I'm scared, too. I'm sure that's obvious. But when I think about it rationally I just don't see how a big crowd of people like that would all turn on us just because we're white."

Erik shrugged. "OK," he said, and bowed and waved his arms toward the intersection as if saying, "after you."

As they got closer they saw two cops—living ones— standing by the squad car. They hadn't noticed them before because they weren't wearing the regular uniforms. They had dark navy cargo pants tucked into combat boots and black t-shirts. They wore their badges on their belts. Vy heard Miranda gasp and saw Haze lying face down on the street next to them with his hands on the back of his head.

"Excuse me, officers!" Miranda said in a high-pitched voice. The officers, one black and one white, looked over at her lazily. "What is this man doing lying on the ground?"

"Why?" the white one said. "You know him?"

"Yes!" Miranda answered.

Then Erik held up his hand, to get her to let him handle it. "Yes sir," he said. "We do know him. He's with us. We've come all the way from the East and he's been a big help."

The officers nodded. "Better tell the sergeant," the white one said. He padded off at a leisurely pace.

"Who is your sergeant?" Erik asked the other one. "Are y'all fifth district?"

"We are," he said, "But the Sarge isn't."

"Where's he from?"

"Third District."

"What's he doing with y'all?"

The cop laughed. "Ain't no Third District no more!"

Erik said, "That's my dad's assignment."

"What's his name?" the cop asked.

Erik said it but the man shook his head. "I don't know," he said.

Miranda was still visibly upset. Probably because it looked like Haze was supposed to keep lying flat on the ground. "That's a pretty cold way to talk about people losing their neighborhoods," she told the cop.

"You don't need to tell me, young lady," he retorted. "I live in the Third District. My whole family, too."

Miranda softened and offered a sympathetic frown. "Are they…were they at your house?"

"No," he said, "they in Mississippi. I think." He nudged Haze in the leg, "OK, you can get up."

"Did you just kick him?" Miranda said with a look of disbelief on her face.

"No, ma'am," he scowled. "I released him. You gonna see a lot worse 'fo you get outta here. I hope you make it outta here. Gon' see people on the ground don't get up."

Haze got to his feet and Miranda gave him a big hug. They just stayed there and hugged for a few seconds. Vy and the other people looked away.

The white officer came back over with an older white man. He wore regular navy police slacks with a yellow stripe but his shirt was just a plain white v-neck undershirt. He had the badge on his belt like the others but wore a Saints cap on his head. He had drawn his sergeant stripes on the sleeve of his undershirt with a sharpie. But he didn't look at Haze, he looked at Erik.

"Mister Fratello?" Erik said.

"Oh my god, Erik!" he said. They hugged—not as long as Haze and Miranda, but long enough for Haze to back away from the squad car and toward the bridge, to the crowd of people all sitting or standing around doing nothing. Miranda followed him. Vy wanted to stay with Erik.

"How's my dad?" Erik asked.

"I don't know son, I don't know," the sergeant said. He seemed really weepy, almost like a scared kid. "God save him and the rest of us, you wanna know the truth."

"You haven't seen him?"

"Not since the flood. We got no communication. We got no idea where the rest of the force is. We're all in these little units where we just ran into each other. I was checking on my mama over here and then got trapped by the flood. Got no idea where my regular unit is. No place to report, no number to call. The chief was just over by here last night. Said to stay put and remain on duty right here."

Erik looked confused. "For how long?" he asked.

"That's the twenty million dollar question, Erik." He glanced at the other officers standing there, then began walking off, motioning at Erik to follow him. Erik followed him and Vy followed Erik. He was going to have to be her lifeline, at least for the immediate future. The idea of being alone in all this was too much to even imagine.

They stopped behind an unmarked Ford Taurus on the other side of the Avenue. "Listen," the sergeant said, grimly, "I don't think we're gonna be able to hold this." He looked like he was ready to cry. His face kept scrunching up like he was trying to hold it back. "They's just too many of them. They looted the Security Sporting Goods, looted the the Wal-Mart on Tchoupitoulas. No telling how much ordnance they got. We'll run out of ammo before they do. They been shooting at us, shooting at rescue helicopters." He was now openly sobbing. "They raping children in the Superdome!" He took a moment to try to compose himself. Then he opened the trunk of the car.

"I know," Erik said. "I mean we got an idea. I saw…we saw…I need to report an officer down."

"You mean killed?" the sergeant asked.

"Yeah," Erik said. "Shot. Gotta be dead."

"Where?"

"Up on Chef Highway."

"What's left of the Third District," he sighed. "They got one of those contractors supposed to be cleaning up over there. Halliburton. Blackwater, somebody."

"Well," Erik wondered. "Is the army or somebody gonna come?"

"Hell no." The sergeant almost laughed. "No, baby, we on our own. Ain't nobody coming."

"Who sent the contractors?"

"Not sure," the sergeant admitted. "Somebody said some company on the Canal hired'em." He dug under a blanket in the trunk and came up with a pistol. He weighed it in his hand and then pressed it into Erik's palm. "Take care of yourself, buddy." They gripped the gun together and looked each other in the eye for a solemn second or two. Then the sergeant dropped his hand and Erik glanced at the gun and stuck it in the back of his waistband. "I don't know how much longer we gonna to be here," the sergeant said.

"What do you mean?" asked Erik.

"Word is, plenty have given up already. People talking about pulling out of the city and letting this-" he waved his hand derisively at the crowd "—kinda work itself out. This could be the end, man." He got a faraway look in his eyes. "End of a great city." He hawked and spit on the ground. "She's worth at least another day or two of fight from me." He patted Erik on the shoulder, said "Good Luck" and got in the Taurus and drove off.

Vy noticed that St. Claude Avenue, at least, had been cleared of debris. It was pushed to the side, forming a short wall of tree branches and miscellaneous detritus against the parked cars along the curb. Erik pointed down St. Claude and said that it ran along a ridge and probably was now the beach road, as it were, for the whole city.

They wandered back toward the old drawbridge where St. Claude crossed over the Industrial Canal, at its narrowest point here, just a few blocks from the river. One of the cops they'd talked to before called over to them, saying, "Y'all know where he went?" Vy supposed they meant the sergeant. She and Erik both shrugged their shoulders.

"Hey," Erik said as they walked, "don't worry about that gun. I'm trained, I'm very safe and careful, and I don't play around."

"OK," she said. "I'm not worried." She was worried—generally—but not specifically about the gun.

"But, uh—" he added, "no need to tell the others about it. They would just probably freak out. You know?"

"I know. I won't." He didn't need to tell her to keep quiet about it. She could tell a gun was a private, secret thing. But she liked that he felt he needed to say all that to her.

The crowd—a couple hundred people, probably, was mostly on the downtown side of Poland Avenue, where St. Claude ramped up to the drawbridge. Many seemed also to be under the bridge, taking advantage of the shade there. They had boxes with them and suitcases, duffel bags, or even garbage bags with clothes falling out. A few were in robes and pajamas, some even in underwear, or an open robe with only underwear beneath. Some people wore wet towels on their heads. There was a handful of children and babies, too. Also, on closer inspection, she noticed they weren't all black. There were a few white people, too, mostly old, most concentrated in a little group close to the squad car.

Everyone seemed peaceful enough at the moment. Trailing down the ramp toward Poland Avenue was something like a line. People mostly sitting, some on the ground, some on boxes or suitcases (one guy on a big square fan)—and some standing—but there was obviously a snaking order to how they were arranged. It became clear when a big tour bus—an old beat-up one—lumbered down St. Claude and stopped at the Poland Avenue corner. The seated people in the line area all got up and picked up their stuff. There were a couple more police officers on that corner whose job was apparently to load the people on the bus. They waved the line forward and people got on. Erik asked somebody where the bus was going and was told the Convention Center. The bus filled up and the long broken line still wound all the way up to the drawbridge. But Vy was even more confused at the bulk of the hundreds of people who didn't even seem interested in the line at all. What were they waiting for?

"Refugees," she said.

"Huh?" said Erik.

"They're refugees."

Ms. Williams had told Haze his dad lived just around the corner from her. She saw him the day before the storm and he said he was staying. But when Haze asked about his family, the one he always assumed he lived with, she seemed confused. "I thought that was y'all," she said.

"No," Haze said, "not lately."

She reported having seen him at another house in the neighborhood that seemed to have kids spilling out of it, but she wasn't sure if that was his family or not. She was fairly certain that he lived alone, in a half-a-shotgun on Miro Street, and had been there for a few years. She thought he worked in a restaurant or hotel in the Quarter. Haze's next question took her by surprise. "He a jailbird?"

But she was forthright in her answer: "Yes."

When Haze asked her what he'd gone in for, she said, "Auto theft." She added, "Might a been some drug stuff before that." She then assured him that he was a sweet man, actually, a good man, but just couldn't see very far past the moment. Haze wondered what people would say at his funeral—which would probably be soon. Or had he died already? Ms. Williams said no, said she saw him leaping from roof to roof toward the higher part of town the morning after the flooding set in.

So Haze was careful to scan the faces of all the thirty- to fortysomething men gathered on and under the St. Claude bridge. He wasn't even sure if he would recognize him. It had been a couple of years since their last meeting. But then he assumed he would, that a light of recognition would click on if only the right face presented itself. But it didn't. So he assumed—though not with a hundred percent certainty—that his dad wasn't there.

He blew soft low tones into his mouthpiece as he wandered up the ramp toward the Industrial Canal, just to get a look at it from the way things used to be, when you saw it from a bridge and the water all stayed inside it.

Miranda followed him. But he felt embarrassed around her, because she'd seen him in that position that his dad must have known so well, and that, up to now, he'd been careful to avoid. It was some kind of destiny, to be lying on your stomach on a dirty street with cops standing around you. And now it seemed to him that spending some time that way might just be unavoidable. What could he do to not draw police attention? Cut his dreds, probably. It was either his color or something in his attitude he wasn't able to suppress. The fact is, walking up to that intersection to scope the scene, he HAD felt guilty. He was slinking around, trying to sneak up and observe the crowd to find out if it was safe for white people. First, when he saw the white cop, he was happy because his white friends—or associates, whatever they were—would feel comfortable. But then that same white cop spotted him and came after him. He couldn't run (his first instinct) so he stood there asking what was wrong. The cop waved him forward, gun drawn, shouting a barrage of unanswerable questions: "Where you been? What you been doing?" As Haze got closer the unanswered questions turned to commands: "Hands on your head! On your head! On the ground!"

The black cop just stood there, quiet as an unplugged fan, watching the whole thing and trying to keep from yawning.

But Miranda seemed more broken up about it than he felt. He knew they weren't going to do anything with him. He knew after they got him on the ground and patted him down, they were just going to let him lie there for a minute and then let him go. They just had to feel like cops. Like they were doing their job. So when Miranda asked him, "Are you OK," he said, "Why would I not be OK? Nothing happened to me." But he was surprised to hear an unintended note of anger in his voice. She just gave him one of her puzzled looks and dropped it.

They had uniforms Haze didn't recognize manning a roadblock at the top of the bridge, on the drawbridge part. They didn't bother much with Haze and Miranda because they were focused on the other side, and with processing people through. Haze read one of their shoulder patches: Louisiana Department of Wildlife and Fisheries. What were they doing in the big city? Hunting?

About fifty yards off, the opposite slope of the bridge dipped into deep water. There was a makeshift marina down there, a flotilla of little boats, like the one they had been in, and a few airboats, too. They kept landing, dropping people off, and heading out again. The rescued people walked up the bridge and waited in line to cross the drawbridge to the Upper Ninth Ward side, where Haze and Miranda stood.

It was strange to watch them. Haze felt like a reporter or a tourist. For some reason, he didn't feel like he was in the same situation as them—but he obviously was. Maybe because he'd been off a boat for a few hours now, and they'd just hit the dry ground seconds ago. Or maybe because he'd been rowing the boat himself? He could see a thought process in these people's faces that made him think *been there done that*. First they were overjoyed to hit dry land, and to see the Upper Ninth Ward side with a dry St. Claude Avenue stretching into the distance. But then, after standing around for a while, they began to question what the next step would be. Stay here? Keep walking? Where? He also watched the faces closely for one, any one, he recognized. Not his dad so much as just anybody from the neighborhood, with news. He thought maybe some neighbor might come through and assure him the flooding wasn't so bad on their street. But he also knew that wish was pure fantasy. It looked like basically ocean for as far as you could see on the Lower Ninth ward side. When he wasn't watching the faces of the newcomers, he couldn't take his eyes off that expanse of water. Out there under that water somewhere was the last sixteen years of his life. He basically had what was on his back. A mouthpiece. A few bucks. A hat. And—the only reason he didn't break down and cry like a baby—his mom, somewhere. The tears were closer than he'd thought, in fact. He had to work hard to choke them back.

He felt Miranda's hand on his arm. He could tell by how she looked at what he looked at, that she knew it had been his neighborhood. Then she looked at his face and when he returned the look she mouthed *sorry*.

He just nodded. Somehow the neighborhood being gone and her standing there seemed related. He couldn't change things, of course, but if he could, he wasn't sure he would. It would be like one of those movies where they raise the dead— it would have terrible consequences. In other words, all this stuff had to happen. There was no way out of it. It was a trial that had to be met. And maybe meeting this girl was some- thing that had to happen—and what possible scenario besides this one would have led to that? Something about her, that way she was like a magic elf, made everything seem weird- ly fated. Even if everything went back to normal—or some version of normal—this moment, the memory of this girl following him around and obviously liking him was precious, golden. Even if it stopped right now, he'd remember it forever.

"They moved back after Betsy," he reassured her.

An old woman overheard him and cackled. "This ain't no Betsy. Ain't nobody be living over there 'cept the fish. But they ain't won. They ain't killed us."

"My house on Lizardi Street," Haze said.

"Lizardi underwater, too," she said "But at least they still got the houses. Over where they set the bomb they ain't even got no houses no more."

Haze puzzled over her mention of a bomb. "Whatchu mean, a bomb?" he asked.

The woman, in a threadbare housedress and slippers, smiled politely at Miranda, as if waiting to be introduced. But Haze just repeated his question about the bomb.

"Yeah, they set a bomb, blew up that levee to clear out the black folks."

"Who?" asked Miranda.

"Who you think?" she huffed. "Same people blow up black churches. Same people blew the levee the last time, for Betsy."

In response to Haze and Miranda's incredulous stares, she added, "Where y'all come from? Y'all couldn't'a been around here and didn't hear that blast."

It didn't take long for Haze to recall that he *did* hear a giant blast, in the hospital, right after the storm passed. He looked at Miranda and saw she was thinking of it, too.

Erik and Vy came up next to them and gazed over at the other side of the Canal. Erik shook his head and said, "I drove right through here every day. Hard to believe now."

Haze had made the same daily trip. "Yeah," he said.

A few white people came through with the next batch and Erik seemed to recognize one of them. "Mister LaBruzzo!" he called, "Mister LaBruzzo!"

An old white man, head and face burned bright red, came through and gave Erik a limp handshake. He was wearing some old workpants with a muscle shirt and flip-flops.

"I thought you was going by your sister's," Erik said to him.

"Decided to stay," he said. "Ooh-whee."

"You all right?"

"They got me out my second floor window."

"Least they got you."

"Yeah." The old man stood there, nodding his head and blocking the path of other people coming through behind him. They just pushed around him, with mild jostling, like zombies or worms, until they got to a more open section of roadway and stood there looking down St. Claude. Then they shook their heads and began asking each other questions. "What now?" was the basic theme.

Erik must have asked this old white man the same thing, because he was explaining how he had just two blocks to walk to get to the house he'd lived in decades ago—and still owned. "I got the key right here," he said, patting his pocket. Then Erik asked a more delicate question: "How's the neighborhood?"

"Aw, Scotty, you got no idea, man." For some reason he called Erik Scotty. Maybe it was his middle name. "They had a oil spill, man. We done. Even if that water goes down, we done."

Erik looked defeated, scared, for the first time Haze could tell. The man must have been talking about one of those big refineries they had out there.

"What, Texaco?" Erik asked.

The old man nodded somberly. Put his hand on Erik's shoulder. "Sorry, buddy." Then he brightened up a bit. "Least we still got the old neighborhood," he exclaimed, pointing down St. Claude. "Your dad went to Jefferson High, right?"

So had Haze, in a way, though the name had been changed to Douglass. Ms. Williams and his own dad had gone there, too—which just proved that Erik's dad was just a few years older than his dad, back when Jefferson still had white students.

"Yeah," Erik said, brightening up as well. "Yeah, he did. Right down there."

"Good luck, son," the old man said, starting down the bridge.

"We got a place, too," Erik said softly to the space where the old man had been. Then he turned to Haze, Miranda, and Vy, as if just remembering. "On Mazant. Or France." His face tensed up in a frown as he scoured his memory. "It's…where we going?"

"The hospital," Haze said.

"Sinai," clarified Miranda.

"Uptown" added Haze.

"Yeah," Erik nodded. "Yeah, it's on the way." He smiled. "So…let's go?"

He started down the bridge and the others followed, threading a path through the standing, seated, and sprawled masses. Then Haze realized why he didn't feel like he was in the same boat with these others: he had a place to go. Not the Dome or the Convention Center, not a general pick-up point for every last penniless hopeless black ass in New Orleans. No, it was his mother's place of employment. A hospital where people would be treated right and not left waiting around forever for nothing.

He turned to say 'see ya' to the old lady who had brought up the explosion and saw she was staring at him in an almost accusing way. "You not from the Ninth Ward," she said.

"I…" But he couldn't figure out what to tell her so he just turned and caught up with the others. Erik was almost bounding through the crowd. Right at the base of the bridge he bumped into a birdcage with parakeets and it fell off the suitcase it had been sitting on. The birds raised a ruckus of chirps but the old white lady they apparently belonged too was nice about it.

"They been through worse," she said, as Erik leaned over to pick up the cage and put it back. Erik apologized but Haze was mildly stunned by what he had seen when Erik bent over:

a handgun tucked into the back of his pants. How long had he had that? He couldn't have gone swimming with it. Where did he get it? It worried Haze but angered him even more. Erik now appeared to him as just another cracker with a gun—like the cop that made him lie in the street. Just another cracker with a gun waiting to use it on a black man. Haze wondered how long it would be before he turned it on him. Miranda was the only reason he didn't take off in another direction right there.

38

Water Erik could deal with, but oil? Couldn't live with it, couldn't live without it. Like fire. Keeping you warm but waiting to burn you. Now his neighborhood would be a superfund site. When he had pictured his house underwater, he'd pictured fish in it, and somehow that consoled him. But with oil in it, there wouldn't be fish, and water that didn't nurture fish had no purpose at all.

But, like Mister LaBruzzo reminded him, this neighborhood right here was the one where he was born and where his mom and dad—and grandparents—were raised. If only he could remember where the old house was. His dad still owned it. They rented it out. He knew he would recognize the immediate area, he just wasn't exactly sure what direction to go in to get to that block or intersection that would refresh his bearings. Of course, unlike Mister LaBruzzo, he didn't have a key.

The other thing Mister LaBruzzo reminded him of, totally unintentionally, was his own grandmother. The one who used to live in this neighborhood right here but was moved—for her own safety—to St. Theresa's, in the heart of St. Bernard Parish. What had they done with her? Had anyone thought of her? His dad had to have thought about her, had her moved. St. Theresa's, if he remembered correctly, didn't have a second floor. They must have evacuated them. Right? But nobody else did anything right for this storm, so why would they have? He wanted to go back to the drawbridge and collar one of those wardens from Wildlife and Fisheries, the closest guy on the state payroll, and pistol whip him, beat him to the ground and make him answer. "Tell me grandma didn't drown in her wheelchair!" And then pummel his face with the sidewalk. "Tell me grandma didn't drown in her wheelchair!"

He had to tear himself away from that whole can of venomous worms, though, because, unless he wanted to commandeer a boat with a motor and pointlessly go out there, there wasn't jack to be done constructively. He forced himself to tighten up and focus: what was in front of him now is all he could do anything about. It was strange, because he wasn't on a distant shore, some other planet, he was right in the old neighborhood that had been hers, his family's, for generations. It would be easier to stay strong, unaffected, effective, in Texas, or Afghanistan.

The neighborhood looked different, though, less shabby than it had when he was a kid. He remembered dusty, bruised bungalows painted a dirty white or some other bland color. Darker shutters—navy or army green. And lots of concrete and hardly any foliage. His dad often referred to the new inhabitants as "weirdos" (the white ones) or more offensive terms, like all the derogatory words for 'gay'. But whatever they were, Erik had to admit they'd done lots in the way of clean-up, decoration, and landscaping. There was more shade now from Crepe Myrtles, the little Magnolia varieties, and a Cypress here and there, all planted along the curbside. A few oaks had been planted, too, but that was a less good idea, since their root systems totally tore up the sidewalk, and probably interfered with gas and water lines underground, too. The electric company had gotten creative and cut out sections of the tall trees that threatened the overhead powerlines. The homes were less sun-bleached than he remembered, too, not just because of more shade, but because the paint jobs were more varied and brighter. Yellow, lime green, sky blue, even pink. Looked like a row of drinks at those shi-shi clubs Ashleigh was so into. Oh, well, she was probably doing it up in Florida right now, Erik out of mind and hanging on the arm of some blond-haired blue-eyed Florida boy with perfect teeth. With a convertible. No—no matter how he tried he couldn't really make himself feel any jealousy or even longing for Ashleigh. Actually, weirdly enough, he couldn't even picture her face that well.

She was part of that former era of a few days ago. But he was done mourning it. Something had clicked in him. Clicked off, or maybe even clicked on. Yes, his house was gone, and Archbishop Leray, too, was under—though at least it was just water there. So what was holding him back? His brothers had already moved on. As long as he could be sure his mom and dad were safe, he was ready to leave it all behind anyway. He had a vague image in his head of him and Vy getting to her house in Marerro and finding no one there—just some note saying everyone was fine—and hopping in a car or motorbike and hauling off to Texas. Vy had said her mom went to Houston—Erik was ready to take her there. What else did he have to do? The one thing he didn't have was money and outside New Orleans money would be required. Even if no one had a use for it here. Maybe he could sell the gun.

But there was a creepy feel in the still air that made him glad he had it. Maybe it was the crude spraypainted messages. Somebody had sprayed 'HELP' in big block letters in the middle of the street. It re-appeared about once a block. They'd even put the word on the walls of some houses. More ominously, another hand had sprayed "U Loot We Shoot" on the big blank stucco wall of an old grocery store, even though the store looked like it had been closed, cleared of groceries, for years, not days.

He saw the sign for Mazant Street—in the old blue-and-white tiles set in the sidewalk—and stopped and took a good look around. Vy was standing right there looking around, too, following his gaze, but Haze and Miranda had hung back a bit. They caught up and sat on a stoop on the corner.

"Is there a reason we're on this forced march?" Miranda asked. "I mean why are we in a hurry more now than we've been before? It's just making us even more thirsty and there's no water." Her voice ground into a rasp toward the end because her throat was so parched. Good, Erik thought, maybe that would make her shut up.

But he was parched, too. And now he was pouring so much sweat he was bound to get dehydrated. He marveled at how the sweat really comes out, not when you're walking, when maybe your body in motion creates something like a breeze, but when you stop. He wanted to wipe his forehead off with something dry but his shirt was soaked through, too. Just from a brisk stroll down the street.

"They ain't even had no water at the bridge," Haze chimed in. "Police, rangers—they can't get no water?"

"Yeah," Erik said. "I'm not sure we want to hang around this town a whole lot more. But there might be water in this house…" He looked up and down Mazant Street again. He thought he recognized the corner—an old tavern with a window on the side they used to buy ice-cups at. Looked like it had been closed for years.

"What house?" Miranda asked.

"This house I used to live at. My grammaw's old house. My dad owns it." He tried to find a reason to convince the others it was worth spending a few minutes looking for. Besides his urge to see something still standing that his family could lay claim to. "If could find it, get in, there might be stuff in it. Food, drinks." He guessed it was toward the river so he took a left on Mazant. Then again, the block in the other direction seemed familiar, too. "Wait," he said. "Y'all just stay here for a second, I'm just going to run to that corner and then I'll know if it's the right direction."

He jogged a block away from the river and, though he

did vaguely recognize the houses, he had a sense they were where they should be: the block next to the one grammaw's had been on. So he turned back, with renewed confidence in his instincts, but was distracted by a shape on the sidewalk across the street.

He stepped cautiously toward it. What appeared first to be a passed-out guy proved to be in fact a dead guy. He was sort of on his side in a too uncomfortable position for even a drunk to sleep in. He wore a white t-shirt and baggy shorts, house slipper on one foot—the other was a few inches away, in the gutter. Black guy. Somebody had thrown a towel over his face. There was a bunch of blood right there under him— dried brown—but no trail. Erik thought, *this guy didn't drown.* He reached behind him and patted the gun nestled there and hurried back to the corner to join his friends.

"It's this block," he said, pointing forward. His first instinct had been the correct one. He had to remember that: just go with first instincts, don't overthink it.

Yes, the block looked familiar. Definitely: there was the old oyster house. It was a two story building with a narrow front balcony and big stable doors on the ground floor. Trucks full of oysters used to back into it and they'd load the oysters into burlap bags and drive out again. Neighbors could get a sack, too, to shuck and suck on their front stoops or right there on the street. The big stable doors were still there, still whitewashed, but there wasn't even the slightest tinge of a seafood aroma, which meant it had to be years since the last oyster had passed through.

Right next door was the house he'd been looking for. The old homestead. It was set back from the street a few feet, behind an old iron gate. It was a long sidehall cottage with a little porch. It was a bit more run down than the average house on the block, but not blighted, either, like some were. He heard movement from the narrow balcony of the old oyster house next door and saw a black man stick his head out of a door up there. He ignored it (remembering he was now armed) and pushed open the gate and entered the small yard. He just felt like he needed to get himself and his charges inside somewhere, off the street, just until that bad, edge of panic feeling went away, so he could think and plan better.

The little strip of front yard was shadier than he remembered, because someone had planted a fig tree. The downside was that the fallen and rotting figs underfoot made it smell somewhat like a restaurant dumpster—and probably attracted rats and roaches. He stepped onto the porch and peered through the windows. Drapes blocked the view. He tried the door, just to cover the easy bases first, but it was locked. He remembered how, when he was a kid, the back door was always open. There was a latched screen door but even the youngest kids figured out how to slide something under the latch and get in. He hopped off the porch and started down the alley, turning back and waving the others forward.

But they seemed highly reluctant. Vy was the only one through the gate at all. Haze and Miranda loitered outside, tossing wary glances up and down the street. Haze said, "I ain't going in 'at alley witchou!"

Then a voice from above cried: "Ain't nobody goin' down that alley! Come on outta there!"

Erik backed out enough to look up and see the barrel of a shotgun pointed at him, in the hands of the man he'd noticed earlier on the old oyster house balcony.

"All a'y'all now," he commanded. "Just get there in a row where I can see you."

Another man—this one white, wiry, and shaved totally bald—crossed from the other side of the street gripping a pistol in both hands, like somebody really planning on using it. It looked a lot like the police-issue Smith and Wesson Erik was carrying. At first Erik wondered whether he was working

with the guy on the balcony or intending to take him out.
Apparently working with him: when he reached the gate he
leveled his weapon at the kids' torsos and barked, "You heard
him. Now lift your hands up, where we can see'em."

One thing Erik didn't contemplate seriously was drawing his own weapon. With two guns pointed at them, one a
shotgun, from above, there would be no doubt one of the four
of them would take a bullet—and Erik's stupid move would be
the cause. If he were alone, he'd drop and roll under the house.
But now his only option was biding his time and hoping they
didn't discover his own .45 caliber secret.

"What are y'all doin' messin' around in there?" said the
skinhead-looking white man.

"It's my house!" Erik called "I own it!"

The man on the street shouted up to the one on the balcony. "You recognize him?"

The black man stuck out his lower lip in contemplation
and shook his head. He said, "They ain't Bruce and Barbara."

"Sure as hell ain't," agreed the skinhead, who looked to
Erik like a stereotypical trigger-happy rookie in a war movie.

Erik heard footsteps behind him and turned to see a
third man coming down the alley. This guy was tall and older,
maybe fifty-something. He had long gray hair and a salt-and-
pepper moustache and goatee. His gun was the most interesting of all: an antique, a .44 or .45. revolver with a long barrel.
The old-timey billowing cotton shirt he wore enhanced the
Jesse James look even more. "What we got here, boys?" he
boomed in a big baritone.

"Looters!" spat the skinhead.

"I told them," Erik protested. "I own the place!"

The tall guy gave them a quick once-over and said, "Don't
live here."

"We rent it," Erik said.

"OK," the tall man replied. "Who's your tenant?"

"Bruce and Barbara?" Erik offered, lamely.

"Nice one!" jeered the skinhead.

"Yeah, he's pretty quick," agreed the guy on the balcony, but in a nicer tone.

"Y'all armed?" asked the gray longhair, apparently the leader.

Erik shook his head. He looked at his travel companions and saw they were all looking at him.

Then Miranda said, "Yes," with a sigh of exasperation or relief—Erik couldn't tell which—"he has a pistol." And she jerked her thumb casually in his direction.

Haze's face looked totally impassive for all of it, but Vy's contorted in anger and she spat at Miranda, "I can't believe you did that!"

The tall man gently patted Erik's back and lifted the gun out. He patted some more and came up with his knife, too. Then he looked up to the balcony and called, "What were they trying to do?"

"Trying to go down the alley," was the reply.

"Well," the tall longhair sighed. "Let's let 'em."

"We take 'em back there, we're gonna have to finish 'em!" cautioned the skinhead.

The tall guy smiled, in a pained way, and said, "You're really liking the Stone Age, aren't ya, Pete?"

Then he stepped to the side and waved the kids into the narrow alley, "Go ahead." He holstered his gun—it was an old-fashioned holster, too. On a belt, with a leather braid dangling from the bottom. "Ladies and children first," he chuckled.

The alley was so tight they had to go single file. Erik went first. He wasn't sure what the order was after that. It was strange to be in this place where he played as a child—like the game where they had to run the length of the alley before getting hit from behind with a dodgeball—in these nasty circumstances. But it seemed too perfectly fate-like that he would actually get killed in the little scrubby backyard of his early childhood. Too perfect, like a movie or a book. Reality didn't play that way. So he consoled himself, anyway.

They all bunched up in the little yard between the back door and the back fence. It was only about twenty square feet, and now it was largely taken up by a magnolia that hadn't been there before. The ground was carpeted with velvety magnolia leaves and cones. The old-timey outlaw with the six-shooter edged past them and kicked a loose board in the back fence. It fell neatly outward and he squinted at Erik and said, "You seem to be the bigshot. Go ahead, take the first stab."

Erik nodded and set his jaw and squeezed through the fence.

He found himself in a wide grassy field that had to take up most of the interior of the block. It was bordered by several back fences on all four sides, but also a few houses whose back doors opened directly onto the green—which gave it the feel of a compound. A couple of abandoned vehicles, one a bright green schoolbus, contributed to the compound vibe. There were quite a few trees, too, but one big one was down, a sycamore. Its carcass took up a whole quarter of the space. It had landed on the back of someone's house, too, totally smashing in the roof in the back. But they had just passed that house on the street, and the damage couldn't be seen from there.

They followed the tall man's waving gray hair to one of the larger structures in the compound, a big rambling mansion with a detached back building. They passed the back building and entered a contained space bordered by the mansion, the smaller house, and a row of crepe myrtles. A giant live oak fanned out toward a fence, behind which, Erik hypothesized, was Burgundy Street. They had one of those big rusty cisterns in the middle of the patio, which was laid with soft mossy French Quarter bricks. The back building had a little balcony, as did the narrow slave quarter attachment stretching out from the rear of the mansion proper. The slave quarter balcony sported a giant skull-and-crossbones flag. From the balcony of the back-building (probably originally a kitchen, Erik deduced from field trip memories) hung a big banner with the words "Independent Republic of Bywater" in meticulous calligraphic hand-lettering.

"Are y-y'all pirates?" asked Erik. He meant it to come across like a sarcastic jibe, but he ended up stuttering.

The tall grayhair let out a booming cackle. "I like you, kid," he slapped Erik on the back. "Hope we don't have to hang you."

Then Erik noticed, dangling from one of the winding oak branches, a noose.

39

Miranda had often fantasized about living in former eras and now she indeed felt like she'd been transported to an earlier time. Only problem was, it wasn't fun. She knew from history books that most people's lives in the past were miserable—especially girls—so maybe there was a lesson in this for her. Provided she lived long enough to absorb it. She was sure Erik was furious at her for ratting him out on the gun. Haze, too, probably, because he's the one who told her and made her swear to not mention she knew. Even Vy hated her, now. But she knew if he pulled a bonehead move like drawing the gun then bloodshed would be definite—better to have it removed from the mix.

Now, at any rate, no guns were out or pointed at anyone. The man from the balcony had come down some rear stairs into the compound without his. The scary hairless white guy had done something with his—at least he didn't seem to have it. And the swashbuckler with the long hair first holstered his, then, on the patio by the mansion, called up to the back building balcony a woman's name—Melody. A willowy pale darkhaired woman came out. "Here," he called, holding up Erik's gun, "got something for safekeeping."

"OK," she said, and went back in, coming out a few seconds later on the ground floor and taking the gun back inside.

She re-appeared on the balcony but this time was followed by…children. Lovely ones, too, a girl of about seven and a boy probably four or so. They both had tumbling reddish golden curls and radiant faces. The boy looked like a smaller, more boyish version of the girl, and the similarity drove up the cute quotient exponentially. They were smiling. They waved. At a nudge from the woman, they sang out in a wobbly unison, "Welcome to Bywater!"

And something ripped and gave way inside Miranda, her own floodwall came tumbling down finally, the tears rushed out. What were beautiful children doing here? She collapsed onto a big oak root—under the noose—and covered her face and sobbed.

She knew everyone was looking at her. So? Girls were supposed to do it. They would all just say, well, she's a girl. Or a kid? Wasn't she still a kid? Not kid enough, like the tots on the balcony, to smile and giggle as if it were just another day to play with mom instead of go to school.

"She's sad, mommy," she heard the girl say.

"Yes," her mom said. "She's sad." Then she chirped, "Who wants to go ride the bus?"

The kids shouted "yay" and "me!" and Miranda heard the planks in the balcony resound with their joyful leaping. She wondered what busses were running and then she realized they meant the old schoolbus in the field, painted like a field itself, with blades of grass and flowers and dragonflies.

"They don't seem dangerous," observed the black man who'd first cornered them. He settled into a festival chair and pulled out a tobacco pouch and rolled a cigarette.

"No," agreed the swashbuckler with a smirk. "But they were trespassing and that's all gotta be ironed out."

The creepy skinhead white guy was pacing in a tight pattern, eyes on the ground, like a caged big cat.

"Take a pill, Pete," advised the swashbuckler.

"Huh?" he stopped but looked seriously confused and aggrieved.

"Relaaax," purred the swashbuckler. "Have a seat. Rest."

The skin yanked up a festival chair and placed it and made a show of slowly lowering himself into it, as if dutifully following a repugnant order. He wasn't much older than Mi-randa. Besides his permanent scowl, as if he were constantly in physical pain, he had big claw-shaped tattoos on his upper shoulders, and, Miranda had noticed during the pacing rou-tine, a German cross on the back of his neck.

A black boy, maybe eight or ten, skipped up to the patio and shouted up to the back building balcony.

"They went in the bus," said the seated black man. The boy ran off in that direction. "How's your grand-daddy do-ing?" shouted the man after him. "He OK," the boy shouted back.

The swashbuckler had been staring at Erik while Erik looked mostly at the ground. He and Vy and Haze were still standing. "Why'ont y'all have a seat?" the man offered.

Haze strolled over to the oak and sat on a root close to Miranda. Vy took a festival chair. Erik remained standing.

The swashbuckler smiled grimly. "OK," he said. "So if you're the owner of 815 Mazant, how come you don't know the tenants?"

"My dad's the owner. Used to be my grammaw. Until she…" A dark cloud passed over his face. "She moved. We rented it out."

"What's your dad's name?"

"Michael Scott Uglesich."

The skinhead guy was suddenly still. He had been bounc-ing his knee up and down like it had a motor in it but then it stopped. The scowl changed somewhat, too, became more of an inquisitive scowl, slightly less aggressive. He looked toward Erik and then got up and walked over and stood in front of him.

"Justin?" he murmured. "Scotty?"

"*Erik*," Erik said, his eyes fixed on the skinhead's, and even taking a step closer to him.

"Whoa, whoa," said the skin. "I remember you. But you

were like a baby."

"Yeah," Erik agreed, with a tone of mock revelation, "I *was* a baby once."

"Good," grinned the swashbuckler. "That's settled. Wasn't in a hanging mood anyway."

"So can I have my weapon back?" pushed Erik.

"Ooh, I'm afraid not," drawled the swashbuckler, shaking his head slowly. "You're not authorized to carry a sidearm."

"Who authorized you to carry one?" retorted Erik. "Buffalo Bill?"

The lounging smoker behind him laughed and pointed at the banner on the back building balcony. "The Independent Republic of Bywater," he intoned, through a haze of blue smoke that hung in the humid air. Then he stood. "I'm André," he said, and he approached Miranda with an extended hand.

Miranda's crying fit had eased. She thought, all in all, that it was true what they said about crying jags. She did feel better. She stood and managed a smile and shook André's proffered hand. "Miranda," she said.

André made the rounds and shook everyone's hand and introduced the others, Pete and the swashbuckler, who was called Captain Davey. Then André said, with a glint in his eye, "Y'all want some water?" Without even waiting for a response, he said, "C'mon then," and they followed him through French doors into the first floor of the back building.

It had obviously once been a kitchen—with a *garconniere* above—because the floor was still brick and there was a big fireplace at one end which had been converted to an entertainment center. It was an open floor plan, one large bright airy room. On the other end from the antebellum kitchen turned high-tech entertainment center was the modern kitchen—a little euro-kitchen behind a counter. On the floor by the counter were two stacked pallets of gallons of water.

"Go ahead," directed André, pointing, "y'all could each take a gallon. That'll be y'all's ration for the day. But tomorrow y'all get less," he chuckled.

Miranda, Haze, Erik and Vy each took a gallon and sat and swilled. Miranda and Haze sat on barstools at the counter, Vy in a chair at a long antique French farm table, and Erik on the bottom step of a spiral staircase leading upstairs. There were kid's things scattered around the room, toy trucks, dolls, legos and other blocks. Smack in the middle of the airy room was a big drum kit, complete with big shiny brass cymbals. Arrayed behind it were congas, bells, woodblocks, and more.

Miranda relished the feel of water sinking into her esophagus. She could feel it working its way down, moistening what she imagined to be her desiccated, cracking insides. Like a drooping plant perking up. Or like an outline of a person getting colored in, literally fleshed out. It worked on her mind, too, her spirit. She felt a psychic filling in and opening up as well. She remembered Ms. Williams' paean to water and heartily agreed. Without water they were nothing. Her awakening mind flowed back over the course of the past few days and she realized that the moment that really changed her, that grew her into a person capable of handling these stresses, was when she got dumped into the canal. She had been terrified of that water, didn't even want to dip a toe into it, but after the shock of going in, of being totally immersed in it and coming out again, the fear went away and the water became more of a bosom spiritual ally, to be cherished and respected. What she wanted now more than anything else, strange as it seemed to her to realize it, was rain. What those dry streets outside really needed was a foot or so of water to humanize them again. Yet more than a foot would drive the humanity away.

Captain Davey had followed them in but Pete remained outside. André had sprawled onto a plush sectional sofa in front of the entertainment center. "I like to just look at it even if I can't turn it on."

"You can watch it tonight," Captain Davey said. "You know the rules."

Miranda wondered what he meant by that. Why would the TV work tonight if not today?

Then Captain Davey said "You could watch something on your laptop, it'll be charged still, unless you already used it."

"Hoh no," said André, "You heard what Liza Jane said. That's strictly for kiddie movies. They don't get their afternoon kiddie movie, they don't take their nap."

"That's his wife," Captain Davey informed then. "Her name's Eliza but my son-in-law here insists on calling her Liza Jane."

Miranda wandered over to the drum kit and tapped a cymbal lightly. "Are you a drummer?" she asked.

"Ever heard of André Noel?" sniffed Captain Davey.

"Never heard'a Captain Davey?" remonstrated André with mock severity.

Miranda shook her head. "Sorry," she said.

"Forget it, André," Captain Davey said. "These kids don't follow New Orleans music. Buncha MTV Target-shopping Americanists, you ask me."

"Americanists?" asked Miranda. "What does that mean?"

"Oh no, oh no," protested André, sitting up and holding up a hand. "Don't get'im started on that."

Captain Davey had gone over to the refrigerator and opened it. He pulled out a can of beer. It seemed cold. There were beads of condensation on it. He pulled the tab and took a swig.

"You sure you wanna get started this early?" cautioned André, though he didn't seem serious.

"I get captain's rations," barked the swashbuckler.

"Are you a musician, too?" asked Miranda.

André snickered. "He's into the psychedelic stuff. Went out with Major Tom back in the seventies and just barely made it back. He likes all that distortion and noise stuff. Now he gotta get back to acoustic. Gotta go in the woodshed with Lightnin' Hopkins or some %#$&."

"He means I play guitar," clarified Captain Davey.

A light knock came at the door.

"Yeah?" André shouted.

It opened and an elderly black man peered in, with gray hair and moustache. "Nanou over here?"

"He in the bus with Letty and Sal," André said. He, too, had a moustache, though his was higher maintenance, neatly trimmed.

The old man started backing up.

"Wait a minute, hol'up Mister Vincent." André popped up and went to the door. "You sure you don't wanna come stay by us?" he asked softly.

"Naw, naw," the old man said, shaking his head. "We all right."

"But that tree got your roof all smashed in. It's probably not safe."

"It's OK in the front."

"We got room, now, OK?"

"We all right."

"But if you change your mind?"

Miranda didn't hear a response as the old man walked off. She knew the tree. She'd seen it down on the house, too. A sycamore. Maybe they weren't strong enough. Especially if they were old and big. All it would take is some termites under it. They could burrow all up inside it and almost totally hollow it out and you would never know. The outside of the tree would show no signs. Until the wind whipped up and *crack*!

André put out some food for them. Old boiled potatoes—which tasted great with just salt. And celery sticks. All conversation ceased while they chomped. Miranda realized that dinner conversation was for people who really weren't that hungry.

For dessert everybody got a Slim Jim—a delicacy Miranda had never envisioned herself partaking of.

"Hey Captain, André!" called Pete from outside. "Ready to patrol?"

André rolled his eyes and Captain Davey knitted his brow.

"We got the parade this evening," Captain Davey shouted at the open door. "That'll be like a patrol."

Miranda heard the sound of something being kicked outside.

"Parade?" said Erik and Haze at the same time.

"Yeah, you know," replied André, "when the going gets tough, the tough start marching."

"To kind of let the universe know we're still here," added Captain Davey.

"And the neighbors," threw in André.

"Any a'y'all play?" asked Captain Davey.

Miranda looked at Haze. He said, "yeah."

"Whaddya play?"

"Trumpet."

"We gotta trumpet lying around, André?"

"Prob'ly." He rose slowly, like a really tired person, and eyed Haze playfully. "Better have his own mouthpiece, though."

Haze coolly produced his mouthpiece.

Both André and Captain Davey were clearly tickled that this kid with apparently nothing more than the shirt on his back was carrying around a mouthpiece.

"Bet that mouthpiece has got stories to tell," ventured Captain Davey.

André rubbed his hands and said, "Well let's get us to the big house, then!

By "Big House," he meant the mansion across the patio, apparently Captain Davey's residence. The ground floor of the slave quarter attached to the rear had been converted into a music studio. They'd sealed all doors and windows and paneled it with soundproofing foam, but, as they explained, they'd undone much of that since the storm, since it got just too hot in there with everything sealed and no cooling. The two sets of French doors were now unsealed and flung open. And Miranda was thankful that, as she'd noticed in the *garconniere* where Andre and his family lived, it really wasn't so unbearably hot. The big live oak's shade went a long way. And there was plenty of airflow through the house and under it, since it was built up on piers the old way. And then she considered that, just possibly, the reason it wasn't so hot was simply that they'd gone days already without air conditioning. It took a few days of withdrawal, but one could, like the ancestors, survive without artificial climate control.

Inside was a drumset, piano, organ, guitars and basses on stands, a big stand-up bass in the corner, and some deep shelves with instrument cases. There was also a big mixing board and mics everywhere. Her old friend Eli would be so jealous.

"Do y'all record in here?" asked Miranda.

"You ever heard of *The Flying Dutchmen*?" asked André.

"Yes," replied Miranda, Erik, and Vy at the same time. They were a hot young band out of LSU just now hitting it nationally.

"Figures," grumbled Captain Davey.

"They got they ticket stamped right here," boasted André, as he sat behind the kit, pulled some sticks out of a hanging quiver and started lightly tapping drums. He did a few soft rolls and then grazed a cymbal.

"For Mardi Gras we get him up on a float so he can do his club tricks," said Captain Davey. "But today has got to be strictly old style."

Erik said, "Don't y'all need like a separate room, like with a glass, to record from?"

"Yeah," said André, "'specially with him around." He jerked a thumb at the swashbuckler.

"You're thinking of Elvis at Sun Studios or something," muttered Captain Davey as he picked up and started tuning a dobro guitar, the kind with a metal plate under the strings on the soundbox. She assumed he was answering Erik's question. "Stuff that's not on TV is a little different," he added.

She thought that was on the rude side, but she figured Erik's hide was thick enough to handle it.

Haze was peering at the cases on the shelves.

"There's a trumpet in there somewhere," Captain Davey said.

Miranda was curious to hear him play a real instrument finally. He pulled out a case and opened it. A gleaming trumpet lay inside.

40

As happy as Haze was to be holding a real trumpet in his hand, he also really wished he was alone with it. At least at first, to warm up, get his chops back. He felt like everybody was looking at him, expecting him to be Satchmo or Kermit or something. Especially Miranda. And he wanted to impress her. He just needed to warm up.

He blew a few long tones into his mouthpiece and then put it in the horn. Then he blew some air through, noiselessly, to warm the instrument (even though it was plenty warm already). "I'm'a take it outside and warm up," he announced. He tried to ignore the look of urgency on Miranda's face, and the smirks on the faces of André and Captain Davey.

He went outside and was happy to have the patio to himself. Just him and the noose. Cute. They obviously weren't hanging anybody with it. He knew it was usually used to scare black people, but André didn't seem too perturbed. Ms. Williams would throw a fit without a doubt, though.

He sat in a festival chair and blew some long low tones. Started on low 'C' and sank down by half-tones, 'B', B-flat', 'A'. Until his lips felt loose as a mule's.

But the festival chair was too deep and saggy. He moved to a metal folding chair that fit his purpose much better. After a few more low tones he made his way slowly up the steps of the 'C' major scale. When he hit the 'C' in the middle of the clef he felt a surge of power and pleasure. He stayed on it, stretching it with a crescendo and decrescendo. Then he dropped down to 'F' and played an 'F' scale. When he got to the top of that one, it felt so good he hit the 'G' above it, then the 'A', but fracked on the 'B-flat'. He tried to go low again but his embrasure was too tight and strained to loosen up for low that fast. He flapped his lips and then started low again.

After a few minutes he started playing tunes—little diddies of his own invention—and felt comfortable enough to play with the others. They were big cats, he knew (even if he didn't recognize their names), so he determined not to be embarrassed. It would be like playing with a teacher.

André came out and said, "Soundin' good. Sound like you can play."

"Alright," Haze said. But when he lowered his horn he found himself looking at the noose again. André noticed and said, "Hope that noose not giving you the willies."

"Naw," Haze assured him, shaking his head, "naw." But then he reflected and figured this was probably a decent time for a black-on-black conversation. He looked back at the house, to confirm they were still alone, and asked, "Whatchu think about that noose? Don't that represent hatin' on black people?"

André snorted. "Black people ain't the only people been hanged. And you don't need a rope for no lynching."

Haze said, "Alright."

André gazed at the noose a bit longer, too. Then he said, "No, you right. You the one right."

"OK," Haze said.

"You know how it go," Andre said. "You hang around white people?"

"Now," Haze replied. "Since the storm."

"Then you know," André said. "They do stuff and they don't mean to be like racist about it, ya heard me? But it's just too much trouble to get all into it. Try to explain everything all the time."

"Yeah you right," Haze said. He was hearing him, too. He had often felt that way, too. As if they didn't know…or did they? It was sometimes hard to know if a white person was saying something intended to be an insult, or a threat, or whether they just didn't know that a black person might take it that way.

"That noose gotta come down," André said, and went into his house across the patio. He came back out with a ladder under one arm and a hand-held saw in the other. He set up the ladder and climbed up it and began sawing at the rope wrapped around the oak branch.

"Why'ontcha play me a tune while I'm up here?"

"Alright," Haze said. He started blowing "Closer Walk with Thee," but André interrupted him immediately. "Naw, naw, don't be playin' no funeral music while I'm up here!"

Haze decided on "Bourbon Street Parade" instead. He had to stand for that one, to feel the mellow swing of it. André approved. "There we go," he said. "That's what Davey means by 'old-style'. Just need a banjo to go with it."

After a chorus the noose fell to the ground and André came down the ladder. "You could play be-bop?" he asked.

"No."

"You need to learn be-bop. That's the emancipation of jazz. Ain't no souvenirs with niggas sitting on cotton bales playing be-bop."

Haze hadn't ever seen any souvenirs like that anyway, but he was sure they used to have them. He'd seen the racist postcards at the tourist places, the re-produced labels from molasses cans and pancake mixes, with the little naked pickaninnies begging for food. Apparently the white tourists just thought they were cute.

"C'mon," André said, heading back to the studio, "I'm'a teach you 'Billy's Bounce.'"

Captain Davey was standing in the doorway idly plucking at his guitar. He looked at the fallen noose and at André with a curious expression but didn't say anything.

"We gon' teach this boy to bop it," Andre announced.

"How'm I s'posed to play bop without my Gibson?"

"Turn on the generator."

"Too frivolous."

"Aren't you the one always saying frivolous is the whole point of New Orleans? The *raison d'etre*?"

"Yeah," Captain Davey admitted sheepishly. "But we got an emergency situation here. Gotta ration the frivolity."

"Cover the keys then," suggested Andre.

"Okayy…" Captain Davey moaned.

But Vy was already sitting at the piano. She plunked a couple of notes.

"You play?" Captain Davey asked.

She nodded.

"Wanna sit in?"

"I don't know jazz," she said.

"Rock'n'roll?" inquired Captain Davey.

"Boogie? Ragtime? Gutbucket?" peppered André.

Vy shook her head. "I don't know," she said, flustered. But she didn't get up. After a second of silence, with everyone staring at her, she played something. It was a classical piece. Sounded to Haze like a tightly woven fabric where you could see different color threads going back and forth and across.

When she was done, André and Captain Davey said, "Nice!"

"Bach, huh?" said André.

"Well-tempered Clavier," said Captain Davey. "The second one, right?"

"I don't know," said Vy, blushing. "It's called prelude in c-minor."

"Oh my God," Miranda gushed, an almost pained expression on her face. "That was so beautiful. I had no idea."

Vy ignored her. She pushed back the bench and got up and walked away from the piano.

Erik stared at her in awe.

Captain Davey and André gawked at each other, like they were wondering what was up with this crowd they'd picked up. "OK," Captain Davey said, and went to the piano and struck a few quick chords in the middle while Andre got situated behind the kit.

"Hey kid," Captain Davey called to Haze, waving him over. "Billie's Bounce, right?" he said to André.

André grinned, kicked the bass a couple of times and kicked the high-hat into a tight fast pulse.

Captain Davey played a melody with his right hand, lots of notes really fast. And never really coming to a stop. "OK?" he said, and played it again.

There was one easy part to latch onto, a repeated "bah-boo-bop" phrase. Haze jumped on that first and just played that part. Captain Davey and André hooted encouragement and he picked up some of the rest. At least he had the basic feel—most of the starts happened on the upbeat, the little phrases ending on the downbeat. And it didn't take much range, it all happened in a little five-note window. It was mainly about rhythm, about feel. He got to where he could feel it and play it and add a note or two, but when they shouted "solo!" he got flustered and lost the groove.

"'S'alright, s'alright," the older musicians consoled him. André was getting set to do another take when the little kids busted into the room. "We wanna play!" they shouted. They made a bee-line for the bottom shelf of the instrument rack, which must have been reserved for them. Their mom came in behind them, telling them they only had a few minutes to play since they had to get ready for the parade. "Parade, parade!" they shouted.

"Where you go to school at?" André asked Haze.

"39."

"Oh, alright," grinned André.

"That's Wilmon's day job, right?" asked Captain Davey.

They were talking about Mister Brice. Haze asked if they knew him.

"Oh yeah," said André.

"He's a monster for sure," opined Captain Davey. Haze knew "monster" meant a cat who could really play.

"I wonder if he's around?" wondered Captain Davey.

"He stay over on Piety Street," said André. "We'll just bring the parade over by him and blow him outta bed."

"Naah," said the Captain, "he woulda left."

"We'll see."

Their conversation was interrupted by a commotion outside. Like lots of people banging on the wooden fence along the sidewalk with big sticks.

"Must be the skeletons," said André's wife. "C'mon kids, let's get y'all in the float."

"Yay!" they cried. They followed her out the door, the girl with a hollow woodblock in the shape of a frog and the boy with a tambourine.

The black boy named Nanou stuck his head in. He was carrying a trumpet.

"Oh yeah," said Captain Davey. "Nanou here blows a trumpet, too."

Haze heard the whomp of a sousaphone and stepped outside to see people gathering where they had opened the gate to the sidewalk. The sousaphone player was a skinny white guy. There was also an older white guy with a straw hat and a beard wearing a washboard. Miranda was helping Eliza lift the kids into this plywood box on wheels—like a little float. The girl had a tiara on and the boy had a little crown. The float had a mosaic on the side made out of old Mardi Gras beads, kind of a swirly paisley pattern. Eliza gave Miranda a strange pointy hat to wear, like a witch hat, but made out of a loud busy fabric with swirly patterns. "Oh my God, it's awesome,"

Miranda told her.

Vy and Erik were standing under the oak watching people line up. Captain Davey went over and gave her a glockenspiel with little mallets. "It's just like a piano," he said, helping her strap it on and plinking a couple of keys to show her. She looked happy about it. Then Captain Davey looked Erik over and scratched at his goatee in thought.

"Give him a samba drum," shouted André behind him.

"Yeah," Captain Davey agreed. "That's the one." He went back inside to get it.

Haze stepped out onto the sidewalk and saw people gathered out there. There were a couple of other black guys out there, too, and close to his own age. One was probably a little younger, a chubby guy with a bass drum strapped on. The other brother had an alto sax and looked familiar. He had long dreds tied back. "You go to 39?" Haze asked him.

"Yeah," he said. They dapped off and the guy said, "Yeah, you just started this year, right?"

"Uh-huh."

"You stay around here?"

Haze said no. He was distracted by the skeleton men. Guys who had t-shirts or chests painted black with white skeleton torsos and oversized papier-mache skulls on their heads. There were four of them. They also carried big animal bones that they knocked on people's fences and doors with.

"They not real skull and bones," whispered André, who'd come up behind him, almost making him jump. "They white people trying to get with the culture."

Haze nodded.

"They alright, though," André added. He had strapped on a snare-drum and now struck it with a few clarion rimshots. The band gathered around him. Captain Davey had come out with a banjo. He'd also changed clothes. Instead of jeans he was now wearing tight leather pants.

"You gon' be a pretty warm cool cat in them leather trousers," André said to him.

"You know I had to wear my Jim Morrison pants," the Captain said.

Turning back to the others, André called "Now we gon' head down as far as the tracks. And then come back. Be mourning on the way down, rejoicing on the way back."

An amen and a hallelujah issued from somewhere behind Haze.

"We'll prob'ly wind around a little bit," André continued. "Ain't got no police escort." Some laughter and a few boos. "Just keep your eye on the marshal," he pointed out his wife standing at the front. She had changed into black silk short-shorts with fish-net stockings and boots. She had a tuxedo jacket with tails, too. It probably wasn't too hot because she wore only a red sequined bra underneath. She carried big colorful feather fans and blew three short bursts into the whistle between her teeth.

Haze looked around for Miranda. She was a few feet away pulling the kid float. In her other hand she had a bright scarf. She was looking at Haze too. She smiled, kind of crooked, but he knew it was because she meant it, and waved the scarf at him.

"This your chance to play 'Closer Walk,'" André told him. "Play it big." He then stepped into the street and started a slow dirge pattern with lots of long rolls. The bass drum punctuated the ends of the rolls and the sousaphone came in on the beats the bass drum hit. They started a slow march down the street. Haze and Nanou took the melody. The boy's pitch was on the flat side, and he didn't hold the notes as long as Haze. But their different ways of playing made their unison a real heartfelt, mournful sound. The alto player from 39 did clarinet-type fills between the main melodic phrases. It was tricky marching, mainly because there was still debris in the streets.

Where there were trees, there were branches, predictable as leaves. And every now and then piles of bricks from walls that failed. Roofing tiles—and nails—pretty much everywhere. And the leaning utility poles and dangling powerlines. When they came to a tree that was totally down, some edged around it on the opposite sidewalk, some climbed over it, and a couple of the skeletons squeezed under. But the tune somehow managed to hold together. Even if individual parts dropped out, the thing as a whole stayed alive and kept up its determined crawl. And then the missing parts re-appeared.

The strangest part, musically, was the glockenspiel. Vy played it very sparingly. She was careful, only striking a note every couple of bars. But it was always the right note. It sounded like starlight, just a touch of gleam to make the tired body of the old hymn shine.

He felt his face rumple up and realized he was weeping. Ever since Miranda did it, he'd been wondering how long he'd be able to hold out. It was the right time, though. He couldn't hassle with wiping his eyes because he had a job, a function, which was, in a way, designed for crying. He just kept playing, or counting beats, and let the tears come down. Tried as much as he could to keep his eyes closed and just place the next foot down methodically in pace with the dirge. The tears eventually stopped, but when he squinted through the red mess they made of his vision, he saw other people in tears, too, as if they figured the way to cry with dignity was to do it together, in the street, with the right music.

He eventually looked back and noticed the crowd had grown a good deal. People had just come out of their houses and followed, like a regular second-line. They all stopped at the tracks at Press Street. There were broad grassy areas on both sides of the tracks. In some blocks these fields were basically used as dumps anyway, but now it seemed to have taken on a new dimension. Great piles of kitchen trash bags had accumulated. The neighbors had obviously agreed this would be a dumpsite, so their waste didn't build up either in their homes or right on the sidewalks out front.

"Smell like a funeral, alright," somebody quipped.

"A funeral for a great city, terrible to see it end this way," said somebody else.

"WHO KILLED NOLA?!" yelled a pierced guy with a mohawk.

"Nola ain't dead, man," countered a black guy in a nice-looking shorts suit. Haze wondered if he heard the parade and then ran and threw on his best to come out.

"Yeah, it is," said somebody else.

"It's the city's own goddam fault," said a middle-aged white woman.

"No it's not," said somebody else.

An middle-aged black woman suggested it was the Lord's plan that New Orleans be washed away.

"He bungled it, then," said somebody else. "He must be as big an idiot as George Bush."

It went on like this for a few minutes. But it was like they ran into each other at the grocery or whatever. They weren't killing each other. They weren't even really complaining a whole lot. Probably they were done with complaining. About half seemed to think that as soon as they could get their rear-ends out of this hellhole they'd been abandoned in, they were never setting foot or sail here again. But the other half vowed they'd never leave, or if they did, it would be out of America altogether. Captain Davey was the loudest on that side. Said New Orleans always represented an alternative vision of life, work, love, and art than anywhere else in America and that's why they didn't give a cheap damn what happened to the degenerates who chose to live there.

"Captain Davey's from California," André ribbed.

"Aw don't start that again," protested the captain.

They lit it up on the way back, and everybody danced hard, malnourished as most of them had to be. First they cut it up with "I'll Fly Away," the post-burial standard. Then somebody started up with "Big Chief" and everybody enthusiastically got on board. The funny thing about it was that Haze had never played "Big Chief" before. He'd heard it a lot, but never played it. But it came out anyway. He just heard it and it went right through his horn and the notes mostly came out right. It was the first time he played something just from ear without thinking about it a lot first and sketching and trying it out. He managed a decent, if spare, solo, too. Then the sax player took one and Haze looked around at the dancers. Erik was on the awkward side but he was trying—probably because of Vy, who was dancing more than playing now, striking a rhythm on a single note, like a drum, from time to time, and kind of swaying neatly, elegantly, side to side.

For Miranda it was all about the scarf. She was pulling the kid float with one hand and waving the scarf in wide patterns with the other, dipping her body down and rising. She gave Haze a big smile and a wink when she saw him looking at her.

The weirdest dancer was Pete, the skinhead white guy. It was like a martial arts routine, with kicking, and chopping with his hand. He had a big empty space around him because he'd probably already barged into other dancers and they'd learned to stay away. Eliza , the marshal, had been winding the route around somewhat, but at one point Pete seemed to wake up from his Jet Li fantasy, and, looking around in alarm, ran up to the front of the parade and had some words with her. Haze didn't hear what it was about, but it must have been about the route, because Eliza blew her whistle and they turned again at the next corner. Probably they were getting too close to St. Claude and he was worried about danger or water, or just bumming people out by reminding them how close they were to the swath of destruction—the whole rest of the city.

They eventually wound back to the compound and the sousaphone did a few parting whomps and André slapped those exclamation marks on the rim of his snare and the music stopped. People stood around and chatted for a while and slowly the second line peeled away, leaving musicians and close entourage only. The sax player from 39 told Haze he was pretty good and asked him if he had a gig with a band. Haze said no and the brother gave him a card. It said, "Bigtime Stompers" and, in smaller print, "for every festive occasion." It had the sax player's name on it, too, DeShaun Schexnaydre.

"That number ain't no good no more," he said. "But if stuff get back to normal, just come by my crib." He told him the address. It was a block away.

"Mr. Brice stay around here?" Haze asked.

"For true," DeShaun said. "We rolled by his place. 'Member that big yellow house with the big palm tree?"

"He didn't come out," Haze observed.

"He prob'ly gone."

They said their goodbyes and dapped out, and Haze walked through the gate into the compound where the others were lounging around under the tree. Erik was drinking a beer. He gave Vy a sip. He heard Eliza ask Miranda if she wanted one, but Miranda said she thought beer tasted awful. She asked for wine but they didn't have any.

André and Captain Davey were passing a joint. They held it up to Haze with raised eyebrows but he declined. Somehow meeting the other cat from 39 made him think that it would survive all this, that Mister Brice would come back, that football, then carnival season, would go on as planned, and that he would have to stay clean to remain in the band. Also he was worried what Miranda would think of him if she saw him smoking.

"'Bout time to kick those generators in," said Captain Davey. André agreed and they went off behind André's building somewhere and Haze heard them pulling on the chord and, after a few coughs and stutters, the motors roared on.

"Who's up for AC and TV?" Captain Davey asked on his return. He was carrying a couple of guns, though, a rifle and a handgun. Haze couldn't figure out why until he handed them to some skeletons who had hung around. They'd taken off their big skull heads and were sipping beers. Captain Davey gave them some quiet instructions and they went off in different directions. Haze thought to look around for Pete but didn't see him.

"Don't wanna let your guard down when those generators are going," Davey said. "The bad guys can hear'em from blocks away."

André came up and took the captain aside. They spoke in hushed tones, but Haze could still hear them. "He ain't right in the head at all," he heard André say. "Ticking time-bomb, man. We don't so something it ain't gon' be nothing nice."

"You thinking about a stroll over to St. Claude. Right?" Captain Davey said.

André said, "Or take him to Father Mike at St. Vincent's."

"Think he can hold him?"

Haze couldn't make out André's response.

"Chickens come home to roost," the Captain said.

"You mean buzzards, man," André corrected.

"Yeah," Captain Davey said. "We might have to."

Then they looked back over at the others and headed into André's place.

Haze was amazed to enter an air-conditioned room, have a cold drink, and watch TV. He started to wonder what the big deal was with the hurricane. These people didn't seem to have it bad at all. They could only get one channel, though, with rabbit-ears (the cable was out). It was CBS. It was national news but it was in New Orleans, on Canal Street. They kept showing clips of people coming out of stores with boxes of stuff. Then clips of helicopters pulling people off the roof. They showed a couple of black women cops loading up a cart with electronics at the Wal-Mart on Tchoupitoulas. Then they had a white talking head saying he didn't think New Orleans would recover, not because of the storm, but because of New Orleanians' reaction to it. He said too many of them were on welfare and now, instead of helping themselves, they were just robbing and stealing and expecting the government to do everything for them.

"Turn that ^$%# off!" shouted Captain Davey.

André did as he said. "TV ain't what it used to be," he groaned.

"OK," Captain Davey said, "we got two rooms for y'all. We got the ac units running in both of them, but in a couple of hours we'll nix the generators and they'll turn off. We run the generators two hours every evening and morning. To keep the refrigerators cool, cool the rooms down a bit, charge devices, and remind ourselves what total &%$holes your regular TV Americans are."

"It's the politicians, too," André interected.

"Yeah, yeah," conceded the Captain. "André's sensitive about TV." He elaborated with a grin: "It's an addict thing, but hey, we got to tolerate each others' foibles, right?" Then he asked how Haze, Miranda, Vy, and Erik wanted to divvy the rooms. "Up to y'all," he said.

Haze looked at Miranda, who was looking at him. But she took a breath and turned away quickly and said, "I guess we'll do girl-girl, boy-boy."

Vy nodded. Eric and Haze exchanged glances, with the predictable "aw, man" look of thwarted hopes, but the fact was that Haze was better with that arrangement, too. He wasn't sure yet how he'd act or what he'd say to her being in the same room overnight. And as to Erik, it's true Haze didn't like him exactly, but he was comfortable with him. Especially when he wasn't armed.

Comfortable enough to share a bed? All they had in the little room was a futon on the floor with a little coffee table next to it. But both he and Erik were too bushed to care, especially given the light cool and hum from the ac unit.

"'Night, man," Haze said, collapsing on one side.

"Yeah, sleep tight," said Erik. Then he asked, "So why don't you go by Rodney?"

Was he serious? He asked him, "Are you serious?"

"Yeah."

"Rodney De—Queer, huh? You want that one at school?"

He snickered. "Why not just Rod?"

""Rod DeCuir, right. Yeah, nice. Thanks for the memories."

Erik's next snicker morphed into a snore. And Haze was out soon after.

41

Vy felt like snapping at Miranda again when she suggested they share a room for the night. But the urge didn't make it to her mouth. She was angry that Miranda ratted out Erik, after all her talk about being on the same team and sticking together. She was ready to let it drop but Miranda must have been lying in wait for the drama of a confrontation. As soon as they got into their room—which was done up like a fancy guestroom with a big four poster bed—Miranda sprung it on her: "Are you mad at me?"

Vy shook her head automatically. It was always her first response to that kind of question. "I'm just sleepy," she said. "I just want to go to bed."

"But you seemed really mad at me when I told them Erik had a gun."

"How did you know he had it?"

"It's pretty obvious," she claimed. "A guy walks different when he has a gun. Everything changes about him."

Vy knew she didn't know Miranda that well. But she was surprised she would have this kind of knowledge. She didn't seem like the kind of girl that was around guys with guns that often.

"You're sure you're not mad at me?" Miranda pressed.

Vy decided the path of least resistance would be honesty. "Yeah. I was mad because I thought you had no right to tell those guys something that was supposed to be a secret. It was, like, not right for the team."

"But didn't things end up OK? Wasn't it good that I told?"

Vy tried to think of why that wasn't a good point. In a

way it was, but how could she have known that when she opened her mouth? "Yeah," Vy admitted, "stuff did work out OK, 'cause these people here are nice. But still you kind of sold us out. You didn't, like, have a conference first and like a vote. You just jumped out and made a choice without consulting any of us."

"Obviously it wasn't the time for a conference or a vote," Miranda sniffed. "But…" She scrunched up her face in thought. "I don't want you to think I'm the kind of person who always thinks she knows what's best for everybody. It's just that guns are serious business. I mean—" she teared up a little "—we've all seen what they do."

Miranda seemed to cry easily. Vy didn't see the point. She also didn't see the point much in talking about stuff like people getting killed. It happened. Stuff was going to happen anyway regardless of if you cried or talked about it or not. It was sort of like just bringing all the bad stuff back to hash over it that way. And a gun didn't seem particularly bad to her unless it was going off on somebody. It seemed like mostly they were used for show, and if they got fired that meant something went wrong.

"These people here have guns," she observed. "If they didn't, people might steal their generators."

"Yeah." Miranda appeared to really think about this. "But they seem to be organized and careful about it."

"Why do you think Erik's not careful?"

Miranda thought some more and then seemed to hit on an idea. "Because he didn't tell us." She nodded. "If he had told us, we could have trusted him. We could have decided, like, what it was for and how it should be used."

Something about the way Miranda wanted to discuss everything bothered Vy. "But it IS his," she said. "Maybe people just get to have stuff. Even secrets. Without big announcements and big…conferences and…debates." She sighed in exasperation.

"Just don't hate me," Miranda pleaded. "I can't handle you hating me right now."

Vy was mildly irritated at Miranda's emotional neediness, but a second later she was impressed by it. What impressed her was how this girl was so open, so willing to trust her and be her friend. She was obviously this smart girl who probably had money, and here they were, stranded together on an island, and this girl was wanting to love and be loved. Like another world, a new world, full of people you never met before, was totally possible. "I don't hate you," she said. "I think you're great." And she meant it, at least partly. She started to feel like she had passed through a huge challenge, like a war, like she had to slog her way through that giant thunderhead she saw creeping across the sky before the storm, but that a magical place, like a fairy tale island, lay on the other side. But old people, like *Ba*, weren't allowed to go. Because it was going to be a totally new place without a history.

"I think you're great, too," Miranda said. "And that's weird for me. I've never been sentimental before. About people."

They lay next to each other on the bed and were soon asleep.

She awoke to a rooster's crowing, and immediately knew she'd been in deep slumber for a while. But she wondered where she was. The lady next door to her grandmother kept chickens, and a rooster, but this one was different, and not as close.

Miranda was sitting up. "Where the heck are we?" she said. "Is that a rooster?"

"Yeah," Vy said.

"I didn't know you could have them in the city."

Vy ran over the past days' events quickly in her mind. "Yeah," she said, "we're in the city," as if just realizing it. It was hard to for her to swallow how far she'd come in just a few days. She'd almost never been actually in the old city of New Orleans before, even though she'd lived in the area her whole life. They usually just drove over it, from the westbank to the east. She knew it was famous and that tourists came from around the world to see it and, now that she was in it, she had to admit it was different-looking than where she spent all her time. It was really like a different city altogether. Like in the *Wizard of Oz*, like the flood took them to another dimension.

The people were also different than what she was used to. She hung around mostly with Vietnamese, and of course black kids at school. She had never really spent much time with regular American white kids before and that was interesting. Miranda was interesting and Erik was, too, though Erik was more of a challenge since he was a boy and she wondered what that was supposed to mean, like should they go out, and, if so, how would that happen?

She thought of her *Ba* again, but it was almost as if they'd already had a funeral and she was buried. Like she was this special quiet place tucked in a corner of her heart that would always be there, a little sad, but natural, too. Before, she had just tried not to think about anything. Just to look straight ahead and get somewhere—like Marrero, and only then she would start thinking about stuff. But how long would that be? Now it seemed to her that she should go ahead and think about what was going on around her and just sort of have a life where she was. Until the next thing, whatever that would be.

But she didn't want to stay where they were. It seemed like they should keep moving. She would end up on the westbank eventually anyway, if she kept moving, so she wouldn't have to feel like she was abandoning her family. She just wouldn't strain herself too much trying to get there fast.

Miranda, Haze, and Erik were also ready to move on.

They had some cold boiled potatoes and Gatorade for breakfast. Captain Davey handed Erik his gun back. "Be careful," Captain Davey said. "The trick is to not use it. Soon as you do…whew." He rolled his eyes and threw up his hands. "Chain of events, man."

"What about my knife?" Erik asked.

"Oh yeah," Captain Davey said, and dug in his pocket and handed it over.

They all said goodbye and hugged. André and Haze did a black handshake. The kids were bouncing crazily on the sofa. But their mom looked really worried. André squeezed her shoulder and she tried to smile.

Miranda wondered aloud if they would ever see each other again. "Up to y'all," the Captain said. "We'll be right here."

They walked out of the gate and headed downtown. After a few blocks they crossed the tracks. Unlike the night before, Vy noticed a few animal carcasses, all in the same spot, like people had agreed that's where they would go. Three cats and a dog, in various states of decomposition.

"Yuck," Miranda said.

"Yeah," Vy agreed.

Haze said, "Bet y'all tired of saying 'yuck' by now, huh?"

He had a pleasant smile on his face, though. Why not? It just didn't seem to sink in anymore. Dead animals, whatever.

"Least it's not us," Erik said.

He was right, too.

Over the next few blocks the neighborhood changed only slightly. The houses got a little closer together and closer to the sidewalk, and they started seeing some grillwork balconies like the famous French Quarter ones on all the postcards. Just like everywhere else, utility poles leaned and powerlines dangled, branches and broken glass and shutters and sometimes whole trees littered the streets. Driving would be hard—

you'd have to get out at least once a block to clear the way, and you might need a chainsaw to do it right. People peered out of windows and doorways every now and then, but the neighborhood seemed mostly empty. Some of the corner balconies had guys with guns, like guards. But people usually waved at them. Or said nothing. Nobody tried to do anything to them.

They crossed the wide boulevard of Elysian Fields and walked under a row of big live oaks reaching over the gate of Washington Square. There was such a mess of downed branches along the sidewalk and in the street that it seemed miraculous that any trees were left at all. But when you looked up, there seemed to be plenty of tree left still—they just looked carefully pruned.

In the middle of the Square was a circle of people. They were holding hands, but other than that it was hard to tell what they were up to. All the gates were locked, so they must have jumped the fence.

They took a left at Frenchmen Street because Miranda wanted to see how the famous clubs were doing. Miranda asked them if they'd ever come down to Frenchmen Street. She said she had an ex-boyfriend who practically lived there.

Erik said he and his friends usually went to Bourbon Street.

Haze said, "We come down and listen sometimes, just through the door. Never went in, though. That cost money."

Vy felt mildly embarrassed because she'd never even heard of it. It was two or three blocks of bars and clubs, all closed, obviously. Some of them had signs out with their schedules. "Look," Miranda joked, "Galactic's playing to-night!"

"We missed the Soul Rebels, though," Haze chimed in, "that was last night."

There was music though—blaring through the open windows of an apartment above one of the clubs. Brass band music, like the style they played last night, but with a rapper.

"Heyyy," Haze said, "that *is* the Soul Rebels."

They walked right under the tall floor-to-ceiling windows the music came screeching out of, but there was no sign of an actual person there—or anywhere they could see. In the next block was a banner, strung from a balcony, that said, "Thank You For Helping Us Help Ourselves!"

They turned up Chartres Street because Miranda said she wanted to walk by the Square—she meant Jackson Square. Vy felt like she was on a walking tour. Years ago, when she was a little kid, her dad had taken them to the French Quarter. The only time, as far as she could remember. They went on a buggy ride. She half expected to see the mules and buggies parked by Jackson Square as usual because, weirdly enough, the Quarter didn't really look that different. There wasn't any debris in the streets. No dangling powerlines either. It was quiet, though, like hardly anyone was around.

Then they saw in the near distance a clutch of people on the sidewalk. As they got closer, the scene became even more improbable. It was a bar. Open for business. There was a guy playing a piano inside, people lined up at the bar, people spilling out. When they looked more closely they saw that most of the customers wore press passes.

"Think they're carding?" Erik said.

"Got any money?" asked Haze.

"They wouldn't charge people during a hurricane would they!?" Erik joked.

"Hurricane way over," Haze said.

They got to Jackson Square and saw it didn't have a thing wrong with it, that Vy could tell. But Miranda and Haze, who knew the Quarter better, concurred.

"Just looks cleaner," Haze said.

Miranda skipped down Pirate's Alley, declaring it one of her favorite places. Vy could see why. With the cracked slate tiles and the stone gutter running down the middle, it really did look like an old alley where pirates might hang out. But further down, behind the cathedral, a giant tree had come down, smashing the gate behind the church and, it looked like, barely missing the Jesus statue, too.

"Oh no!" Miranda moaned. "This was one of the most beautiful places!"

"Now, now," Erik said, "Let's keep some perspective: be happy it's not underwater."

They turned down Royal Street and Miranda said the only thing needed to complete their afternoon in the Quarter was an ice cream cone. The strangest thing was that her statement didn't seem crazy. Here in the Quarter, the storm and the war that raged on everywhere surrounding it seemed suspended, like they were in some bubble. Like the giant black thunderhead in the sky surrounded the place but didn't touch it.

The next people they noticed, conspicuous a block away, was a couple at a little cafe table on the sidewalk, under an awning. There was a bottle of wine and some crackers on the table. An older, graying man in white pants and shirt, and a stiff, elegant straw hat. The woman wore a loose-fitting sleeveless linen dress with big pastel flowers on it. She also wore a straw hat, but it was floppier (in a stylish way). She seemed a bit younger than the guy, like thirty-something.

As they walked by, Miranda slowed down and seemed to catch the woman's eye. The woman said, "Heyy…," and lowered her sunglasses. "Miranda Maitre?"

42

"Ms. Godowsky?"

This latest twist of fate threw Miranda into a kind of swoon. The kind of state she used to strive for in her chair in front of the window at home. *Reeling—-thro endless summer days, from Inns of Molten Blue.* But a totally opposite path got her here. Instead of utter stillness until the filters dropped away, it was roller-coaster twists and turns of constant movement that brought her to this woozy alertness. Like driving a fast car on a curvy road. But it was too intense. She had no idea what to say to Ms. Godowsky! Even though she'd been wanting to see her again since the morning Ms. Barnigal showed up in class instead of her, announcing that the more interesting woman would not be coming back.

Ms. Godowsky chuckled. "I think under these circumstances, call me Martine."

Miranda smiled and tried to think of something not utterly stupid to say.

"Won't you join us?" Ms. Godowsky offered, with an inclusive glance at Haze, Eric, and Vy.

The older gentleman next to her didn't say anything. Just sat staring at the table.

"Oh, don't mind him," Ms. Godowsky purred. "He's having a terrible time!"

The man seemed to try to smile at them. Then he touched his hat brim.

Ms. Godowsky said, "We have…salami," she glanced at the man, "yes?"

He nodded.

Erik and Haze mumbled, "Yeah, OK, thanks," and ev-eryone stood a little closer. There were only the two already occupied chairs.

"Come, dear," Ms. Godowsy said, stroking the man's fore-arm, "Let's get more chairs out of the restaurant."

He got up and jangled some keys and opened the glass door behind him and went in.

"I have to prod him a little," Ms. Godowsky confessed. "He really is despondent."

"Because of the storm?" Miranda asked.

Ms. Godowsky nodded. Then, as if reproaching her-self for not introducing him earlier, she sighed and pointed behind her, "His name's on the window. He thinks everybody knows it anyway."

There in a wide picture window, in a gold and black cur-sive arch, read: "*Simon Pitot's*," and under it, in a horizontal line of smaller, print letters: "Restaurant."

Simon Pitot came out presently with three chairs—cane-back cafe chairs like the ones he and Ms. Godowsky sat on. He placed them neatly and went back inside.

Widening her eyes, Ms. Godowsky said, "However on earth, dear Miranda." It was a question.

Miranda wanted to explain how she felt about every-thing. She wanted to analyze everything that happened to her and show Ms. Godowsky what a changed thing she was from the goofy awkward geeky weird girl sitting at her desk a year ago. But she knew a clean narration is what she wanted.

"Well," she considered, then launched into it, "We were all evacuated to the hospital where my dad works, and their dads—or moms. Except Vy—that's her—we got her on her roof later. But earlier we tried to leave the hospital but our helicopter crashed and we were stranded. Erik here, who is a really brave guy—"

Erik beamed, in frank surprise.

"—he swam and got a boat for us. So we rowed away and tried to spend a night in an abandoned school. But, well, I kind of almost got raped there—"

"Oh my God!" cried Ms. Godowsky.

"—well, not really, nothing happened. Well, I stabbed him."

"Oh my God!" she said again.

"But he was OK. We saw him later and he killed a guy, a cop."

"Oh…" Ms. Godowsky covered her mouth. "Where have you been?"

Simon Pitot came out with a napkin over his arm and a basket. He pulled out of the basket a small cutting board, knife, and a salami. He put these down, laid a napkin alongside them, and set down the basket, which contained crostini (of necessity, of course, considering the date of the last bread delivery).

Then he pulled his chair out from the table a bit, to provide room for the others, and sat down again.

"Just," Miranda continued, "all around the city. We got Vy from her roof. She plays the piano! She's great. And we crossed the Industrial Canal. They're trying to plug that breach but I don't think it's going to work."

"I knew that crackpot scheme wasn't gon' fly," growled Simon Pitot.

"Then we spent the night with one of Haze's teachers. She told us an old story about old New Orleans. It was…what was that guy's name?"

"Juan San Malo," Haze said. "Or Jean St. Malo, the French way."

"Yes," continued Miranda, "and Haze—" she pointed at him and felt herself smile beyond control, the tip of giddiness "—is a GREAT trumpet player. He goes to McDonogh 39— you've seen them at Carnival, right?"

Ms. Godowsky and her apparent consort both gave Haze a respectful nod.

"We were in a parade last night."

"Really?" grinned Ms. Godowsky.

"Yeah, with these…guys that pulled guns on us and took us to their compound. Then they had a parade. They were like…vigilante musicians."

"Simon," Ms. Godowsky sighed. "We need to get out of the Quarter."

"Yeah, risk your own neck," was his brusque response. "We hear the gunshots every night. Y'all see any bodies?"

They were silent. And then they all nodded.

"Uh huh," grunted Simon Pitot as he took a big swill of red wine from his glass. It was one of those short glasses, not stemware. Miranda had seen them in Europe.

"And then we had a lovely walk in the Quarter!" she added.

"You kids must be thirsty," Ms. Godowsky said.

Pitot got up and went back inside again and came out with a stack of go-cups and a liter of water. It was a German sparkling water. Miranda found it quite refreshing, even though it was on the warm side. It scoured the throat more than still water, gave it a clean feeling.

"Would you like some wine?" Ms. Godowsky asked the table, surveying their faces politely.

Erik said, "Got any beer?"

Pitot shook his head. "Sorry. Traded it. For lack of a better term."

"I don't care for red that much," Miranda said.

"I've got some nice whites back in the apartment," offered Ms. Godowsky. "What do you like?"

Miranda strained to remember the glass she had for her sixteenth birthday last holidays in Paris. "Vouvray," she recalled. "I like Vouvray."

Ms. Godowsky beamed. "I have a fabulous Vouvray! It's in the pool. Come, accompany me," she said, standing and holding out her arm to Miranda.

She unlocked an iron gate and they walked down a narrow cool brick alleyway into a shady courtyard. It had big pots with palmettoes and elephant ears, a cast iron table and chairs, and a narrow pool. "This part of the pool," Ms. Godowsky said, squeezing an arm through two potted palms, "never gets any sunlight at all." She had a net in the water with bottles in it. "*C'est voila*," she exclaimed, coming up with the bottle of Vouvray.

Then a look of concern flashed over her face, and she said, "Come, let us say hello to MiMi." She turned into a door facing the pool and Miranda followed her into a cozy living room. MiMi was apparently the fat calico cat sprawling on the cool polished slate floor.

"Oozh, tsk, tsk, she is from Montreal." Ms. Godowsky picked up a mister from the counter between the living room and kitchenette, and sprayed it. Not directly at MiMi, but a few feet over her. The mist, lilac scented, drifted down slowly and eventually landed on MiMi, who seemed to adore it.

Miranda surveyed the room and was intrigued by a strange object on a marble sideboard against the wall opposite the patio and pool. It was some kind of aquarium that shifted back and forth slowly on some kind of lever under the middle. The left side would settle down, then come up, as the right side did the opposite. It was filled with a clear liquid, like water, and a thicker, blue liquid. They kept flowing against each other back and forth over and over again. Never mixing but always undulating in harmony, like an intimate partner dance where they lean all over each other and dip a lot. The wall behind it was glass bricks, so the filtered sunlight came through and put an iridescent shine on the liquids as they flitted on the stage in their limpid way.

"Oil and water," Ms. Godowsky said. "Have you seen it before?"

Miranda wasn't sure how to answer. "Yes," she finally said. "But it was never this pretty."

"Probably the color," mused the older woman.

Miranda sat on the coffee table—it was the closest thing—and lost herself in the rippling iridescent blue.

Ms. Godowsky sat next to her. "They don't mix, no, but, the way they are together. They respond to each other. Man and woman, maybe?" She laughed. "Depends, as always, on the man and woman in question. These," she squinted and twirled her hand in front of the tank, "they are not the same, but that is precisely why they are able to embrace each other. Or see each other. As through a mirror. Man and woman, or each of us and all others."

She thought about her comments and then her face seemed to reject them. "But this kind of thing is an Apollonian fantasy." She rose. "One settles for rougher equations in life. My Pitot?" she sniffed. "He's a strange man. And he is too demanding. But a boring life is the worst, right? Perhaps some spice, maybe too much? Better than no spice at all. And without friction, where would the excitement come, hm?"

Miranda rose, too. Gave the see-saw tank one more long stare, and turned to follow Ms. Godowsky back through the cool alleyway.

"Ms. Godowsky-"

"Martine, please, we will share a bottle!"

"Yes…Martine."

"The cause of my sudden disappearance from your school last year?"

"Precisely," Miranda grinned.

"The colleagues and I, well, like oil and water, yes, but we never found a way to dance. And the parents made a fuss."

"What about?"

"I was in a movie once—very tasteful—but of dubious moral value. It featured depictions of a sexual nature and no one was punished in the end. One of the parents shared a clip with that horrid Barnigal witch—excuse me, I shouldn't…" she touched Miranda's shoulder. "And the board took a furtive gander, too, and…" she waved her hand around in a search for words. "They spun a tale of fear and shame involving students and youtube." She emitted a light, airy laugh, and said, "They apparently wanted me to apologize. A young board member, a man, apparently taken by my performance, returned often to the term 'youthful indiscretion'. But I defended my virtue by asserting that there was no indiscretion, not until the artifact in question was hauled before unwilling eyes by a parent of the school. When they failed to convince me to cower in shame and beg forgiveness, they washed their hands, as it were, complaining that I wasn't making it easy for them. Then they sent me a letter, the cowards."

"I'm sorry that happened to you," Miranda consoled her.

"Ah, the twists and turns of life, the vicissitudes of fortune. Maximize the good, my dear…and to hell with the bad."

"You were my favorite teacher, for what it's worth. You seemed to want to really make things mean something, instead, of, you know, 'you have to learn this for college.'"

"Hm!" she chirped. "Dancing through the bureaucracy. A depressing game, the whole business—and it's not just school. When you're done with school, then comes employment, which is even more deadening. A rat race, but one is forced to participate." She sighed in resignation, then brightened up. "Until along comes a cataclysm to freshen our viewpoints again!"

They arrived at the iron gate to the sidewalk. Before pushing the gate open, Ms. Godowsky sighed, "Oh, my dear," and gave Miranda a hug. "I hope I'm not depressing you. Life is really a whole lot more fun than I'm making it sound." Then she pushed open the gate and they exited the cool walkway.

Simon Pitot and the others were apparently in a heated discussion about the city's future.

"Who's coming to a restaurant in this damn hell town anymore?" Pitot demanded to know. "Wait a minute! Y'all haven't seen a TV, have you?"

"We saw one last night," Erik said.

Pitot nodded and threw up a hand. "They're never coming back. The storm was one thing, challenge enough, but the media is finishing the job. Goddam firing squad."

"But…" Miranda ventured. "The Quarter and everything is still beautiful. It's practically untouched. Isn't that what the tourists come for?"

"Yeah, but people gotta live here, too," Haze said. "Can't everybody live in the Quarter."

"Yeah," Erik agreed, "the places where people live are toast. Where are they gonna live?" He shook his head. "Doesn't look good."

"But it's not just the Quarter," Miranda countered, "where we were last night, this morning, all of that's fine."

"And y'all got a house, there, right?" Haze asked Erik.

"Yeah, but—"Erik said. "Not everybody wants to live in an area like that."

"What do you mean?" Miranda asked.

"Like people want different things. Not everybody wants to live in hipster land."

"I'm not sure what you mean," Miranda said, but she was more sure than she was comfortable with. Her conclusion was that he was basically intolerant. "I mean, if you're talking about St. Bernard Parish, that's sad, but that's not really New Orleans."

Erik's face reddened. "Why not?" he said, in a quiet but charged tone. "Everybody that lives there's got roots in the city go back a hundred years."

"But it just looks like," Miranda groped for words, knowing she was treading on risky terrain but feeling entitled to say her piece, "I mean, didn't it look like, just a regular suburb?"

"What do you mean by regular suburb?" challenged Erik.

"I think I know what Erik means," Vy softly interjected, "Some people like more space, like for a garden."

"New Orleans isn't just the fancy buildings in the Quarter that the tourists come to see, it's people who live around here," Erik said. "But I don't care much anymore, to be honest. Doesn't seem to be nothing for me anymore. And you know what else? This city was going down before the storm hit anyway."

"Got that right," barked Pitot.

Ms. Godowsky jumped in: "Of course the city will never be the same again. It will sink back into the primordial mud, never to be heard from again. Except, of course, in song." She raised her glass. "But that is precisely why there is no more worthwhile place to be right now. And I will always be thankful that my personal sojourn dallied here for so long."

Miranda didn't like what she was hearing. "You mean you're going to leave?"

"I don't want to leave too soon," Ms. Godowsky assured her. "Things are quite interesting right now. But, if the pendulum swings back to something more normal—it seems like this moment would be great as a final chapter. It would be anti-climactic to stay."

"Doesn't anybody want to stay and help the city?" Miranda exploded. "Help it heal and get better? It's like you love someone until they have an accident and then you're like, 'you're too much trouble, now, see you later'. I mean, that's sooo cold and selfish."

Ms. Godowsky looked at her with a quizzical expression. Then placed her hand over hers. "You remind me of why I loved New Orleans in the first place, Miranda. People like you, speaking of a city in the terms of a lover."

Haze said, "I'm staying."

"I'll tell you one thing," Pitot asserted, "'back to normal' is the exact development that'll drive me out screaming."

Erik grunted agreement. "That's what I was saying."

"You're right," Pitot said, "But everything that was going wrong before is just gonna get worse, now. And you're right, too," he said with a glance at Miranda, "the buildings are still here but the tourists are gonna be too scared to come after seeing all that rampaging on Canal Street for days on end. Looks like a damn race war on TV."

Erik nodded at this, and kept nodding. Then he said, "Well, it kind of is." Emboldened by an affirmative raise of the eyebrows from Pitot, he continued. "And it's been a long time coming, kinda. I mean, you think about it, who messed up the city in the first place? And who's giving it a black eye now?"

The table was engulfed by sudden silence. Miranda looked at Haze, who was frowning and apparently trying to think of something to say. Then she heard an unmistakable sound in the distance. Galloping horses. Looking up Royal Street she saw, wavy in the heat haze, a couple of riders hoofing it towards them.

"What's that?" she said.

"The *gendarmes*, I imagine," mused Ms. Godowsky.

She was correct. They were mounted NOPD. They weren't riding toward them, but they stopped when they saw them. One rider passed them and the other halted his mount alongside them. Then the one who had passed turned his horse around and cantered back.

"What are y'all doing still here?" one of them barked.

"We live here," said Pitot flatly.

"Not anymore you don't. Nobody lives here anymore. We're clearing the city."

"Oh my," said Ms. Godowsky.

"Too bad the Constitution doesn't allow it," countered Pitot.

"You don't need the Constitution, you need a raft," said the cop. "You could be under eight feet of water this time tomorrow."

"I don't believe that," asserted Pitot.

Erik jumped in: "The water's already going down. We've seen it."

"Not what I heard," said the cop. "And water's not the only thing you gotta worry about. There's a rampage going on."

"But we're not the ones being a problem," Erik argued.

"Yeah," Haze said, looking at Erik, "*We* are not causing a problem."

"If you're still here tomorrow you'll be arrested."

"But how are we supposed to get out?" asked Pitot. "Can we borrow your horse?"

"Assemble at the Convention Center. Busses are coming."

"A deportation party?" said Ms. Godowsky in a bubbly voice. "Delightful."

The cop glared at her and spit on the ground. Then he spurred his horse and continued down Royal Street. The other followed.

"Great," said Erik, "First they ruin the city and then they kick the good people out."

"Yeah," said Haze slowly. "Those cops sure are something."

"You know I don't mean the cops," Erik said.

"Who you mean, then?"

"You know who I mean, brah-"

"Why you callin' ME bruh?"

"Just admit it," Erik admonished, his voice rising, "the brothers ruined the city. Admit it."

"When?" Haze demanded. "When they came over in

chains and BUILT the damn city? Or when they couldn't vote for a hundred years?"

"Yeah?" Erik said, "You're right. We shoulda picked our own damn cotton."

"Straight," Haze agreed. "You shoulda."

"Don't even bring all that up like y'all always do," Erik went on. "My people weren't even over here when all that happened. We came on purpose to help. The country and the city. And that's what we been doing!"

"Until you don't like the way something go," Haze retorted, "then you get all mad and start shouting at people."

After a second of strained silence, Erik said, "You're right. No point in shouting." He pushed his chair back and stood. He looked at Vy. "Had enough conversation?"

She looked confused and upset and didn't say anything.

Miranda asked where he—or they—were going.

Again, Erik looked at Vy. "The west bank?" he said.

After a pause she nodded.

"Oh," Miranda sighed. She felt terrible. "Are you sure?"

"It's the first stop to get the hell away from this &$%* city," Erik said.

Vy stood up and said, "My house is over there."

After an awkward moment of looking at each other—everyone that is, except Haze and Erik—they walked off quickly.

Haze shouted after them, "Be nice to the brothers, now, ya heard me? They might do something for you."

"Oh," groaned Miranda, burying her face in her hands. She couldn't accept how fast this new family she had tried to nurture fell apart. She tried not to blame New Orleans, but it seemed that maybe New Orleans was to blame after all. Minutes ago, she was flush with love for everything around her. And now here was everything crumbled to dust again. She felt a hand on her shoulder. It was Ms. Godowsky's. Then a hand on her other shoulder—Haze's. "We gon' be alright," he assured her.

"It didn't work!" Miranda blubbered.

After a few respectful seconds, a confused Haze said, "What didn't work?"

Then she reasoned that whatever didn't work wasn't even noticed by anyone but her, so it couldn't have been that significant. She dried her eyes and simply said. "Yeah." She nodded her head, squeezed Haze's hand. "Yeah."

But she wondered what the next twist would be. Something had happened between her and Haze since the first time they held hands—that obituary prayer on the overpass in New Orleans East. But what? She still didn't know. "Boyfriend" and "going out" seemed like such empty, trivial designations. Maybe he was just a friend. If that were so, she had been mistaken all her life about what the word 'friend' meant. If only she could talk it over with her dad. Yes, her dad. It all came rushing back to her. That she had a dad and a mom who had to be worried sick over her. "We have to get to Sinai," she said.

"Where…are you going?" Ms. Godowsky asked.

"Sinai Hospital."

"Yeah," Haze agreed, nodding. "We been at this enough."

"Been at what?" asked Ms. Godowsky.

"I don't know," Haze said.

Miranda answered: "Adventure."

43

Erik felt bad about the whole altercation with Haze, he wished it hadn't come to that. Haze was a nice guy, etc. But why couldn't they face facts and admit they have problems? And he was worried Vy thought he was a racist.

"I'm not a racist," he told her. "You know that, right?"

"Slow down," she said, hurrying to keep up with him.

He slowed his pace and repeated what he said.

"Why are you worried about that?" she asked.

"Because I said black folks ruined the city, some people would probably think that's racist."

"Did they?"

Erik worried she was trying to trick him into saying something wrong, so she could indignantly dump him (if she were his girlfriend, which she wasn't). Then he reflected that he was probably being paranoid, too slow to trust people. And she'd given him no reason not to trust her. So he decided to just speak his mind rather than try to figure out the right thing to say. "Did the black people ruin the city? That's your question?"

"Yeah, did they?"

"What do you think?"

"I don't know. I really don't!" she assured him. "I didn't even know it was ruined. I mean, before the storm."

"A lot of people think it was."

"It was like, worse than other places in America?"

"I think so."

"I asked my dad once and he said Marrero was pretty much like most of America. I've only been to Houston and

San Diego besides here."

So she didn't think he was a racist. Good, that was his worry. But he didn't want to tell her if black people ruined the city or not because that was something she'd have to decide for herself after looking around and making her own judgment. Telling it to Haze was different. Man to man, face to face debate. But he took it the wrong way. Predictable.

They arrived at Canal Street and it was hands-down the busiest street in town. Looked like a van convention. Vans with satellite dishes parked all up and down the neutral ground. Men and women in L.L. Bean attire talking into microphones—why weren't they wearing ties? They had catering vans, too. He and Vy gaped at the donuts and cold drinks and finger sandwiches. Erik began to wonder how they got all this stuff into the city. And if the city was to be abandoned, were the reporters going to stay? They might as well help themselves to the finest hotels. Ah, yes, he noticed, as they passed the Ritz-Carlton: they had! It was the city's last gasp as an international destination. Going out in style. The big story everywhere, the dying city, and luxury accommodations for the messengers. If you missed it, too bad. She was quite a town.

"Hey," Vy said, "there's CNN."

"Yeah, they're all here."

"Let's walk behind that guy and wave at the camera."

"Why?"

"Maybe our families are watching?"

Erik thought it was a great idea, so they strolled up quietly behind the reporter and silently waved and mouthed "I love you" and "We're OK." But they got shooed off. The cameraman lowered the camera and frowned and some other goon said, "C'mon, this is a serious story."

"Just taking a walk in our own town," Erik said. But then he realized: it really wasn't his town anymore.

The CBD was more peopled than the other areas they'd

seen. Lots of officials, law enforcement, everybody wearing some tag. And the roads had been cleared and vehicles were moving around. In a few blocks they'd hit an on-ramp to the Crescent City Connection, and start their trek over the river. But something seemed too easy about it. Just walking over the bridge. He was sure other people had already thought to do this. Had they succeeded?

As they approached the on-ramp, Erik blinked at what looked like a herd of some kind of animals in the shade under the high bridge. When one of them got up and sniffed in their direction he saw it was a dog. Another one stood up and looked at them too. About twenty stray dogs, all in a pack. Different shapes, sizes, but all bearing the marks of street life: scars, bit-off tails and ears, matted fur. Erik had seen packs of strays before, but never this large and never so close to the re-spectable parts of town. Some growling ensued and it dawned on Erik that they might, in fact, be in danger.

"Would they actually hurt us?" Vy asked, grasping his arm and angling herself behind him.

"Maybe," he said.

The first dog to stand up began padding slowly toward them. Other dogs stood and they started barking. "Let's back slowly off," Erik said, in disbelief that these dogs were going to force him to walk blocks to another on-ramp.

The dogs were almost all up now, and some, it seemed, were walking off with the intent of circling around behind them. Erik drew his gun and pointed it at the closest dog, the one who had started the whole thing. He seemed to recognize it. He dipped his head and turned and moved back. The other dogs were barking wildly now and lunging forward and back, but none came closer. Erik kept the gun drawn and pointed, and edged around the pack to the foot of the on-ramp. He and Vy hopped over the railing and started walking up. There was a half-hearted barricade in the middle of the road, but it was easy enough to step around—they didn't even have to climb over it.

When the on-ramp joined the main span, Erik felt a deep sense of relief. They were already high over the city, and the bridge would keep climbing to almost two-hundred feet. "Nick of time, huh?" he said. "Wow. Wild dogs, huh? Whoa." He tried to laugh.

"Have you gone hunting?" Vy asked.

"Yeah," he said, but without the pride he usually felt. "A dog's different."

Erik soon saw he was right that they weren't the only ones to think of this way out. While there wasn't a single car, there was an increasing crowd of pedestrians, all trudging up the high bridge. Erik noted, with a sinking stomach, that almost every one of them was black.

The view from the top was so impressive, it was hard not to stop and admire, no matter how urgent the journey. What was so special was to be able to stand there and take in the scenery at such a leisurely pace. You usually saw it speeding by in a car. Vy said the same thing. She had gone over the bridge countless times, in all types of weather and all times of year.

"They should have a festival for this," she said. "Close the bridge and let people walk on it once a year."

"If we ever get out of this," Erik grinned, "don't tell anybody your idea. They'd love to have another excuse to shut down the city and drive away business."

The skyline looked mostly normal, except, on closer inspection, the blown-out windows. And the white rubber skin stretching over the Superdome roof was shredded and hanging over the side. In the near and far distance, swarms of helicopters still buzzed around. And pillars of gray smoke dotted the sky. As if flooding and killing weren't enough, God added fire to his efforts. Erik pictured thunderbolts from the heavens, or meteors, and a booming voice flinging curses along with the brimstone.

But what befuddled Erik most was what he didn't see, especially in the river. Where was the battleship with the US of A flag pouring troops over the side to secure this major city? Maybe the senior hippie from Bywater had been right: *they don't give a damn about New Orleans.* But that wasn't because of people like Erik. Didn't they know normal hard-working Americans lived here, too?

But the most tell-tale sign of all was the growing river of people flowing over the bridge, not under it, all rushing for the same destination: the hell out.

It was less strenuous on the downslope but Erik was confused because people seemed to not be moving forward anymore. The river of people widened and pooled, but he could see open empty road beyond them. The culprit was a roadblock. He heard the crack of a .22 rifle. The crowd rippled like water with a rock thrown in it. There was screaming and some people ran back toward Erik and Vy, yelling, "They shooting, they shooting!"

Erik saw uniformed law enforcement, squad cars, an armored car, and horses. But they weren't NOPD. It was Jefferson Parish Sheriffs. St. Bernard Parish was underwater. Orleans Parish was descending into hell—whether or not it was deserved, destined, whatever. And Jefferson just put up a wall and said stay the %$#@ out.

"Neighborly, huh?" he said to Vy.

"They're not letting people go?"

"Not letting them *come*," he corrected.

"Why not?"

"They think we're all black."

"I guess so."

"And that's not a racist comment!"

"I know."

And Erik just didn't know who to be mad at anymore. Apparently everybody deserved it. He felt like shouting, "Hey, it's not just black people down here! You're making a big mistake!" But he could see Haze's look after he said it. That look he did of "*What did you say?*" Here Erik was on this bridge high in the sky, a black planet, and he and Vy were the only surviving examples of every other race on the earth. But it didn't matter: baby out with the bathwater. Which meant that's how black people must feel, too. That's what Haze's look meant. It meant "*here I am looking at you, are you talking about me?*"

"Let's head back," Erik said. "It's just doom down there."

44

Now that the easy way to the westbank was blocked, Vy had no idea how she'd get back to the family home. If only they still had the boat. Of course, there was no guarantee that anybody would be there, anyway. Given what was on the TV, her mom wouldn't be rushing back from Houston anytime soon. She probably should have stayed at her *Ba*'s. Probably her dad and brother came back in a boat and were shocked to find her gone, to find she had abandoned her own grandmother. With the Crescent City Connection closed, it probably made more sense now to head back to the east, to her church, Mary, Queen of Vietnam. Probably everyone was gathering there— if it was dry. But why would it be? That's where her grandmother would have gone. Probably, since they were already in the east, that's where her dad and brother would end up. If it was dry. If they were alive. It didn't seem at all possible that they would have drowned—they both spent more time on the water than on land, it seemed to her (free time, anyway).

She mentioned heading back east to Erik but he didn't like the idea. "Going back in the direction you came from… that's depressing," he said. "Your mom's in Houston?"

"Yeah. With my other brother."

"Busses are coming to the Convention Center. I bet they're taking people at least as far as Baton Rouge. But maybe Houston, too. From the looks of this mess, Baton Rouge is prob'ly already full by now."

"Houston seems like a far way to go." It had taken them so long just to get across New Orleans. At the same rate, it would take them a year to get to Texas. She knew that calculation didn't make sense, but she didn't know how to make sense any more. Even basic math seemed no longer relevant. Her mind was muddled by that same gray cloud that flipped everything upside down and in reverse.

"Gotta brother in Baton Rouge," Erik said. "I could drop in on him, tell him everything's OK. And then borrow his car."

It seemed like as good a plan as any to Vy—since she didn't have one. Driving on the open road seemed downright blissful. But she didn't expect anything to go according to plan, of course. The crux of the weird situation was not being able to call people. If she could just phone her mom, like on a regular night to say she'd be out a little later than agreed, that would take a load off her shoulders. She figured the phones had to work in Baton Rouge. It was only a little over an hour on the interstate. It was amazing how the easiest things had become impossible.

She assumed Erik could make it happen, though, if anybody could. If he couldn't find a bus, he'd probably commandeer a tugboat and head up the river.

She wondered if he thought she was his girlfriend. After all this, he probably did. He was her protector, her guardian. She didn't mind if he wanted to be her boyfriend. Her mom said the main thing was that a boy be catholic, that he didn't necessarily have to be Asian (as long as not black, because, she'd explained, of the place they occupied in the society). Her mom's sister had married an American guy (white). Their kids were fun and good-looking. But Vy hoped Erik wouldn't get too heavy about it, too future-oriented. She just wanted to have a cute guy friend, a guy she was with, and who was with her—even if she couldn't show him off to anyone she knew. If he wanted to kiss or whatever, well, whatever. But they were so dirty. Obviously they'd have to wait for all this to be over—and it was hard to imagine it being over. It was starting to seem like the new way the world was going to be. Like they were going to have to set up their own compound and scavenge and try to help humanity survive. It was hard to believe all this chaos ended at the city limits. So where did it end?

Deep below the bridge they saw one of the biggest crowds they'd seen so far. It filled up a wide street for blocks and then disappeared under the bridge. They could hear shouts and wailing when the breeze blew in the right direction—what little of it there was.

"Convention Center," Erik informed her.

"Oh," she said. "That's where we're going?"

"They said there'd be busses."

Vy was getting thirsty again. "I wonder if they have water?"

"Well," Erik said, "we were officially directed to go there, so…if there's water anywhere, I guess that's where it is."

"It looks really crowded."

"The trick is to stay on the edge, never get tangled up in it."

The crowd that had been trying to cross the bridge was now starting to drift back to the east bank. "We better keep moving," Erik said. "We've only got a few hours in the day left. If busses don't come, we don't want to be down around all that in the dark."

Vy waited for him to finish his thought. She hoped that wasn't the end of it. "I don't know, we'll find a park or something, construction site," he suggested. "With half the city all bunched up in that spot, it leaves lots of room for everybody else."

"Why are they all down there?" asked Vy.

"They think somebody's going to help them."

Vy knew then what Erik had to be thinking. No busses were coming.

45

"I'm sorry about what Erik said," Miranda told him as she squeezed his shoulder. "That must have been hurtful."

"If he think it's the truth, he oughtta say it." He hoped she didn't think she had to console him, that he was like some girl with her feelings hurt. He found it more interesting, illuminating, than insulting. He and Ms. Williams, in fact, had had a very similar conversation at her place. She got all weepy about how they finally had their chance—black folks—and blew it. He found Erik's remarks offensive, yes, but not a shock. In a way, Miranda's attempt to comfort him was worse.

"For real, Miranda, I mean it," he said, "somebody making a general statement about black people isn't gon' break my heart OR my legs."

"But it seems rude to say things like he did."

"It ain't polite, that's true, but look around," he swept his arm at the French Quarter street in front of him (which was actually well kept and in good condition), and said, "what use for 'polite' does anybody got now? Prob'ly better to go ahead and jaw it out."

"I guess I'm just not used to those kinds of conversations, where it's so personal and also about history and everything."

"You wanna know why black people causin' problems right now?" Haze challenged. "I know."

"But I'm sure white people are causing problems, too-"

He cut her off: "I know, I know, but we talkin' about black now. Black people causin' problems now 'cause they po', a lot of 'em."

"But Ms. Williams wasn't causing anybody any problems.

I bet if you counted all the African-Americans in the city now, a lot less than half would be a danger or a burden."

"Well," Haze began. He was mildly annoyed that she, too, didn't seem to get it. "I know that."

A different, more engaged, part of his mind was puzzling over the issue of the city's future, or, more specifically, the future of people he had met recently. Namely Miranda. He hadn't realized, until he'd heard her talk about healing the city, that he was committed to staying. For a while it had seemed that everyone was looking for a way out, and that the city's long history was finally coming to an end. Yet this girl was all about staying, no matter what. He was, too. The thing he'd always wanted—marching through the neighborhoods playing his horn—he wasn't sure they did that anywhere else. Ms. Williams, too, had announced that she wasn't going anywhere. So, great, he'd see Ms. Williams, look up his bandmate about that gig—whatever went down with 39. But what about Miranda? Was he supposed to look her up, too? It just didn't seem imaginable, in a more normal world. She was going to *Back That Azz Up* at the block party? Go to church with him? Or was he supposed to go into her world? On what planet?

He grounded himself by stressing the plan: they were going to Sinai Hospital. If they kept walking, they'd be there in just a couple of hours, probably. They'd be re-united with their families, exchange numbers (in case the phones started working again) and think about what might/could/should/would happen between them another day. But by the time he and his mom figured out where and how they were going to live, he most likely would remember Miranda like some dream he had a long time ago.

But a couple of hours seemed so short. And he'd just really gotten used to this exotic island of a life. He tested the waters: "We prob'ly hit Sinai in a couple hours."

"Yeah," she said, her quiet smile fading into a businesslike frown. "That's like really soon. Hard to believe it's so close."

"Yup," he said. "City's really not all that big. If you don't count the watery parts."

She gave a polite laugh. "I'm getting thirsty again."

"You must be used to that by now."

"You think they'll have water by the Convention Center?"

"They'll have it at Sinai if they got it anywhere," he answered. But he knew her concern wasn't really about water. She obviously wanted to stretch out the time they had together by taking a detour.

"It might be wild over there," Haze warned. "If they telling everybody to go there."

"It might be interesting to see if they actually are bussing people out or not."

"What, you a reporter now?"

"Kinda," she grinned.

"Or a tourist?"

"Hey!" She punched his arm. "That's below the belt."

He squelched his vulgar rejoinder before it hit his mouth.

Canal Street was main street again, apparently. News trucks lining the avenue for blocks, on both sides and in the middle. Plenty of cops, too. It was like the Green Zone in Baghdad, the secured area from which they went on forays and ambushes. The palm trees they'd put in a year or so ago held up OK. A few had trouble standing up, but most were still vertical. They didn't see any looters. Probably they'd already all been shooed away. Which explained why the footage they saw the night before seemed to be the same images over and over. There was no water in the street, either, and on the TV there had been.

The Convention Center looked pretty much like the other staging areas they'd come across so far—the High Rise, the St. Claude Bridge—except multiplied by a lot. Probably twenty times the people at Poland and St. Claude, at least. It was hard to tell. They walked along the edge for a few blocks but the crowd just kept stretching into the distance still. It was like they were waiting for a parade, but in a less festive mood. Most people were underdressed the same as the other stranded groups they'd seen. Like they'd woken up in bed with the water tickling their ears and had to run up to the roof. They had lots of sick people too, with IV tubes and oxygen tanks that probably weren't working anymore. At least a couple of wheelchairs per block. There also seemed to be some dead people. A guy under a blanket on the thin strip of neutral ground down Convention Center Boulevard. A lady in a wheelchair by one of the service doors, also with a blanket over her head.

Lots of people praying. In little circles or alone, on their knees.

People had set up little camps. Families around a couple of folding chairs and some flattened cardboard boxes with sheets and pillows. There were a few little grills along the curb, too, but he didn't see any that were smoking. Pretty much all ages. The very old and very young seemed to be having the hardest time. There was one old couple in lawn chairs holding hands but the man really looked dead to Haze. He didn't want to stare long enough to be sure. Some sick babies, too. Expressionless, dull eyes, heads lolling on their necks. There was one woman on her knees sobbing and crying to Jesus, holding a wrapped-up bundle that looked like a baby, but the way its head was covered—especially in that heat—Haze thought it probably wasn't alive anymore.

Every now and then some altercation would break out, there'd be shouting and pushing from somewhere deep in the crowd. You could tell by how the outer edges responded, how they all looked in a particular direction and stepped back. But, seconds later, it was hard to know what had actually happened. There was an air of bad things going on—besides the smell of body odor and feces and death—but it was hard to know what specific things were happening at a given time. One thing they overheard a lot were warnings not to go inside. People, even girls, who needed to pee, just got their friends or family to form a circle around them on the curb. They came across one relatively empty patch, next to a service door, and realized why no one had camped in the immediate vicinity: it had been turned into an open-air latrine. Human feces, swarming with flies, spilling off the sidewalk and reaching into the middle of the street.

"Let's go to Jamaica next time," Haze quipped.

"Yeah," Miranda said, a look of horrified absorption on her face.

Every few blocks was a Hummer with a few very nervous-looking soldiers. Louisiana National Guard. "Yes, Ma'am, we've been told busses are en route," they heard one of them tell a pleading old couple, the guy leaning on a walker.

That's when Haze noticed, in fact, a bus just a few yards away. A beat-up school bus. Haze thought there'd be a line of them, a fleet. But here was just one. He assumed at first it just happened to be parked there when the storm hit, though it didn't make much sense, it being in the middle lane. The engine sputtered on and he wondered why people weren't racing to board it.

They walked alongside it and saw there were a few seats taken, but not all by any stretch. Maybe they were reserved? They heard the National Guardsmen explaining to the old couple, "That bus is not authorized. You get on there, it's your own risk."

Haze peered into the door and saw a man sitting behind the wheel staring straight ahead with a set jaw. He looked tired. Or drunk. His eyes were dark and glazed.

"This bus leavin' out?" he asked.

The man barely glanced at him. "Baton Rouge," he said.

The voice, and how he turned his head, struck a chord.

Haze had to get him to say something else. "When you leaving?"

The man turned and surveyed the half-empty seats. "Soon as it fill up."

Yes. It was his dad. But he didn't seem to recognize his son. "How you get out the city?" Haze asked.

"Metairie Road." He sucked his teeth and leaned out the driver's side window and spit. "Only way."

"You did it already once?"

"This be my third time, coming up." He glanced back at Haze and did a double take. But it was because Miranda was standing behind him.

"We don't need to go to Baton Rouge," Miranda said. "We're staying."

They stepped aside to allow a few old people to get on. They struggled up the steps and down the aisle with pillows and old brown grocery bags stuffed with sheets and clothes.

"When you get to Baton Rouge, where you take'em?" Haze asked.

"Bus station," he said. "They got plenty people there. They finding shelters for'em."

Haze turned and asked the closest grouping of people if they were getting on.

"I don't wanna go to no Baton Rouge," said a young woman in a headrag. "I wanna go to Jackson."

"I'm tryna get to Houston," said a man sitting on the curb.

But another woman, attached to a different group, said, "That man crazy. I ain't fool enough to get on that bus." The people around her nodded and said 'hm-m'. One of them said, "He stole that bus. They prob'ly arrest him and everybody on it."

Haze turned back to his dad with another question.

"How long it take to get to Baton Rouge?"

"'Bout a hour. Ain't no traffic." After a pause he looked down at Haze again. "You coming or not?"

Haze took a deep breath, exhaled, and said, "Naw. I'm alright."

His dad nodded once and the door pulled shut with a screech. The bus lurched and slowly started off.

Miranda looked into his eyes with a curious expression.

"I knew the man," Haze said. "I recognized him."

"Where from?"

"He didn't recognize me, though."

"From where?"

Haze looked at her. Thought about telling her. But didn't want to go all into it until he figured out how he felt. "From the old neighborhood."

Miranda said, "OK," but with a doubtful tone.

Haze had dated a few girls before, but in a way this seemed more like marriage. She was constantly looking at him, trying to figure out he felt, pressing him to explain what was going on in his head. It's because they spent every second together. There was no kiss goodnight and I'll call you. If only he could take a break and figure out how he felt—about her and lots of other things.

"It's getting kind of depressing around here," said Miranda.

"Got that right."

They took one last long gaze at the exhausted mass, both ready to put it behind them. But Haze saw another face that seemed familiar, and he couldn't tear himself away before he figured out who it was. A large, beefy brother with a bald head. Better-dressed than most, too. Brand-new jeans with the big pockets down low in the back. Pricey brand-new limited edition Reeboks. And a colorful oversize silk dress shirt. But all Haze had to do to place him was to picture him in

Dickies and a white T. With a stiff bloodstain on it. As soon as he realized who it was, he stepped behind a skinny tree on the neutral ground, pulling Miranda with him.

"What?" she said.

"It's y'boy from that school."

"Oh my God, you mean-"

"Yep, that's the one. It's alright, he don't know we're here. He recognize you faster than me, though."

She glared at him playfully.

"Yeah, you kinda stick out."

"Where is he?"

It was too hard to explain, to point him out. "He in there. 'S'alright, we going."

But he didn't move. Green was looking at someone else. Intently. Haze tried to see where he was looking and saw a white guy, first just the arm of a white guy between the other people. He knew before seeing the rest of him that it was Erik. Did he know this guy was staring at him? And where was Vy?

"Oh, Erik!" Miranda called out.

"Shh!" Haze insisted.

"Does he see that guy?"

Some people in the crowd shifted and Haze saw that Erik did see Green. "Yeah," he said softly. "He sees him." Actually they were both staring right at each other. He saw Erik smile, nod, and wave at Green. What was he up to? Trying to get killed?

Green started working his way, quickly, through the crowd towards Erik. Where was Vy?

"It's Vy!" Miranda said.

Vy was just at the next Crepe Myrtle over from theirs, on the thin strip of neutral ground on the edge of the crowd. She had been watching Erik, too, and called out to him.

Erik was running now. He crossed the neutral ground a few yards away from Vy, but turned and held up his palm and mouthed "stay" at her. Then he hot-footed it down a side-street. Green followed close behind.

"Uh-oh," Haze grunted. "I don't like that." And he took off running, too.

"Haze!" Miranda yelled.

He shouted "stay" at her but she didn't listen. But she didn't run as fast either.

He followed Green, who was chasing Erik, about two blocks. Green never looked back, apparently didn't even hear Haze's feet behind him. Erik turned into an alley, followed quickly by Green. Haze got there seconds later, but didn't go barging in. He slipped behind a car on the other side of the street to scope the situation.

But it looked like Erik needed help fast. He was standing there begging for his life, saying, "C'mon, man, don't shoot me. I got a family, man."

Haze shouted "Police!"

Green wheeled around, but, when he saw Haze's head ducking behind the car, he laughed. "Oh, lord, it's ya little friend ain't it?" He seemed to savor the moment. "I'm comin' for you next!" he yelled at Haze. Turning to Erik, he said, "You dead, bitch," and raised his gun.

But Erik was already holding his own gun. He fired and Green spun around, pistol flying from his hand, clattering over a car hood, and landing in the street. Erik fired again and Green fell to the pavement. He lay there on the sidewalk squirming, trying to get up. Erik walked over to him, the gun still in his hand.

"Wait!" Haze shouted, darting from his hiding spot.

"What?" called Erik, "You wanna be on the jury too?"

Haze sidestepped the gun in the street and met Erik on the sidewalk next to Green. Miranda and Vy stood staring a few yards off.

"The worm isn't dead yet," Erik growled. "Should we cut

him in half?"

Green gripped his right arm above the elbow and tried to get up, but he couldn't bear any weight on his left leg.

"What the *&$% you up to?" Haze demanded. "I'm not gon' stand here and watch you kill a black man!"

"No!" cried Miranda, hurrying over and forcing herself in front of Haze.

"He's not black," Erik contended. "He's the color of puke."

Green's lips were curled back and his eyes wide. He sucked in rapid, shallow breaths through clenched teeth. He glared at Miranda and said, "You the bitch who stabbed me!"

"Yeah," Miranda said. "Hi!"

"Too bad she didn't finish the job," said Erik.

"I'm trying to save your life," Miranda told Green, "you could at least be polite."

Green started to say something but gave up after a grunt and a cough.

Haze leveled as steady a gaze as he could on Erik's face and spoke softly. "You not killing no black man. Not today."

"But it would be OK if he was white?"

"No," said Haze, shaking his head. "That wouldn't be OK either." It wasn't that Haze had a particular issue with a black man, more than a white one, getting killed, it was that Erik seemed to think black was more killable, more deserving or easier to get away with or more used to it. But Haze didn't have the energy or the time to figure out how to phrase all that at this particular moment.

"We leave him here, he'll prob'ly die anyway," Erik reasoned. "Like the cop he left to die."

"Maybe not," Miranda said. "He's not bleeding like… y'know, the other guy did."

"Maybe Haze wants to carry him to Charity on his back," Erik taunted.

"Ain't no Charity," Green wheezed.

"Guess we gotta drag him all the way to Sinai, then," mocked Erik.

"Ain't no Sinai, either," said Green.

Haze wondered what he meant by that.

Miranda asked him what he meant.

"Ain't no hospitals at all." A smile seemed to dance somewhere behind his pained grimace. "They done shut'em all down. Everybody leaving the city."

Haze's mind mulled that possibility in an exhausted, barely coherent way. It seemed to him that it was possible, at least, that Green spoke the truth. "Where you heard that?" he asked.

"Man, everybody know that," Green spat. "Just %@#$ing kill me or get the %#$& out my face!"

"OK," Erik said, pointing the gun at his head.

"Man, quit it!" Haze said, pushing him.

"STOP!" Miranda shouted. She looked around for Vy, who kept a few feet of distance. "Vy," she cried, "tell Erik he doesn't want to kill some guy and be a murderer!"

Vy came a couple of feet closer and said, "Yeah. She's right."

Erik looked over to her and they stared at each other for a couple of seconds. "Yeah, yeah," Erik finally conceded. "Yeah, I know." He returned his gun the back of his pants.

"And YOU two," Miranda continued, looking from Erik to Haze, "need, need, NEED to get along."

Haze just kept his gaze locked on Erik and said nothing. Get along. Sure. Until one of them killed the other.

"At least until we…get out of this," Miranda added. But it was clear from the sinking features on her face that she was no longer able to imagine a world beyond or different than "this." Haze was having the same problem.

"Are y'all gonna shake hands?"

Over a black man's writhing body? Haze wondered if she

even saw the man lying at their feet.

"I'll shake hands," Erik offered.

"Naw, I ain't shaking hands," said Haze.

Miranda's face looked tired, resigned. Haze couldn't tell if she was looking at the ground or at Green. "So what she would do about him?" she asked.

"You heard him," Erik said. "Nothing to do."

Miranda crouched down closer to him. "Can you walk if we help you up?" she asked.

"%#$@ you!" he hissed.

"Hey Haze," said Erik. "You gonna get his gun?"

"What I want with a gun?"

"Safer," argued Erik.

"Not for no black man. See what happen to a black man with a gun?"

"Now, now," Miranda said. But she wasn't looking at them. She was surveying the area, looking for something specific. She wandered back into the alley Erik had been cornered in, to a dumpster and a pile of construction debris.

"She's right," Vy ventured, inching a bit closer. "Y'all need to chill."

"Which one of us?" Haze inquired in amazement.

Vy said, "I don't know," and shook her head and put up her hand, to signal regret at being involved at all.

Miranda came back with a two-by-four, about five feet long. "We'll help you up and get you propped on this," Miranda told Green. "Then you can hobble back to the Convention Center and seek medical attention."

"From who?" he wanted to know.

"We'll go ahead of you and tell the guardsmen you're coming."

She leaned the two-by-four against a car and looked at Haze and Erik, raising her eyebrows and pantomiming lifting Green up.

Haze nodded and crouched and tried to figure out how best to lift him.

But an aghast Erik said, "Whoa! I'm not touching that puddle a' diarrhea!"

Miranda glared at him. "Great, Erik," she said. "I'll do it. I'll get his blood all over *me* again." Her face drooped and then tightened. "You @#$%ing coward," she yelled, voice rising to a shriek. "Be a #$%*ing MAN!" Her face was burning red and her eyes had gone nuclear. She was shaking.

Erik looked bewildered and almost cowed. He glared right back at her a few seconds, then glanced over to Vy, who stood there with folded arms and seemed to be crying. Then he shrugged and got down on one knee and slid his arm under Green's shoulder. "Let's try to just prop him up against the car first," he said. "One, two…"

They got a good grip and hoisted him up onto his good leg and leaned him against the car. Then Erik took the two-by-four and wedged it up under his good arm. The other arm and leg had been hit, but apparently no arteries because the blood was just oozing rather than gushing.

"OK?" Miranda said, looking at Green matter-of-factly.

He didn't say anything. Just stared at the ground.

Erik went into the street and got the stray gun. He picked it up by the tip of the barrel. "This is evidence."

They started back toward the Convention Center. After a block Haze looked back and saw Green struggling along behind them.

Erik said, "I don't wanna carry this thing around."

"Don't look at me," said Haze.

"Two guns is too many," Erik muttered. He stopped suddenly at a mailbox and dropped Green's gun in. "I can tell'em where it is later."

Haze saw a sudden ray of opportunity and acted immediately. He slammed Erik into the mailbox, pulled the gun out of his rear waistband, darted a foot in front of Erik's leg and pushed, knocking him to the ground.

"What are you-?" Miranda cried. Vy gasped.

Erik twisted around onto his butt and stared up at Haze, who gripped the pistol deliberately in his right hand. Erik's look went from disbelief to strained amusement to terror.

"Uh-huh," Haze grumbled. He opened the mailbox and dropped the gun in.

46

Miranda was getting dizzy from the war of moods inside her. The city was at its own throat and so was she. One feeling would rise up on the back of another and stay there until the next coup. She couldn't take it anymore. At one point she adored Haze and loathed Erik, but now she feared, even kind of hated Haze, and pitied Erik. Vy she used to admire. Now she thought she was pathetic. The new world before her struck her once as shimmering, rippling with fullness and promise. Now it was a cockroach world, a dung pile for insects to jostle each other in. She couldn't believe this day wouldn't just be over. One more flip of her overheated consciousness and she would faint, just lie down on the sidewalk and pass out—but, of course, never, ever sleep again. Not with both eyes closed.

Pain—has an element of Blank—Miranda took a deep breath and resolved to get there—to the Blank. It was the only place she could function.

Erik rose slowly, pointlessly opened the mail slot and peered inside, nodded his head, sighed. "You owe me for that gun," he said.

"How much you paid for it?" asked Haze.

"Not relevant."

"Seem to me like that police on St. Claude *gave* it to you, and pinned a little deputy badge on you, for keeping the brothers in line," Haze said coolly. "Not no more, though."

Erik and Haze both looked at Miranda, like they expected her to referee. But she had no intention. She was done.

The wounded Green was gaining on them, however slowly. Miranda heard the thud and drag of the makeshift crutch, like the mummy.

So they kept walking. What else could they do? Erik and Haze in front, evidently not done with their conversation, and Vy and Miranda behind. Miranda was happy to be with the one who didn't talk. She wondered whether Vy suffered torments in her quiet head or just, cow-like, ruminated serenely on the wonders of creation.

"So you think," Erik talked at Haze, "there's some, like, *conspiracy*, with white people, to keep black people down?"

"Not like that," Haze replied, "more like, I don't know— an instinct."

"But I hope you don't think *I* think all black people are the same."

"I gotta think about that one." They'd reached a corner and Haze paused, pointed to the right, and turned, saying, "We don't need to go back that way." He meant the Convention Center.

"Second that," Erik agreed. So, again, their tracks turned uptown. Miranda was happy about that. In just a few blocks the battered brick of the old warehouses would give way to the soft leafy lanes of the Garden District.

"No," Haze continued, "I don't think you think black people are all the same, I think you think *black people* think they're all the same."

Erik chewed that over as they plodded a few more feet. Miranda realized how tired she was, physically and in every other way.

Erik said, "You're the one called the scumbag back there a 'black man,' instead of a scumbag or a low-life or a punk or whatever. That's bringing up race."

"You shouldn't be killing anybody, man. The reason I said it was about him being a black man is, it seems to me, like white people think they can decide what happens to a brother, like that's they job, they prerogative."

"You mean all white people or just me?"

"Man, you the only white brother I ever hung with this much!" Haze exclaimed. "I never hung with white people this long before!"

Vy said, "Me, either."

Erik tossed a smile back to her and Miranda realized that he wasn't really on edge, aggressive, anxious. For that matter, Haze seemed fairly nonchalant, too.

"Haze," Erik said, slowing down and turning toward him, "you're the only one I…lemme see. I mean we got black kids at my school, and I've played lots of sports with'em. But you're the only one I've, like, talked to about this stuff. I don't mean no offense, man, I swear."

"I ain't offended," Haze insisted. "Just glad you don't have a gun."

"You snagging my gun, though," Erik reflected, "That makes me wonder whose side you're on."

"Why it's always gotta be some side versus the other side?" Haze asked. "Why can't it be just people trying to get by? You talk like there's always a war on."

Erik didn't respond. He seemed to be thinking. They were all silent for a few blocks as the neighborhood shifted from concrete and windowless brick and flat roofs to sloped roofs, iron gates, porches, and narrow front gardens. The trees made a comeback, too, but they had no more need of shade since the sun was already down, leaving only afterglow.

Miranda felt a twinkling of contentment, even almost joy, when they reached Coliseum Square. It was not actually a square but a long and somewhat winding park, about a block wide, but spanning several blocks in length. The great quiet oaks abided, chastened by the loss of many a limb, but still very much intact. Homes ranging from magnificent to humbly graceful lined the uneven rectangular "square" on both sides.

But the peace of the scene was disrupted by an exceedingly rare sight since the storm: headlights, racing toward them. It was a big SUV, running roughshod over the scattered branches littering the street. When it got alongside them it screeched to a halt and the window rolled down. A head stuck out, but before it said anything, Miranda heard a dissonant chorus of mewing, hissing, and caterwauling. Stacked up in the back seat and trunk area were cat cages, stuffed to the brim with complaining felines. Painted in sloppy white letters on the side windows were the words "Animal Rescue."

"Have you guys seen any pets?" came the gruff request from the driver. He was a youngish man with wire-rimmed glasses. A woman, with hair a bit too gray for her age, sat in the passenger seat and waited intently for an answer.

Miranda and the others looked at each other. Haze and Erik said, "Uh, no."

"You got any water?" Vy asked, but they didn't hear her, were already speeding off.

"Got some dogs under the bridge need rescuing!" Erik shouted after them. Then he said, "Wow—a car."

They kept walking along the sidewalk bordering the old park, kicking at the mess of downed branches. "I always wanted a house on Coliseum Square," Miranda said. The others turned and looked at her like they'd forgotten she was there.

"Better start making money, then," Erik said, eyeing a rambling ornate manse.

"Not for that one," Haze countered, pointing to one of several more dilapidated structures, a center hall with a wide gallery that had apparently been broken into apartments. Next to that was a long battered single shotgun listing to one side.

As they continued their trek up the length of the

Coliseum Street parkway, they saw that many of the houses, maybe almost half, were in varying stages of renovation. Haze stopped in front of one of these and stood there until the others stopped, too. He turned to Miranda and asked, in a serious tone, "How about this one?"

"What about it?" she said. It was a moderate specimen, an Anglo-American townhome with porch and second-floor gallery neatly stacked on square columns. The first floor was boarded up with plywood, but the second floor windows and doors—all the same size, stretching from the floor almost to the ceiling—gaped open. No plywood, glass, framing, anything.

In the park across the street someone had tied a rope around an oak branch to make a swing—but if there had once been a board knotted at the bottom, it was long gone. The rope just hung there, as if lonely for kids to swing on it.

"Looks nice and breezy up there," Erik observed. "Up higher than the bugs, too," he added, slapping at a mosquito.

"But…" Miranda felt obliged to point out, "if we keep walking we'd probably get to Sinai in just like an hour."

Everyone was silent for a few seconds.

"That what you wanna do?" Haze asked.

It took her a moment to digest the magnitude of his question. It was really, "Do you want this to end now?" And, maybe, "Are you ready to say goodbye to me, all of us, now?"

Erik and Vy were looking at each other, quietly mulling the same choices.

The twists and turns. Though dizzying, they were also awesome to behold. For most of her life she fantasized about a home overlooking this park—and now, under the most unpredictable circumstances, was an invitation to try one out. Complete with a swing in the park adjacent that just needed a board. She had always, in an unquestioned and unexplored way, pictured a husband somewhere near as she reposed on the gallery overlooking the green—and kids on the swing? Was Haze in this picture? No wonder she had never filled that portrait in—her unschooled imagination would have rebelled.

"I bet the view's gorgeous from up there," she said, gazing at the second floor gallery, with its high awning, already painted pale blue on the underside.

Erik and Vy stood facing each other still—just inches apart. Erik said, "Whaddya think? Wanna squat?"

She frowned—playfully, it seemed—and punched his arm.

Haze was already jumping the low iron fence and peering down a side alley. The others followed. The rear yard was all sand, but the adjoining yards were richly planted. All the first floor windows were boarded up, but under the rear porch, the bottom rungs of a ladder stuck out.

"Score," Erik exclaimed, as he pulled it out. Haze gave him a hand. It was a long house-painter's ladder, easily able to reach the high second story. Haze and Erik grabbed opposite ends and yanked it to its full length. It looked heavy and awkward to upright and lean against the side of the house. But they accomplished it, and each waved the other on to climb up.

"What?" Erik grinned, "You not worried about turning your back, huh?"

"No," Haze said, "I ain't worried," and started up the ladder. Miranda went next, then Vy, then Erik.

They came into what would one day be a kitchen. It had a long granite island in the middle, and a counter along one side. New track lights along the ceiling. No appliances yet, though, just cut-out squares and rectangles in the granite, pipes and wires sticking out of the walls. The floors were original—wide reddish brown wooden planks.

The rest of the place was less re-done than the kitchen: just a series of high, wide, white-washed empty rooms, with dusty chandeliers hanging from peeling rococo plaster medallions. The tall windows, filled with the pale blue of the evening sky, were like dim panes of light, brightening the gray of the large empty rooms. There was a bathroom, but it was hazardous—the subfloor hadn't been laid yet, so it was just piers and a drop into an equally unfinished bathroom some twenty feet below. The shape of the room and the PVC piping were the only clue that it was a bathroom at all.

They wandered back into the kitchen and, since there was no furniture, hopped up onto the countertops and sat.

"Nice place," Haze said. "All we need is a table, some chairs, a refrigerator, stove, some food…beds?"

"And an entertainment center and a jacuzzi," Erik added.

Vy said she just wished they had food.

Erik sniffed at the air. "Smells like…?" He jumped down from the counter and went to a window. "Figs?"

The others went and looked, too. He was right: there was a fig tree next door.

"Figs it is," said Haze, with a reluctant grimace.

They all made their way back down the ladder and found a way to climb over the wooden fence to the neighboring yard. Miranda was the last to make it over. As she dropped to the ground she heard Erik exclaim "Whoa! Jackpot!" and a squeal of joy from Vy.

They had landed in a backyard vegetable patch. Tomatoes, cucumbers. Big leafy greens. "These collards?" Haze wondered aloud.

Erik was smelling another green plant. "What's this?" he asked. "Is this food?"

"It's basil," Vy laughed.

"Got us a grocery cart here," Haze said, dumping old cans out of a blue recycling bin.

Just as Miranda wondered what other sort of manna would fall from the sky to bless them, she spotted a big yellowish thing against the far fence, looking like a giant egg in the twilight. "Oh my God," she gasped, "a watermelon!"

The others had been yanking at plants and tossing things into the bin, but now all motion stopped and all eyes followed Miranda's.

Erik strode over to it, flipping open his knife and saying, "Let's just have a picnic right here." He cut the twiney vines connecting it to the earth and then plunged the knife in. The blade wasn't long enough to cut all the way across, so he just cut around the circumference and then dug his fingers in the gash and ripped it apart, then did the same with the two halves, ending up with four big chunks. They all sat in the dirt and sucked up their portions—more drinking than eating—until they were all gnawing on rind. By then the mosquitoes had found them. What's more, they heard movement in the house in front of them. So they stood, chucked a couple more cucumbers, tomatoes, and basil sprigs in the bin, and scaled the wall back, just as a window opened onto the garden. It was a second-floor window, so Miranda consoled herself that, in the darkness, their theft wouldn't be discovered.

Back in the kitchen, Erik gave Vy his knife and she chopped the cucumbers, tomatoes, and basil into a messy salad that they consumed with their fingers right off the granite counter.

Erik belched and said, "That just leaves the beds."

"Got that covered," Haze assured them.

They looked at him and waited for an explanation.

"Y'all saw all them roofing tiles packed up back there?"

They all continued staring. Finally Erik said, "What, sleeping on roofs is part of the culture now?"

"No man," Haze grinned. "They wrapped in cardboard."

Miranda should have noticed that, too. They'd seen so many cardboard sleeping arrangements around town, there must be something to it.

Haze and Erik descended the ladder again to tear strips of cardboard from the packaged roofing tile, while Miranda and Vy watched from the high window.

"Wow," Vy said, with the most natural smile Miranda had seen on her so far, "They're like, waiting on us."

It seemed true, but not waiting on them like paid help—another way. Haze had been so solicitous of her wants, so gently inquisitive about her emotional state, so self-effacing and attentive—but in a firm, sure, proud manner. Everything she always fancied, in her childish antebellum fantasies, a true Garden District gentleman would be. Everything but the bowing—and the duels.

47

After supper, Miranda suggested they sit on the front gallery. Haze was all for it. He was a big new fan of porch breezes. They took some cardboard mats out and sat, leaning against the wall and looking out over the city. The stars came out big again, and there was a bright moon, too. It made the park and the houses around it look blue, and clearly defined, like somebody drew it all. Past the rooftops you could see the cranes and rigging of ships on the river. Haze wondered what they were doing. Must have gotten stranded because of the storm coming. Were their crews on board? The Crescent City Connection loomed to the left, a dark skeleton without its lights. Somewhere over there was the west bank, where people were going about their normal business.

He saw a form moving across the park toward them. As it got closer he saw it was an old lady, blue-haired white lady in a worn-out housecoat. She was lugging along something heavy. As she crossed the street he saw it was an orange gas canister.

"Guess somebody still got gas," he said.

Miranda called out a big "Hi!" and waved, but the lady ignored her, didn't even glance up, and went in the house next door.

"Uh-oh," Erik said. "Hope she's not wanting that watermelon."

Haze figured the moral department was Miranda's, and she seemed to be thinking about it.

"We should knock in the morning and see if she's OK," she suggested.

They all nodded, happy to not think about it anymore.

But it itched at Haze a bit longer, because the last time he saw somebody toting gas cans it ended up bad—the guy on the roof of the hospital, who obviously drained the fuel out of the chopper and wrecked them, killing a man. The vague suggestion in his head that he was somehow culpable, for not saying anything, was too unpleasant to dwell on. Besides, he didn't have the energy.

"What day is it?" Vy asked.

After counting back, they concluded it was Friday night.

"Wow," Vy said. "So if this hadn't happened, what would we be doing?"

"Football game," Erik said.

"Yeah," agreed Haze. "At Pan-Am stadium. Was gonna be my first time on the field. You on the team?" he asked Erik.

"Naw," he answered. "I take that back—I wouldn't be at the game."

"Nothing exciting from me," Miranda said. "I'd probably just be at home. Or the Penny Post."

"What's that?" they all asked.

"A coffeehouse? on Daneel? Lots of kids…that I know— hang out there. Open mics and stuff." She looked at Vy. "What about you?"

Vy's smile faded. After a pause, she said, "Sometimes I went out with friends, you know. Like Oakwood?"

That was a mall on the west bank—Haze had been there.

"But usually," she continued, so quiet he could barely hear her, "we went to my grandmother's house."

Erik cast his eyes down, like she'd said something tragic.

After another pause she said, "My grandmother died."

Haze nodded. "Yeah. Mines passed last year."

They sat there in silence until Vy said, "Mine died…a couple days ago. The day after the storm."

She was in that house, Haze knew, where they'd picked

Vy up.

Erik made a weird grunt, with a little tremor in it. Then he said, "Mine was at St. Theresa's."

Haze knew that was a nursing home, but he wasn't sure where it was.

Erik didn't seem to want to talk about it anymore so Vy continued. "It was just really hot up there. But she made it seem not so bad. Then she kind of closed her eyes and she just didn't move for a while. I thought she was…you know, gone. But I wasn't really sure. But she stayed like that, just kind of lying down?" She stopped, swallowed. "But then she, you know, got kind of hard. That was when y'all were there, that… morning. She told me she didn't want to go anywhere."

"My-" Erik started again. It looked like he was trying hard to keep his face together. "She might be still with us. Not sure, you know."

Sounded to Haze like he was more sure than he let on: she wasn't.

Haze thought Miranda would say something. He wished she would. But since she didn't, he thought he should try. "Well," he ventured, "old people pass."

Vy nodded. "My grandmother said that, too."

Haze heard a familiar sound rising up somewhere around the house—he used to hear it this time of evening from the Florida Canal, muted chirping like dripping water in a trippy cave.

"Y'all hear them frogs?" he said.

The others nodded.

"Reminds me of by my house."

All the others said "Me too."

"Guess the frogs made out alright."

But Erik said, "Long as they not in the oil slick."

Haze thought of something else to say. He said it quickly, so he wouldn't change his mind about it. "My dad passed."

Miranda stirred from her trance, turned to him.

"When?" Erik asked.

"In the storm." He didn't want to spill it all out at once. Didn't seem respectful to rush out the details.

A few seconds later, Miranda muttered, so softly it was almost a whisper, like it was dangerous to say it too loud: "Katrina?"

"Naw, naw." He changed his mind because he didn't want saddle them with an obligation to help him grieve. "Back in Georges."

"Where was he?" Erik asked.

"Offshore."

"On a rig?"

"He was doing rescue. For the Navy."

Haze was thinking about something else, too, that he didn't want to say. How, yes, old people pass, but what had been going on in this storm wasn't natural like that. If Erik's granmaw drowned and Vy's baked to death, that wasn't the natural time for them to go, even if they were old. Not to mention the other people dropping like flies around them. The cop at the gas station—a man with kids, probably—that baby at the Convention Center. His dad's passing was more natural than those, since, basically, to Haze, he was imaginary anyway. It was like Santa Claus passing, or the Easter Bunny. It was just time. A circled date on the calendar he finally got to. He said it happened in Georges because he didn't want to cheapen the mourning of these people who just lost some-body real. But for him, and in future tellings, his dad would be on the long list of Katrina casualties.

Haze took a deep breath and when he exhaled, just like Ms. Williams told him, all the trouble and the heavy cross and the scars from the lashes just evaporated right out of him. He felt good.

But not about the other people. And did that mean

Green—if he didn't make it? Or was that one natural? Living and dying by the sword? Erik had tried to convince Haze, when they were cutting strips of cardboard for bedding, that he hadn't meant to kill Green at all, that he intended only to do what he did, wound him, scare him. He said he didn't have much choice, the guy recognized him and came after him. But Haze couldn't buy all that because he'd seen Erik grinning and taunting the man at the Convention Center, and then leading him into a trap in that alley. Underhanded. Maybe he hadn't meant to kill him, but shooting him was something he obviously planned and carried out. But the main thing Erik tried to convince Haze was that he wasn't a racist, whatever that was supposed to mean. Whatever it meant, it meant a lot to Erik—just to not have that word associated with him. If the word meant hating on all black people, Haze was sure it didn't apply, he could tell Erik wasn't like that. But if it meant thinking things about black people that might not be totally correct, he wasn't sure. Of course, you could say that about a lot of people. Haze figured Erik might be more the kind who just didn't know any better. He tried to explain to Haze that the cop they saw get killed on Chef Highway was a black man, too, so he was actually avenging one black man as much as punishing another one. But Haze thought that cop had been Spanish, Cuban or Honduran or something. Anyway, Haze had countered, black people didn't need white people to come protect the good black folks from the bad ones. He figured white people's hands should be full dealing with their own bad eggs—the ones running the country.

The frogs had the airwaves to themselves until Miranda said, "I wonder what time it is." She pulled out her cellphone and turned it on. Amazingly, it lit up and sounded the company jingle. "Wow," Miranda marveled. "It works."

Erik and Haze pulled out theirs, too.

Vy said, "I forgot mine."

"9:30," Miranda announced. Then it sounded the tone for a text message. "Hmm," she said, "never heard that before."

"You got a text?" Vy asked.

"Is that one of those message things?"

"You got a text?" Haze repeated.

She shrugged her shoulders and handed him the phone. The battery indicator was already blinking. He went to the messaging menu and pulled up the text. He didn't want to read her private stuff, but he was pulled in because it was so mean. He didn't even want to give it back to her. It was from somebody named Jess: "F u bigtime. Lakeview safe? Hell. F u n ur f-ing city 2. Hope u both die. Never cming back dont call me ever."

Miranda looked at him anxiously. "What is it?"

He reluctantly handed her the phone. He watched as she frowned at it. Her face went through a few moods, and then she said, "Oh well, guess somebody hates me." She smirked and snapped a finger, then shut the phone.

Erik's messaging signal went off, too. He opened his phone and whistled.

"Wow," Vy said, peeking at the screen, "Twenty new messages?"

Erik hastily snapped it shut. "Yeah, just my mom."

"Don't you wanna answer?"

"I mean my granma-"

"But you said-"

"My aunt…I mean."

Sounded to Haze like he meant 'girlfriend' but didn't feel like Vy knowing about it. You could tell because all the fake people he mentioned—who probably didn't text anyway— were females. Haze suppressed a chuckle and saw he had a message, too. From his cousin. It said "Wer r u?" Haze texted back: "OK. Sinai 2morrow." He clicked send and, after a moment, the checkmark appeared: "Message Sent."

Miranda asked if he had just sent a message.

"Yeah," he said, slowly, because he was still convincing himself of it.

"Guess that means it's almost over," she said.

"Yeah."

Erik and Vy got up, picked up their palettes, and went inside.

"Whew," Miranda breathed. "Exhausted. I want to talk. But I can't." She got up on a knee and re-arranged her cardboard further from the wall, then lay flat on it. She took a deep breath and closed her eyes. Haze watched her lie there, her hair splayed out under her head, her face relaxing into a smooth, soft surface, like a fresh tablecloth. He put his cardboard alongside hers and lay on his side next to her. He gently placed his hand on her stomach. She put one of her hands on top of his, and slid the other along the floor until it touched him at his bent knee.

48

Erik's arm was still across her when Vy woke up. The window was getting brighter. Another morning in the world beyond. And she didn't really want to leave. But the whole point about this place was that you couldn't stay. It was inside this moving cloud. The cloud would evaporate, and there'd be a different world. Not like the one before, but more like the one before than like this one, this bridge.

She saw in front of her, in the little slice of world in the unadorned slab of window, wisps of gray cloud, close, as if strands were already peeling off and dropping. There was more. The cloud seemed to be getting thicker rather than dissipating, like they were driving deeper into it instead of finally falling out. And it had an acrid smell: of burning. In seconds it had come into their secret hiding place and made it hard to breathe.

Erik awoke. "Huh? What the-!" He jumped up and grabbed Vy by the arm. "C'mon." He grabbed his pants and pulled them on as he staggered with her toward the kitchen.

They heard a shout behind them. "Naw, don't go in there!"

It was Haze, standing in the opposite doorway with Miranda, waving them toward the front.

The smoke was thick now, and carried heat. Felt like the inside of a barbecue. Erik pulled her to the ground and they crawled back toward Haze and Miranda.

The next room was less smoky so they rose and ran through the two other big rooms to the balcony.

Haze and Miranda were searching along the sides for

a way down. The ceilings were so high in this place that the second floor was almost like a third floor in a more common, modern house.

"They got a drainpipe on the side?" Erik called to Haze. He shook his head.

The house next door, the one with the vegetable garden in back, where Vy had said a quiet prayer for *Ba* the night before, was totally engulfed. Big thick blasts of fire were coming out of it and licking at the house they were on. Back in the rooms they'd just vacated, they could already see flames taking shape in the thick blue haze. And that barbecue feeling came out to the balcony, like when you hold your hand over a grill—but it was her whole backside feeling it, head to foot. She pressed herself against the railing and looked down. The only thing that made *Ba* OK with dying was that Vy was sup-posed to live—that's what she'd said.

Erik said, "Broken leg's better than getting charred." They were all looking over the side now, trying to get up the cour-age. But they also all knew there was no one to help get them anywhere if they all broke their legs.

"What about that tree?" Miranda said, pointing at an oak branch that stretched across Coliseum Street from the park. "Look!" She pointed lower.

It had a rope swing on it, on the same branch but on the other side of the street, closer to the trunk.

"Wish that was over here," Erik said. Then he turned to Haze, looked him over and asked how tall he was.

"Yeah," Haze said. "I know." He looked back into the smoke-clogged room behind them, then back at the branch. "OK."

But the branch was quite a few feet from the balcony. Haze and Erik must have decided Haze had the best reach, being the tallest, and the best chance of landing a hand on it and holding on.

Haze did a few stationary jumps, straight into the air. He stuck his hand straight up while he did them, like he was trying to slap the ceiling. "OK," he repeated.

He smiled at Miranda and did a fist-pump for confidence. She just stared at him with wide eyes, but tried to look like she was OK. She looked like she was fighting back the urge to tell him not to try it.

He got up on the railing in the corner closest to the oak branch, steadying himself on the column. Then he edged away from the column, leaving one hand on it—then just a finger— for balance. He bent his knees and straightened up a couple of times. Then he let out kind of a bloodcurdling deep-throated groan and was in the air, hands flailing in front of him.

He must have caught hold of something because he ended up hanging from the tree with both hands. He just hung there for a second and then, with a smaller grunt than before, swung a leg up, and then pulled his whole body up, until he was sitting on the branch facing them.

Erik shouted, "The brother can JUMP! %#$* yeah!"

Haze shook his fist at him, like to chastise him, but he couldn't help smiling. He slid down the long branch, tearing off a few smaller ones on the way, until he got to the swing. It was tied kind of loose, staying in place because of a branch sticking up behind it. So it seemed not that hard for Haze to slide it up the long limb over the street—which got narrower and narrower as it neared the burning house.

But the flames were already licking out of the windows and doors. The palette Haze and Miranda had been lying on the night before was on fire. Erik picked it up and through it over the side, but that didn't mean much, considering the inferno eating up the whole house behind them. They crowded together in the last little unconsumed corner.

Haze had hit an obstacle. A branch too big to get the looped rope around, and also too big to break. The ground under him was littered with fallen branches—but this one had held out. He tried to stretch out so he could kick at the stubborn holdout. Because of the slope of the big limb over the street, he was almost upside down, gripping the bark with his hands and wildly kicking at this one branch. When that didn't work, he gripped it and swung from it. His weight ripped it at the base and he barely grabbed the big limb in time to not fall to the ground. Then the little wiry branch was bent enough for him to grapple with his hands and peel off. It finally fell down to the soft pile of firewood the hurricane had made of the street.

Miranda was already standing on the railing, Erik holding one of her hands and the other leaning on the corner column. "OK!" she called. She must have figured Haze was close enough. He swung the rope toward the house. It swung back. "OK," Miranda called again. "Just keep doing it."

With more tries, the arc got wider, and the rope got closer to the house. It actually didn't have a swing or a tire or anything on the bottom. Just frayed out and stopped.

Miranda jumped, with a scream. The scream turned into a grunt when she hit the rope and held on. Then she slid down quickly and dropped to the street. She landed in a thicket of branches but she stood up quickly and started clearing the spot. Moving around in quick circles and tossing the branches to the side.

"OK," Erik said, taking Vy by the arm. The way he said it took some of her fear away. Like he was a professional skydiving coach and this was all in a day's routine.

She flew into the air and heard a little yelp coming from her own throat. When she hit the rope her hands knew what to do. Like it was instinctive. They just wrapped around it and tightened. Then she folded her legs around and slid down. The trip burned her hands, thighs, and the back of one of her heels, but then she was hanging there at the bottom of the rope. She wasn't sure how far away the ground was, but when she dropped, it seemed like nothing, like dropping from a swing at a playground.

Haze started the rope swinging again. Erik stood on bent knees on the railing, arms stretched out at his sides. He had a look on his face like a football player, or a guy getting ready to punch somebody. He went in the air and landed on the rope without a sound. Then he hung there for a while, hugging the rope, before sliding down. He crossed himself and found his way to the ground.

Haze came down the rope, too, and they all stood in a circle of asphalt with branches piled up around them, looking at the big old house that gave them food and rest go up in flames.

The gallery was totally engulfed now. The fire snatched at the tree they'd escaped on and continued its march to the next house over.

Other people had gathered in the park behind them. Middle-aged white people, two couples. The guys were in shorts and polo shirts and the women in work-out outfits with their hair pulled back. One of the guys, in a wide-brim floppy canvas hat, called out to them, asking if they'd lived in one of the burning houses.

They all shook their heads.

Then one of the women asked if they were OK.

They all said yes and thank you.

Then the old folks left them alone, even though they looked at them like they were either curious or suspicious of them—Vy would be, too, if she saw people as raggedy as they must have looked, loitering around. They were all standing close enough that Vy could hear their conversation, about the fire, like they knew what started it. "Think it was Mrs. Hed-dinger?"

"You know they took her cats?"

"Yes, unbelievable. Took 'em right out from under her, like she wasn't there."

"And that was the whole reason she stayed."

"Think she's still in there?"

A big sigh came from one of them. "If she is, she wanted to be."

"We should have raided her garden before it all got burned up."

After a pause, another one said, "I really don't think that's funny or appropriate."

"They tried to get in our house, too, they heard Duke barking."

"Yeah, they wanted to know if we had any cats. When Robert said that wasn't their business they gave us a lecture about how the city wasn't safe for animals."

"I know one thing," one of the men said, "after they clear out all the cats they better come back for the rats."

They stopped talking when a siren started wailing toward them. It was a medium-sized fire truck crunching over all the branches in Coliseum Street and lurching to a halt in front of the burning houses—it was almost the whole block. The driver jumped out and a few other firemen jumped off or just stood up in the back and looked at the fire. They waved at Vy and her friends and at the other people. "Anybody in there?" they asked.

"Not in that one," Erik pointed at the one they'd been in.

"There might be someone in 1015," one of the ladies behind them called.

But that one was already collapsing. The firemen told Vy and the others to step back. They walked into the middle of the block-wide park, back around where the older couples were, but not right next to them. The grass was still wet with dew. It felt pleasant on Vy's bare feet—they were all barefoot. Erik was shirtless.

The firemen didn't really do anything. Just stood there. Even though a fire hydrant was right there plain to see on the curb.

"Y'all gonna put it out?" Erik called.

A fireman turned around slowly. "No water pressure," he said, flicking a hand at the hydrant. Then he and the others went to work with wide shovels, pushing the fallen branches away from the burning houses.

They heard a helicopter approaching. It had a big sack hanging from a cable, like the sandbags they were dropping in the canal breach. It hovered directly over the fire but instead of the bag snapping loose and dropping, like at the canal, it just opened, and a torrent of water fell down onto the fire. The chopper banked off, toward the river, and another came up, with the same apparatus, and dumped more.

"They getting it from the river?" Haze asked.

"I guess so," said Erik, scratching his chest.

It didn't seem to Vy like they'd be able to put it out that way. But it was doing something. She realized they weren't pouring on the houses that were already blazing, but on the next one in line, that had just started smoking. Their house—where they'd spent the night—would be a total loss, a sacrifice. But at least they were stopping it from spreading.

It was like a bridge burning behind them, erasing the tracks that brought them to where they were, and making return impossible.

From what the people behind them said, that old grandmother had started it. It's like what Ms. Williams had said, about every time a girl turns grandmother age, a big thing like Katrina happens. It was like the grandmothers themselves, after planting their gardens, called up the cloud—thunder, vapor, or smoke—to be like a boat to take them to the next stage. And it ended up changing the people left behind, too. And that was how the world changed, and how people changed.

The people behind them, teary-eyed, shook their heads and walked off.

Haze said, "Y'all ready to walk?"

They all nodded.

"Dang, Erik," he grinned, "looks like you finally lost the shirt off your back."

"Yeah," Erik grunted, "Tarzan never needed one."

"Didn't need shoes neither."

Miranda stopped and looked back one more time at the collapsing ash of their old historic home. "Guess we're all maroons now," she said.

49

Erik thought about that, about them being maroons, and it sounded like the truest thing Miranda had ever said. Whatever they had been before mattered less and less. Now they were all the same nation, at war with some elusive enemy that was always tracking them. That enemy could be black or white—or Asian—just like them. Watching that block of houses burn down, it convinced him more than ever that there was nothing for him here anymore. Everything he touched here had to be left behind. If only he could take Vy. Form their own colony, far away, and guard it well.

They saw a steady stream of vehicles a few blocks away. Army personnel trucks, headed downtown.

Haze said, "They on St. Charles, huh?"

They drifted in that direction—it was close enough to Sinai to not be a detour. They noticed, closer to the Avenue, that more streets had been swept of debris, made more drivable. When they came across a busted-up corner grocery, Erik was sure they all had the same idea as him. They all glanced up and down the street and strolled over to the door, a glass door that had been smashed in. In fact, it was still locked.

Erik was the first to duck under the bar in the middle of the door and venture in. The snack racks up front—not to mention the booze and smokes behind the counter—had been picked clean. The register was on the floor, bashed up and pried open. Erik wondered what kind of knucklehead would waste his time beating on a cash register in a closed store. Did they think they left the money in it?

The others had come in behind him, but they couldn't advance very far because broken glass—and a disgusting sticky residue—pretty well covered the floor. Too hazardous for bare feet. What they needed was a shoe store. They sighed a collective "naah," and turned to go. But they paused when they heard the squeal of brakes outside and a car door slam. They exchanged glances mixed with apprehension and defiance and Haze crept out first.

Erik heard somebody asking a question and then heard Haze say, "Man, %$#* you!" That was followed by the scuffle of quick feet and some thuds of flesh on flesh. Miranda ran out screaming and Erik edged past Vy and got out next.

One guy was standing by the car, in the street by the driver's side door. The passenger door was open and another guy was wailing on Haze up against the wall of the store. Had him in a choke hold and kept punching him in the side.

Miranda was standing there screaming "Stop! Stop it!"

That's OK, it was Erik's turn now. It was an NOPD squad car but who knew who was a real cop anymore? They weren't in uniform. It wasn't right the way they were beating down Haze, anyway. He looked around calmly and the environment they'd learned to survive in easily met his needs. The cash drawer from the register lay in the gutter right in front of the store. It was aluminum but the front end was heavy, it had a nasty edge on it, and it was easy enough to wield. He strode over and bopped Haze's assailant one on the head. "Get the @#$% offa him!" he yelled, slamming the guy in the face as he wheeled around. He went down and Erik got him one in the kidney.

He stopped when he heard a gun go off. For a split-second he tried to figure out if he'd been hit. Apparently not.

The voice behind him barked, "Turn around punk, so you can see the bullet coming!"

The voice sounded oddly familiar. Like a late-night movie star. He turned around slowly.

The cop had the gun trained on him over the roof of the car. He loosened his grip and raised his head. "Erik?"

It was his dad. Erik knew that much. But he didn't know what to do. Everybody else had stopped moving. "Dad…" Erik started. He gestured at Haze. "I know the guy."

His dad holstered his weapon and started walking around the front of the car. First slowly, then faster. Erik worried for a vague second that he was going to get whupped in front of his new friends.

But his dad lurched into him with a suffocating bear hug instead. "Thank you God, thank you God," he keened. He repeated it softly and rocked there from foot to foot squeezing him for what seemed a few minutes. Erik decided it was too much to feel at the moment. He needed to work up to it. Probably he'd break down like a baby when he saw his mom. Even if his dad was doing it now. He felt the man's tears on his neck.

"I love you dad," he managed. But had to stop, because his own tears were seeping through the gates he'd locked so tight against them.

His dad let him go and tried to get professional, in a red-eyed, soft-spoken way. The guy he was with—not his regular partner—had apparently figured out the situation and stood off to the side shutting up and looking away.

Haze was up, too, leaning against the store with Miranda under his arm.

Vy crept out through the door of the grocery, red shock of hair first, then her little body. Like when he first saw her in the East.

His dad was looking at Haze. "Rodney DeCuir?" he said.

"Yeah," Erik grinned. "That's the name."

"Miranda Maitre?"

She nodded.

Then he turned to Vy, lifting his finger and dropping it again. "Uh," he muttered, glancing back at Erik.

But Erik had no idea what to say. So he just said her name.

50

I Like a look of Agony, Because I know it's true—. But she didn't. Didn't like it, even though she knew it was true. She had a much clearer idea of truth now and, yes, it looked a lot like agony—sometimes. What she was still unclear on was what she liked. She'd soon have lots of time to mull it all over in her own room. She would have to re-arrange it, of course, whether or not the sycamore still stood. She wanted to clear it of everything, leave it high and airy and open, empty, with nothing but a window and a cardboard palette on the floor.

The four of them piled into the back of the squad car. The door slammed and she looked out through the bars at the battered, exhausted city streets. They turned on St. Charles Avenue and drove uptown toward Sinai Hospital. It was only five minutes in a car.

Erik told his dad he'd been thinking a lot about Texas. His dad nodded. "We might end up there, who knows?" he said.

She and Haze were scrunched up right next to each other but they kept their hands in their laps. They both had thinking to do, had places to go where they couldn't go together—physically and mentally. She knew he was pulling back. They had to. For now. He'd said last night he sometimes couldn't figure out whether she was daydream or real. She'd said, "Maybe reality is for people who can't handle daydreams." But they both knew such a cavalier attitude would crumble as soon as civilization returned—and it appeared, for them, at least, that it had.

For the city, too, if civilization could be equated with

trucks bearing armed men. As they coursed uptown, the other side of the streetcar tracks bore a steady stream of canvas covered green trucks, full of soldiers, moving in to restore order. She wondered what their mission was, exactly. To forcibly remove the holdouts? She wondered who would shoot at them to stay put in their neighborhoods. Simon Pitot? Captain Davey? Not Ms. Williams. She would just give them a cold stare and they would turn around and go. Ms. Godowsky would accomplish it with smiles and teases.

Maybe the next time she would see Haze would be right here, on the Avenue. She in her family's usual parade spot, him high-stepping in a 39 uniform on the route.

He was obviously already focused on his practical immediate future—texting someone.

She pulled her phone out and turned it on. A text came through—from Haze. It said, "Now u got my #."

She smiled at him, and he smiled back, but in a cool teen way, like kids flirting, which meant so little, nothing like what they had already earned together. But then again, that was a daydream bounded by water and fire, not something that could thrive in the regular boring safe world they all desperately wanted back.

St. Charles Avenue had been cleaned up pretty well already. The differences from before the storm were subtle. The sun peeking through the live oak canopy above was much stronger, more voluminous than before the storm. Less shade. If you hadn't seen them before, the trees looked perfectly full, healthy. If you had seen them before, there was no doubt: they were scragglier. Harder to hide under. Less like the primordial swamp, not the scene of elicit romance and vampires and serpents. More like the trees in Bible pictures, with solemn men in robes under them trying to explain everything. Why %@$# happens. Who's responsible. The city was going to be an altogether different kind of grove now. At least until the green canopy between them and the sky fleshed out again.

Miranda's parents were on the sidewalk out front as they pulled up to Sinai Hospital. They were sharing a cigarette. Miranda had never known them to smoke before. She wasn't shocked, but they just didn't look much like the parents she remembered. She had expected them to look different, of course. Specifically, a few years older.

But they didn't. They looked younger.

Six Weeks Later

From: 504 861-0066

Hi from ur daydream friend. Have gotten hng of txtng.
Hear 39 2 open 4 Jan. Us 2. What 2 do till then? Creole crmry
is open. Never got that ice crm in qrter. Wanna?

Received:
Thu Oct 21, 8:11 p

From: Haze

U dnt have hng txtng yet. But crl crmry str8. When?

Received:
Thu Oct 21, 8:12 p

From: Miranda

2morrow 3?

Received:
Thu Oct 21, 8:25 p

From: Haze

K

Received:
Thu Oct 21, 8:26 p

About the Author

C.W. Cannon is a native New Orleanian who has published a wide variety of fiction and non-fiction about the city. His first novel was *Soul Resin*, an experimental ghost story published in 2002. His work has appeared in *Other Voices*, *Third Coast*, *Exquisite Corpse*, *American Book Review*, *Constance*, *Louisiana Cultural Vistas*, *New Orleans Review*, *The Rumpus*, and the New Orleans *Times-Picayune*. He is also a frequent contributor to *The Lens* (thelensnola.org), where he writes on New Orleans culture, the south, and race. His essays in *The Lens* earned him the 2014 New Orleans Press Club Award for Best Column. He teaches writing and New Orleans Studies at Loyola University and resides in Faubourg Marigny with his wife, kids, cat, and chickens.

www.ingramcontent.com/pod-product-compliance
Lightning Source LLC
Chambersburg PA
CBHW061012120726
47910CB00006B/1899